"I might remind you, Sloan Calder, that pretending to be a happily married couple was not my idea!"

Katherine challenged.

"For God's sake, keep your voice down," he whispered.

"Maybe I don't want to. Maybe I don't care. Maybe I want—" She stopped in time, aware of the tension tightening between them; Sloan was staring intently at her, his mouth a breath away from hers.

But the kiss she'd expected, wanted and hoped for didn't happen. For seconds she watched in amazement as Sloan seemed to struggle for control. His face and eyes took on a guarded and distant expression.

"Are you afraid to kiss me?" she whispered.

"Terrified."

"But why?"

"Because I know where kissing you would lead. And that can't happen. Damn it, I won't let it."

Dear Reader:

We at Silhouette are very excited to bring you this reading **Sensation**. *Look out for the four books which appear in our Silhouette* **Sensation** *series every month. These stories will have the high quality you have come to expect from Silhouette, and their varied and provocative plots will encourage you to explore the wonder of falling in love – again and again!*

Emotions run high in these drama-filled novels. Greater sensual detail and an extra edge of realism intensify the hero and heroine's relationship so that you cannot help but be caught up in their every change of mood.

We hope you enjoy this **Sensation** *– and will go on to enjoy many more.*

We would love to hear your comments and encourage you to write to us:

Jane Nicholls
Silhouette Books
PO Box 236
Thornton Road
Croydon
Surrey
CR9 3RU

DEE HOLMES

Without Price

Silhouette Sensation

*First published in Great Britain in 1994
by Silhouette Books, Eton House, 18-24 Paradise Road,
Richmond, Surrey TW9 1SR*

© Nancy Harwood Bulk 1992

Silhouette, Silhouette Sensation and Colophon are
Trade Marks of Harlequin Enterprises B.V.

ISBN 0 373 59229 9

18-9406

Made and printed in Great Britain

Other novels by Dee Holmes

To my parents: Dick and Jane.
And to my better-than-any in-laws:
Reinier, Sr. and Elizabeth.
And to Reinier,
who keeps reminding me he is never wrong.

Prologue

Katherine Brewster awakened instantly.

She lay still, her sleepy mind trying to focus on what had disturbed her. She'd heard something. Not Danny; should the baby awaken at night, his sounds were always familiar, a soft stirring or a crying out. This was more of a shuffling sound or a muffled scrape.

Slowly and carefully silent, she pushed back the sheet and slipped out of bed. A fluorescent 2:25 blinked at her from the digital clock. The windows were open, the May night cool and starless. Close by, she heard the crickets commune and from the distance came the cloying scent of a passing skunk.

Amid the outdoor sounds, her ground-floor apartment suddenly seemed excruciatingly quiet. Barefoot and wearing her white cotton batiste thigh-length nightie, she crossed the carpet and went to her open bedroom door.

She peeked out, trying to locate anything that looked out of place. The room seemed orderly, the faint smells of Danny's talcum powder mingled with the scent of roses arranged in a nearby crystal vase.

Then the noise came again. A definite shuffling in the hollow darkness. Katherine squeezed her arms against her body and tasted the cakey pulse beat of fear. Swallowing, she didn't bother to remind herself to stay calm. It was too late for that.

Hastily her logic searched for an explanation other than the one clawing through her mind. Perhaps a mouse in the walls? But that would be more of a scratching. A nocturnal animal; maybe the skunk she'd smelled a few minutes ago? God, she'd even welcome a skunk in preference to the direction her mind was heading.

She stood perfectly still, her bare toes gripping the carpet as if she were balanced over a gaping abyss. Another sound. A muffled cough. Her heart pounded as the cold sweat of terror broke out across the back of her neck.

Someone was in the apartment.

Immediately her mind raced. Get Danny and run. Although her throat felt full and tight, she took a shaky breath. Pretend you're calm, she reminded herself, more than a little frantic. Hadn't she just read somewhere that keeping composed could save you if you were overpowered by a robber or a rapist?

Just the thought of an encounter with either scared her, negating whatever benefits the objective points on calm and composed might have had.

She listened. Her instinct to run across the living room and into the nursery was so great she could barely contain it. The baby had made no sound, and she quickly prayed he was still deep in sleep.

She took a breath and began to rationalize. If it were a robber, and she didn't panic, he'd take what he wanted and leave. Still she didn't like the idea of the living room separating her from Danny. Should he awaken and cry, the intruder might get scared and then...God, she didn't want to think about those possibilities.

Then she remembered. Call 9-1-1. She almost groaned with the relief.

The rose pink carpet muted her steps as she hurried around the bed to the phone on the nightstand. She picked up the receiver, carefully holding the base of the phone so it wouldn't make any noise. Thank goodness for the all-purpose emergency number, she thought. She couldn't concentrate enough to recall the police station's number or, if she had, to even push the corresponding digits that would be required to summon them.

Quickly, she punched 9-1-1 and waited.

Nothing.

She tried again, an encroaching fear making her fingers all but useless. Still no sound. *Nothing but a dead phone.*

She pressed the receiver tight against her ear, as if the dial tone was there but her hearing were gone. Had her phone line been cut? She tried to tell herself that was ridiculous, something out of the movies or television. She hung up the phone, her imagination latching onto an image of a helpless woman in a nightgown, the phone lines cut, turning suddenly to see a grotesque face in the doorway.

Like a terrifying echo, she heard herself whisper "Please, no" as she spun around toward her own door.

No one was there. Only the darkness enveloping the vague shapes of her living-room furniture. She pressed her icy fingers to her mouth. Terrific, she thought, you're not only *not* calm but you're getting close to losing it.

Maybe the phone lines weren't cut. Maybe, for some reason, the instrument just wasn't working. Maybe she hadn't hooked the kitchen extension's receiver on completely after her sister had called earlier in the evening. Yes, that had to be the problem. The receiver was off the hook in the kitchen. She felt such sudden relief at the certainty that she went weak. If she could get to the kitchen...

Katherine lifted her robe off the chair by her bed, slid her arms into the sleeves and belted it tightly around her. Taking a deep breath, she ventured gingerly out into the living room.

No sign of anyone, she thought with an almost gushy relief. The moonlight outlined the Victorian furnishings with seemingly nothing amiss. Maybe the sound had come from outside. Sounds traveled in the night and were sometimes distorted. Perhaps someone walking near one of the windows had made a noise or a dog was wrestling with something from a neighbor's trash can.

Wanting to check on Danny, she crossed the living room and approached the guest room that had been turned into a nursery when her one-year-old nephew and her sister, Jennifer, had come to live with her.

Katherine was almost to the door of the baby's room when a figure loomed up in front of her, filling the doorway.

For timeless seconds she tried to fit the figure to the room. A maroon shirt hanging out of dark chinos didn't belong. Nor did the odor of beer and cologne.

She screamed.

The sound pierced the night and just as abruptly died when the figure clamped a hand over her mouth. All her nerves tightened, the blood pumping and centralizing in her heart. The man whirled her around so she couldn't see him and slammed her tight against him.

Despite a kind of squishy feel to his body, she knew better than to underestimate his strength. His hand felt clammy and hot. The boozy-smoky smell of some bar clung to him. With his palm still wedged against her mouth, he pressed her head against his chest. A necklace or chain dug into her scalp.

From behind her she heard Danny begin to cry. The intruder bent his head and spoke with a croaky slur. "I'm not gonna hurt you. I'll take my hand away if you don't scream."

She nodded. Her lips ached from being pressed against her teeth and the sweaty taste of his skin made her stomach churn sickly. Only because Danny was in the apartment had she complied. She knew if she'd been alone, her instinct would have been to scream until her lungs ached.

Slowly he released the pressure against her mouth.

Immediately she begged, "Please, let me go and check on the baby."

He didn't answer her, but shoved her forward into the moonlighted area, toward the living-room couch. "Sit down and keep your mouth shut."

She stumbled, almost falling onto the plump flowered cushions. "Please, I have some money you can take," she pleaded desperately. "There isn't anything here of value." Besides Danny, she thought, her eyes darting around for some weapon she could use if the man headed for the baby.

Her purse lay out in plain sight, her credit cards and money clearly visible, yet he was moving away from it and back toward Danny's room. Frantic, Katherine leaped off the couch, her hand sweeping up a brass candlestick.

Rushing at him, she wielded the weapon, yelling, "No!"

He flung his arm up and she heard the sick sound of hard metal hitting flesh and bone. With an economy of movement, he grabbed and squeezed her wrist until she dropped the candlestick.

He gritted his teeth together, dragging her so close she had to turn her face away from his foul breath. "You little bitch. I told you to sit down and shut up."

"You can't touch the baby. Please, you can't."

"I can!"

He stepped near the window and into some reflected street light. She saw the full lower lip and the whiskery cast on his cheeks that her sister had once thought was sexy. But then she saw his eyes. Too coldly blue, too sharply fierce and void of any mercy.

Six months had passed since Katherine had last seen him, but she instantly recognized Danny's father. "Oh, my God."

Gerald Graham growled warningly. "Stay out of my way."

His words echoed around the room. She didn't know if it was because she'd recognized him or if it was just the knowledge that he'd obviously been drinking, but to her surprise she felt a lessening of the tension in her muscles.

Jennifer had ended her relationship with Gerald some time ago, and as far as Katherine knew he hadn't seen her sister or his son for a few months. Jennifer had gone to Australia on a photo assignment and no doubt Gerald, having gotten a little drunk, was feeling sorry for himself and had decided to take advantage of her sister's absence to see his son. Breaking into her apartment wasn't legal or excusable, but knowing who he was at least alleviated some of Katherine's earlier fear. On the heels of that thought, unbidden, two questions suddenly surfaced. How did he know Jennifer was gone? And why had he chosen tonight? She shook them away. This wasn't the time to analyze. She had to get rid of him.

"Look, I don't know what you think this will accomplish. I know if must be difficult not seeing Danny—" Her sister had been adamant about Gerald staying away from his son.

"Shut up," he snapped, obviously not happy that she was no longer quaking with fear. "Your sister thought she could just say 'get outta my life' and I'd leave. Well, I gotta surprise for her. No more time to be nice and patient, I gotta make my move. Now get over there and sit down or I'll have to tie you up."

She didn't move.

"Do what I tell you, damn it!"

Afterward she was never sure what caused it—whether it was his threatening tone, or some sixth sense that told her Gerald wasn't babbling and rambling from too many drinks—but whatever it was, Katherine went cold with new fear.

Before she could move, he bore down on her again, his eyes glistening and bitter. He snarled, his words cutting and precise. "I don't like gutsy broads with big mouths. I want my son. Your sister can't stop me and by God, you won't, either."

Danny began to cry louder.

Katherine made her voice stay even. "Please, let me go to him," she said. "He's frightened."

Gerald looked in the direction of Danny's room and for an instant Katherine thought she detected a glimpse of concern in his expression, but then it was gone. Suddenly he grabbed her arm and wrenched it so that she yelped in pain.

"I told you to shut up!"

He twisted her arm up behind her, forcing her forward. She winced, the pain making her eyes water. She tried to think. He wasn't taking Danny; whatever she had to do, she would do, but she would not allow Danny to be kidnapped.

Gerald hauled her into the baby's room and shoved her down into the rocking chair. Her arm ached where he'd twisted it. She started to get up, but he pushed her back down. He swung toward the crib, reached in and plucked out a screeching Danny.

For the tiniest of seconds, he held him, staring at the baby's contorted face. Then, as if realizing what he was doing, he shoved Danny at Katherine. "Stop him from crying," he ordered.

Danny trembled, sucking in air around his wailing. Katherine pressed him tight against her, whispering soothing words. His dark curls were damp and she stroked her hand gently from his head down his small back. Gerald went to the door and listened, obviously to determine if the crying had roused any attention.

Katherine bent her head to the baby's ear. "Shh, sweetheart, shh," she murmured even as she realized what would happen if she made him cry harder.

She gulped. Though she knew he wouldn't understand, she whispered, "Sweetheart, I'm sorry that I'm going to hurt you, just remember that I hate doing it." Even as she uttered the words she was having difficulty with the idea of purposely hurting the baby. But the alternative—this man taking Danny and running off to God knew where—was even more monstrous. And realistically, she knew that was exactly what would happen. Gerald was physically strong enough and if some twisted revenge against Jennifer was his motive, no amount of cool reasoning was going to change his mind.

She gripped Danny tighter, her palm absorbing the heaving sobs in his small body. He wore summer-light blue pajamas with a tiny circus tent motif. Just a few hours ago he'd giggled happily when she'd played This Little Piggie as she'd snapped him into the cotton pajamas. Now she squeezed her eyes closed and touched her fingers to the chubbiest part of his thigh. Forgive me, Danny, she prayed. Then she pinched his leg.

He let out a screech that cut through the room like a missile.

"What the hell are you doing?" Gerald roared, then instantly realized the volume of his own voice.

Katherine hugged Danny to her, feeling miserable that she'd had to resort to hurting him.

Suddenly a loud knocking on her front door had Gerald whirling around. He cursed. "You dumb bitch. Now look what you've done. Give me the kid."

"No!"

The knocking came again, this time insistent and accompanied by voices. Gerald cursed foully and muttered something about nothing he wanted that was important ever turning out right. Faintly Katherine could hear her name being called. It was her upstairs neighbors, the Irwin sisters, Marion and Nina.

Silently she prayed that not answering would make the women suspicious that the crying wasn't just the normal sounds of a baby at night.

"Get up," Gerald snarled.

"What?"

"I said get the hell up. Go to the door and tell whoever it is that everything is okay. The kid had a nightmare or something."

When she didn't move, Gerald took her arm and hauled her to her feet. Danny clutched at her, tears streaming down his cheeks.

"You're frightening your son," she said, deliberately making the paternal connection in hopes of touching some cord in him.

He went very still for a moment, as if considering her words and the prospect of taking a screaming baby out of the apartment.

"Put him back in the crib."

"No, please, let me hold him. I'll go to the door and tell whoever it is that everything is all right." Katherine knew that if she had Danny, Gerald would have no leverage. Once she got to the door, she would have at least enough time to shove Danny into another pair of arms.

He jerked her chin up, his eyes hot with anger and desperation. "So you can hand him to whoever that is?"

Katherine swallowed, her face paling. She'd underestimated him. He might be drunk and desperate to get Danny, but he wasn't stupid.

He gave her an unpleasantly superior smile. "Put him in the crib."

She knew if she let go of Danny, crying or not, Gerald would take him and go out the back door. She didn't need to stare into his eyes too long to know that he was both driven and desperate. He would take Danny.

A distant siren had Gerald whirling toward the window. Instantly Katherine took advantage of the second and fled the room. Behind her, she heard him swear and stumble against the rocking chair.

She raced across the living room, gripping a trembling Danny, and flung open her front door.

By that time more of her neighbors had converged in the hall. The Irwin sisters' white poodle yipped and struggled to get in the door. Katherine sagged with relief.

"Katherine, what is going on?" Marion Irwin asked with concern, immediately taking Danny into her arms. "We heard you scream and then that terrified yowl from Danny. Poor child." Marion soothed the baby, rocking him against her matronly bosom.

Nina immediately put her arm around Katherine. "Come, my dear. Tell us what happened. You're as white as a sheet."

From behind her she heard her back door slam. She sank into Nina's generous arms, her own fear releasing itself in tears of relief. Gerald was gone. Danny was safe.

At least for now.

Chapter 1

Sloan Calder pulled off his sunglasses as he stepped inside the Harbor Bay police station. His eyes still felt gritty from lack of sleep, or second thoughts about taking the Brewster case—he wasn't sure which—but he'd promised the police chief he'd be here. Despite his misgivings, Sloan didn't break promises.

Behind the front desk the sergeant sat huddled in front of a computer terminal. On a napkin near his elbow sat a steaming mug of coffee and a half-eaten jelly doughnut. He punched in a command on the keyboard before he glanced up and grinned. "Hey, Sloan. Been hearin' good stuff on that private investigatin' business of yours. Sure am glad you're in on this deal. Nothin' like a handy ex-cop when you gotta go outside the department. The chief couldn't have picked a better guy."

Sloan hung his glasses on his shirt placket. "Better hold your evaluation for when this is over, Newman."

"That's what I've always liked about you. None of that overconfident stuff—just thorough and cautious."

Not always, Sloan recalled grimly. He would have sold his soul for the chance to go back in time and be more thorough, more cautious. "Is she here yet?"

"Nope, but you know women. She probably saw a dress on sale or stopped to gossip with some neighbor," Sergeant Newman said offhandedly, as if his opinion was some standardized reasoning on the way women functioned.

"Maybe she's wondering what in hell is going on," Sloan said, finding himself annoyed at the sergeant's assuming tone. He'd first heard it when Joe Drummond, the police chief, had approached him about the short-term protection arrangement, and now here it was again.

Sloan sighed. Maybe his more than suspicious nature was at work, but getting called to come down to the police station on the pretext of *discussing* an arrest would have raised a few questions in his mind. Surely such a request had at least made her wonder why the police were talking and not acting.

He tapped on the door marked Chief of Police.

"Yeah, come on in," Drummond called.

Inside hot coffee scented the air. Sloan noted the beige walls and a large wall clock with black hands that read ten o'clock. The American and Rhode Island state flags stood in dusty folds in the office corners on either side of Drummond's desk.

Framed, gold-lettered certificates and wood-backed brass plaques awarded to Drummond and his department had been strategically placed so that anyone sitting across from the chief would glean the impression that Harbor Bay's finest not only served and protected its citizens, but did so flawlessly.

Sloan knew there had been a few not-so-flawless investigations. Mistakes in officer assignments, charging a suspect on flimsy evidence because someone got overanxious, political maneuverings—nothing that was unusual for any police department. Yet because the Harbor Bay force was small, Drummond was very aware of the judgment calls he made.

If the chief had made the right one when he'd contacted Sloan would be known shortly. Or whether he'd made the wrong one, Sloan decided with cynicism.

Logically he realized that whether he or Katherine arrived first made little difference. However, he did have reservations about the way things were starting off. At least he knew the score. Katherine didn't. Not yet, anyway. Technically he supposed he was overreacting, but he'd learned the hard way that assumption could be costly. And Drummond had assumed a hell of a lot when he'd gone ahead and set the plan as if there wasn't a chance she'd refuse.

Sloan had seriously considered calling her, but had decided against it. For one thing, he'd had no contact with her for more than three years and an out-of-the-blue phone call might really have alarmed her. Besides, the entire issue was far too complex, too secretive and too dangerous to be chewed out over the telephone. All logical reasons. Or excuses.

He dragged his hand down his face, grimly reminding himself not to get personally involved. Do the job, don't leave loose ends and collect the fee. Leave the heart-and-soul stuff for the movies and TV.

"Ms. Brewster must be on her way. I just had a call put in to her apartment and we got her answering machine," the chief said, closing the office door after Sloan. Drummond was stocky, with a face as leathery and seamy as a catcher's mitt. Dressed in a suit, his jacket was open and the tie loosened. His eyes were alert and probing. Despite the professional persona, Sloan knew the police chief was worried.

For months, the department had been embroiled in an internal investigation of mob influence on police recruits. Recently the police had identified Gerald Graham as a major player. But his recent attempt to snatch his son had created a dilemma for the police. Arrest Gerald and risk their own case because the evidence wasn't yet strong enough, or chance Gerald disappearing with Danny. Since getting Gerald convicted both helped the department and assured Danny's safety, Drummond had come up with a plan. Hire Sloan to protect Katherine and Danny for the next few weeks while the police completed their investigation.

Sloan glanced at the chief. "You wouldn't be having a few second thoughts on this brainstorm idea of yours, would you?"

"Don't talk about second thoughts. I'm still wrestling with the first ones," Drummond said. "If we move too soon and don't have strong evidence for a grand jury, Graham will be free. But if he gets that kid and runs, I'm gonna have to live with that on my conscience, not to mention that I'll have the city council on me like buzzards on a corpse for not protecting a citizen.'' He waved Sloan toward the coffee carafe. ''Get yourself some.''

Sloan poured himself a mug and added two packets of sugar. ''Any clue as to why Graham picked now to play the outraged father?''

''We've been hearing rumors from a few stoolies that Gerald is trying to break from some of his mob cronies and go on his own in a new place. New identity, fresh start, that sort of thing.''

Sloan scowled. ''And he figured his son would make a good addition to a new image?''

''Yeah. And in a twisted way that's a plus for us. If Danny isn't here, he's either got to abandon the idea or he'll hang around until he can make another snatching attempt.''

''And you're betting he'll hang around.''

Drummond nodded. ''The station shrink did a psychological workup on Graham from the info we have, as well as what Katherine Brewster said happened the other night. The shrink says Graham wants to be a father in a bad way. So, yeah, we're pretty sure he's not going to leave Harbor Bay without his son.'' Drummond sighed heavily. ''How I'd love to skip the mind-probing stuff and just haul Graham in here and lock him up. When I think of those recruits who accepted Graham's bribes—hell, I hate that word—of money and sex.'' He snorted in disgust. ''That trick is so old—''

''So old it works,'' Sloan said grimly. ''The mob sniffing around for inside information on raids and arrests was going on way before I was in the department five years ago. When you think about it, the mob paying Gerald to get friendly with a vulnerable fresh-faced recruit, then inviting him on a seemingly innocent weekend vacation with gambling, booze and the kind of sex he's only dreamed about is pretty powerful stuff.''

''Well, it's not going to work anymore,'' the chief said confidently. He jammed his hands into his pants' pockets and stared up at his wall of awards and certificates, as if drawing courage from past accomplishments. Without looking at Sloan, he said, "You did a helluva job on that case involving the labor relations board. Very impressive."

Sloan knew the comment was Drummond's way of saying he wanted to be impressed with the way Sloan handled protecting Katherine Brewster.

"Impressive maybe, but also very boring," Sloan said, suddenly realizing that most of the cases he'd worked on of late bored him. In fact, despite a sense of foreboding and edginess over getting involved in this deal, the reactions were also the first genuine feelings he'd had in a long time.

Drummond paced to the window, over to the door to glance out and then back to the window. Finally he sighed. "Maybe we'll get lucky and this whole thing will work without any hitches."

"No one gets that lucky," Sloan said dryly, knowing Drummond was doing what every cop did. Hoping for the best while expecting the worst. Reality was reality. Even on the best days and what seemed like the easiest of jobs, the unpredictable could happen. Sloan had learned that growing up in the inner city, again while he'd been a cop, and definitely as a private investigator. No arrangement involving even potential confrontation was foolproof. Gerald Graham certainly fell into the potential confrontation category.

Drummond gave him a long measured look. "She'll go along with this. Given the circumstances, she has no choice."

Sloan raised an eyebrow at that. "The lady definitely has a choice. She can say no, then she can get herself a lawyer to find out why the police are stonewalling on protecting a citizen. After her experience the other night, it could look as if the cops care more about finishing their own investigation than protecting a baby. Not so good for the Serve And Protect motto, Joe."

"And our solution to the serve and protect problem is you." Drummond gave him an intense stare. "You having second thoughts about doing this, Sloan? If you don't think you can handle it, tell me now."

Sloan poured himself another mug of coffee. He knew Drummond meant protecting Danny and Katherine. Since his wife's death more than a year ago, Sloan had been plagued with guilt. He'd been the target of an old grudge from his police days, but a fatal error had been made when the killer, in the guise of a hit-and-run driver, rammed into Sloan's car. Angela had used his car that day. She'd died in the crash that should have killed him. The days after that were little more than a blur of sleepless nights and too much whiskey. He still had memory gaps from those dark days, both before and after the funeral. The months that had followed had been racked with a deep sorrow that had fed his guilt and locked all the emotional doors on his soul.

Finally he'd hauled himself out of his self-imposed hell and grimly rememorized a few of the golden rules for people in his profession: never underestimate the bad guy; never stop looking over your shoulder and never, ever, allow anything to come between you and total focus on the case at hand. To do any less would endanger innocent lives. He'd also made a single, yet to be broken promise to himself: never again would he get personally involved with a woman. The price was too high, too costly, and too devastating.

Repeating that vow in his mind now, he kept his voice low and unemotional. "Second thoughts keep me alert. If I was too sure of myself, I wouldn't be here."

Drummond nodded briskly. "Just what I wanted to hear. I hate cockiness." To show that the issue was settled, Drummond peered out the open office door, obviously impatient at the delay.

Sloan crossed to the window. Traffic on Broad Street was heavy for a May morning. The doughnut shop was doing a brisk early season tourist and trucker business. A battered pickup skidded to a stop when a woman stepped into the crosswalk.

Sloan sipped his coffee as he watched Katherine Brewster. She walked quickly across, her purse swinging from one shoulder, a firmly gripped toddler in her arms. Sloan had recognized her instantly, but then watching people was what he did for a living. His first impressions were often right, and Katherine had made one at their first meeting more than three years ago. He'd sensed in her an almost desperate need to trust against all the evidence that pointed otherwise. He wondered now if that were still true.

Studying her, he noted changes. A more determined walk, more sophistication that gave her an air of independence. Just as he'd changed radically in three years, she, too, was different. Her brown hair was longer now and she'd pulled it back in a ponytail at her nape. He could see just the edges of a white bow. She wore a light blue suit with a slim skirt and a jacket that was open enough to reveal a white silky blouse.

Physically, she didn't have that incredibly flawless beauty that Angela had possessed. In fact, Katherine reminded him of the girl next door who'd moved away in a burst of energized innocence and then suddenly returned, years later, with her idealism defiantly intact. Sophisticated, but still soft. And something else, he realized with a frown at the flow of unexpected and unwieldy thoughts. Katherine Brewster had a kind of lavish mystique about her that a man explored at his own risk.

Sloan checked the immediate response of denying his reaction. No, better to acknowledge it and then dismiss it as mere curiosity.

Comparing and contrasting women had never been his style. And to compare Katherine to Angela . . .

Hell, what did he think he was doing? They didn't *compare or contrast*, nor should they even coexist in the same part of his mind.

Angela had been his wife.

Katherine and the baby were part of a case that required nothing from him but his professional expertise.

Sloan put the coffee mug on the windowsill, his eyes thoughtful as he recalled that first meeting with Katherine Brewster. More than three years had passed since she'd sat in his office at the Calder Investigation Agency and said she'd wanted her fiancé followed.

She'd been nervous and tearful and desperate, asking Sloan over and over again if he thought she was being too possessive, too paranoid, too suspicious. She'd suspected that her fiancé was seeing another woman, and she'd been torn between wanting to know and bracing herself for the worst.

Sloan had followed him for a month, gathering information and taking pictures of the subject with his flashy redheaded companion. The woman, in Sloan's opinion, was a definite zero compared to Katherine Brewster, but then Sloan hadn't been impressed by the obvious sexual come-on approach since his late teens. Katherine's fiancé, however, had not only been impressed, but obsessed.

Sloan remembered her widened eyes and pale cheeks when he'd told her what he'd learned. The written report had been thorough and concise and factual, but she'd tucked it into her purse and told him that she'd read it when she got home. She'd wanted his verbal opinion based on his professional experience and what he'd observed. He'd explained that he wasn't a counselor nor was he an expert on male-female relationships, but she'd insisted. Sloan had kept the lurid details at the gloss-over level, finally assuring her that as painful as the truth was, she was far better off knowing it now before she married the guy.

She'd listened, asking an occasional question or two, and when Sloan had finished, he'd had the damnedest urge to get up, round the desk and draw her into his arms. He'd known that his urge didn't go beyond that of comfort or reassurance, and yet his reaction had puzzled him. Never in his experience as a private investigator had that happened. But she'd looked so mortified and vulnerable that he'd found himself fighting the "urge" to find the fiancé and deck the unfaithful jerk. But he hadn't. Nor had he touched her or given any overt indications of sympathy beyond those professionally acceptable, yet he'd never quite forgotten her, either. She'd paid him, then left the office. The last thing he remembered had been the almost defiant lift of her head.

His opinion then had been that the lady had guts, and he couldn't help his curiosity now as to how she would react to Drummond's proposal.

Moments later Drummond opened the door wider at the sound of her knock, and Sloan had to smile at the flourish. The only thing missing was the drumroll.

"Ms. Brewster, please come in," Chief Drummond said.

In an out-of-breath voice with an underlying soft huskiness that wove into Sloan's mind like a lingering echo, she
said, "I apologize for being late, but I had to stop by Stems
'n Petals for a few minutes." As she spoke, she balanced the
toddler on one hip while she tried to untangle her purse from
where it had twisted behind her. The purse was a soft floppy
drawstring bag. A toy giraffe had been stuffed into the
gathered top.

Sloan had stepped back and, with all the commotion by
the door, knew she hadn't yet seen him. Scowling, he realized that he'd forgotten she owned a flower shop. He didn't
like forgetting details, but then his last experience with the
Harbor Bay florists had been Angela's funeral. The bouquets and wreaths from Angela's family, their friends and
his clients had been massive. Sloan recalled few of them except for the cascade of jasmine and tulips that had been
draped over the top of the casket. He'd had one hell of a
time getting the jasmine and tulips. Had she been one of the
florists he'd called? He closed his eyes for a moment, trying to think, wrestling uselessly with the thick dark past, but
he couldn't remember. The nightmare of those days remained a black hole.

Suddenly an overwhelming sense of being forced back
into the inky depths swept over him, and he had to stop
himself from bolting past the others and out of the station.

Despite his inner shudder, he made himself stay. It's just
the unexpected tie to the funeral, he rationalized. He'd been
unprepared, caught off guard. It probably wasn't her florist shop anyway.

Concentrate on the present.

Drummond was saying, "Would you like Sergeant Newman to take Danny? That way you can relax and have some
coffee."

She hesitated, and Drummond patted her shoulder as if
to reassure her the baby would be perfectly safe. The chief
added, "He'll be fine. There are some games and blocks we
keep for kids."

"I don't want him to be a bother. He's just beginning to
walk and doesn't like to sit still."

Drummond assured her that Danny wouldn't be a bother and again that he would be safe. Finally she nodded. But when she tried to hand Danny to him, the baby clutched at Katherine, his lower lip trembling. She raised apologetic eyes. "After the other night, he's been uneasy about anyone but me holding him. Perhaps I better keep him with me."

Newman appeared. "Hey, Danny! How 'bout we play some ball?"

Danny's eyes widened as the sergeant pushed the red beach ball down the hall toward where Katherine had kneeled down with the child. Newman made no attempt to pick Danny up, and, in fact, kept the emphasis on the red ball. After some coaxing, the one-year-old let go of Katherine, his chubby legs hesitant as he tested his walking ability. Then, apparently deciding he could get to the ball quicker by crawling, he fell to his hands and knees and scrambled toward the sergeant.

She watched for a few moments, obviously waiting to see if Danny would discover that he'd been seduced away from her. When she heard him squeal with laughter, Sloan saw her relax.

Turning to the chief, she asked, "Is it all right if I leave the door open in case he cries?"

"Of course," Drummond said as he urged her further into the office. Sloan took the few seconds before she saw him to assess her closely.

He knew she was thirty-two and still single. Apparently she'd dumped the fiancé after Sloan's report, which told Sloan she wasn't some pushover, or worse, took the attitude that if she loved the guy enough, she could change him. He found himself impressed by her good sense.

Sloan didn't need to be any expert on maternal instincts to know Katherine had them. Although Danny was her sister's son, Sloan saw a fierce determination in her manner that said she would do anything to keep Gerald Graham from trying to snatch him. No doubt that determination had been tuned sharply after finding Gerald in her apartment.

Before Drummond had a chance to make any introductions, Katherine glanced toward the shadowed corner where

Sloan stood. She blinked, tipping her head sideways in momentary confusion.

"Sloan? Sloan Calder?" Her voice was a strange mixture of surprise and curiosity. "What are you doing here? Chief Drummond didn't say anything about a private investigator." Coming a few steps closer to Sloan, she studied him as though trying to fill in the blanks.

Sloan met her gaze, telling himself her eyes weren't a spectacular amber color. "We're going to work together on this, Katherine."

"Together? I don't understand." She turned to Drummond, who was now sitting behind his desk. "Why is Sloan here?"

"Please have a seat, Ms. Brewster, and I'll explain."

She sank into a chair, obviously a little stunned by this turn of events. Her eyes darted back and forth between Drummond and Sloan, her body rigidly straight.

Watching her, sensing her questions, her uneasiness and no doubt a very real fear of Gerald Graham, Sloan realized the wisdom of nonrelationships with clients. If at any point in the past there had been something personal between himself and Katherine, he would have said no to Drummond based on a conflict of interest. Not because it would have made a difference as far as protecting the baby from Gerald Graham, but because Sloan wasn't stupid. Trying to maintain a business relationship *after* there'd been a personal one would be as insane and dangerous as combining business and pleasure. The women who'd hired Sloan had remained just that; clients with problems that required his services. No sexual or emotional involvement.

"I'm beginning to feel as if I'm caught in some sort of intrigue where I'm either the target or the only player who doesn't know the rules," Katherine said.

Drummond raised his eyebrows at her obvious savvy. For the first time since he'd entered the office, Sloan let the corners of his mouth lift in amusement. If Drummond had thought he was dealing with a pliable, ditzy female who needed pampering and stroking, he'd just learned differently.

* * *

Katherine placed her purse beside the chair closest to the door. She'd been unsure exactly what was going on from the moment Chief Drummond had called and asked her to come down to the station.

Her phone had just been repaired for Gerald had indeed cut the outside lines. How he'd gotten into the apartment was still a mystery, but then anyone who'd plan to the point of cutting phone lines probably knew how to break in without being too obvious about it. The police had come, looked around, asked a lot of questions and had said they'd investigate. That had been three days ago.

When Chief Drummond had summoned her, she'd assumed they had arrested Gerald and they needed her to identify him.

But when she'd seen Sloan, her puzzlement had quickly changed to astonishment.

If it hadn't been for the muscled leanness and his incredibly black hair, she might not have remembered him. The gray-green eyes that had been so sympathetic when she'd gone to him about Robert were now hard and devoid of warmth. A guarded distance that wasn't confined to just his eyes, but to his entire demeanor. Stress had carved deep lines around his mouth and his body language redefined the words restraint and reserve. The softest things about him were his clothes: the black denim jeans—beltless, snug and smooth from wear—gray cotton fatigue shirt with the sleeves pushed up to just below his elbows. His dark glasses hung on the shirt's placket, which was unbuttoned and exposed a nest of dark chest hair. Katherine stared despite the warning alarm in her mind.

What was she doing? she wondered frantically. This was no time to be thinking that she'd always found chest hair incredibly sexy. And it was certainly inappropriate to be thinking it in connection to Sloan Calder.

She redirected her thoughts to Danny and her responsibility for him. Glancing out the door to make sure her nephew was all right, she felt her heart fill with love, even as she reminded herself that Jennifer should be here.

Going to Australia to shoot photos for a national magazine was a huge break professionally for her younger sister, and Katherine was delighted for her. What didn't delight her was Jennifer's tendency to be irresponsible and depend, far too often, on Katherine to bail her out of some mess. Like taking the assignment first and then tearfully begging Katherine to keep Danny.

It wasn't keeping the baby that annoyed her, it was the assumption that her life was so routine, so uncomplicated, that baby-sitting wouldn't be a problem.

She'd been trying to reach Jennifer since Gerald's snatching attempt, was still trying. She'd left messages at her sister's hotel to return the call, but so far she'd heard nothing.

Deep down Katherine wasn't sure what her sister would do. Although she knew Jennifer loved Danny, Katherine felt her sister tended to view life the same way she took pictures: through a single lens. The relationship with Gerald had ended abruptly, but obviously Gerald didn't agree. Admittedly Katherine knew little about what had happened to cause their breakup and now damned herself for being so respectful of Jennifer's privacy. Now, however, given the snatching attempt a few nights ago, she had a lot of questions.

And that disturbed her, because the questions were about her sister as well as what had really happened with Gerald Graham.

Katherine glanced at Sloan.

He sat sprawled in one of the chairs, his long legs out straight, his booted feet crossed at the ankles. He watched her intensely and with what appeared to be a touch of curiosity. For no reason that made any sense, she suddenly felt a thread of kinship with him, but decided to dismiss the feeling. Just because he'd seen her at one of her worst moments—tearful and vulnerable over a man—and he hadn't patronizingly tried to offer her comfort, didn't mean they'd shared . . . My God, she'd seen him vulnerable, too. Had he forgotten? Chosen not to remember?

Not wishing to stir up bad memories just to find out, she diverted her train of thoughts. She lifted her chin, hoping she sounded firm and aggressive. "You were about to explain why Sloan is here, weren't you, Chief Drummond?"

The chief turned to Sloan, who shook his head. "This is all yours, Joe."

Drummond shifted in his chair, as if not sure whether to stand and pace or sit and explain. "The reason we asked you to come down here, Ms. Brewster, is to explain why we can't act on your complaint against Graham."

"Won't, Joe. Not can't," Sloan added.

Drummond scowled. "I'm explaining this, remember?"

Sloan said darkly, "Then make sure the facts are clear."

Katherine glanced from one to the other, sure she'd misunderstood. "You aren't going to arrest Gerald?"

"Not just yet," Drummond said. "However, we want to present a plan to you that will insure yours and Danny's safety in the meantime."

But Katherine's mind latched onto the first part of the statement. "I don't understand."

The chief gave her a bland smile. "I can't give you a lot of details because it's an ongoing investigation, but we're gathering evidence that connects Graham to some rather nasty people doing a lot of illegal activities. To bring him in for questioning on your complaint could make those people suspicious. It would do irreparable damage to our investigation."

Sloan rolled his eyes, "Good job, Joe. That was as clear as mud."

Katherine thought it was deliberately evasive. "In other words, you're telling me that Danny being kidnapped is less important than Gerald's connection to another investigation?"

The chief obviously hadn't expected her to catch on so quickly. Clearing his throat, he mumbled, "It's more a matter of timing, Ms. Brewster."

"Timing? You're not serious. Gerald was in my apartment. *In Danny's room.* What possible connection to another investigation could be more important than a baby being snatched?"

"I'm sorry, I'm not at liberty..." Drummond looked stricken. "I know I sound callous, and believe me that isn't my intent. Of course the police are concerned about Danny..." He dragged a hand down his face. "We're working as fast as we can. We've tried to make this as painless as possible for you by hiring Sloan."

Katherine blinked. "Hiring Sloan?" She'd hired Sloan to follow Robert. "Did you hire him to watch Gerald?" Drummond looked confused for a moment, but she rushed on. "Is that what is supposed to make this painless for me? Sloan watching Gerald? And what if something goes wrong? What if Sloan makes a mistake and Gerald gets away?"

She glanced in Sloan's direction in time to see the color drain from his face. "See," she added, "even Sloan acknowledges that's a possibility. Gerald snatches Danny and runs off to God knows where. Then the police put Danny on a priority list. Is that what you're telling me? First the crime has to be committed and *then* the police do something?"

"Let me assure you, Ms. Brewster," Drummond said in a calming voice, "We aren't minimizing the danger."

She glanced at Sloan again. He looked decidedly uncomfortable, but he kept silent. Katherine turned her attention back to Drummond. "Of course you're minimizing the danger. Or perhaps I'm still too idealistic. I thought the police were supposed to help people, not tell them that their complaint isn't important enough to act on." She knew she sounded frantic and impatient, but since Danny's safety was the issue, she didn't much care about their opinion of her.

Drummond looked at Sloan, who still hadn't moved.

Katherine had had enough. She got up and went to the chair by the office door. Lifting her purse and swinging it onto her shoulder, she turned to Sloan, her frustration plainly visible. "And what have you learned about Gerald, Sloan? Did you peer in his windows or follow him down some dark alleys? Did you write a detailed report from which the police have concluded that arresting Gerald isn't as important as some other investigation?"

She didn't wait for an answer, because she didn't want to hear the truth. For no reason that was easily explainable, she wanted Sloan on her side. The moment she'd seen him, a part of her had breathed a sigh of relief. She knew he was one of the best private investigators in the state and had no doubts he would do his best to keep close tabs on Gerald. But what if he didn't? What if something went wrong? In her opinion Gerald should be locked up, not allowed to run free as if all he'd done was break into her apartment to borrow a cup of sugar.

Perhaps she would just pack Danny up and go somewhere. Going into hiding sounded overly dramatic, but realistically that would be what she had to do. She pulled open the door.

"Wait! Please, Ms. Brewster!" Drummond came out of his chair quickly, rounding the desk to stand in the doorway and block her exit.

Sloan came to his feet and was across the room instantly, his hand on Drummond's wrist.

"She can't leave, Sloan."

"Yeah, she can."

Drummond stared hard. "You know damn well what's at stake."

"I also know you're walking a thin line when it comes to regulations. She's got choices and she can choose to tell you what to do with the plan the department has come up with."

"Then do something," Drummond urged. "You said this wouldn't be a problem for you." He took a long shaky breath, as if to say more, but changed his mind.

Sloan's eyes had darkened to a deep stormy green. "Back off, Joe. If you were seriously worried about my part in this you never would have hired me. This is Katherine's call and *her* decision."

Katherine looked from one to the other, suddenly aware that the conversation was no longer about Gerald snatching Danny. "What's going on?"

Neither answered her, but there was no doubt as to where the shift in power had gone. Drummond seemed to shrink a little before her eyes.

"My apologies, Ms. Brewster. Sloan's right. You have every right to leave," Drummond said.

But Katherine didn't leave. Instead her eyes followed Sloan as he walked over to the window and stood with his back to her. He braced one hand high on the wall and even though a few feet separated them, Katherine could still feel the rawness of his fury at the chief.

In a voice that could have turned water to ice, Sloan said, "Spell it out for her, Joe. I want her absolutely sure and absolutely clear on what in hell she's getting into."

Drummond walked back to his desk and sat down in his chair as though exhausted. "Arrangements have been made to protect you and Danny. You'll be going to a safe house on Cape Cod until we finish up this investigation and arrest Graham. Sloan is going with you." He paused and drew in a long breath. "To make sure the cover is secure and that the three of you won't raise any needless questions for the next few weeks, you'll be posing as Mr. and Mrs. Calder and their son Danny."

Chapter 2

Two hours later, in the living room of her apartment, Katherine settled Danny in the playpen. She watched the baby drag his blanket up to his face and rub the satiny blue edge against his cheek.

She wished there was some tactile thing she could take comfort from. Or better yet, something substantial such as someone telling her the entire truth. When it had happened, she hadn't pressed her sister as to why she'd broken off with Gerald because she'd respected Jennifer's right to privacy. Katherine knew that sense of mortification; she'd dealt with it herself after she'd learned Robert had cheated on her. Now, however, given her own terrifying encounter with Gerald, Katherine decided the better question was why her sister had gotten involved in the first place.

Now the police were being evasive because of some mysterious investigation they refused to explain and yet they expected her to simply accept their premise that they couldn't arrest Gerald.

And even if she hadn't sensed it, Sloan's attitude had convinced her that this wasn't standard police procedure.

But then again, she thought with a deepening frown, he hadn't been very forthcoming with information, either.

Surely he knew why the police had hired him—the details behind the stall. Admittedly she didn't know Sloan all that well, but from the way he'd acted in Drummond's office, she doubted he'd allow himself to be hired as a fake husband and father without valid and clearly defined reasons.

Katherine readily acknowledged that it was disconcerting, the thought of having a man hired to be her husband, but perhaps it was the police chief's assumption that she'd entrust herself to someone just because she was told to, that rankled so much. Yet keeping Gerald from snatching Danny was an out-of-the-ordinary circumstance, she reminded herself.

Suddenly chilled, she tried to rub warmth into her arms. Goose bumps of fear, she'd begun calling the too familiar reaction to her apartment. No longer did she enjoy the coziness, the artfully combined shades of green and blue, the furnishings that she'd chosen individually and with care since she'd found the converted Victorian home. Now, because of her frightening encounter with Gerald, nothing here held any pleasure. All she felt was an ominous sense of violation, of breached privacy, and a deep anger that showed little sign of lessening.

She'd tried to act normal and upbeat with Danny. Yet she couldn't help but wonder if the child sensed the ruse. His difficulty in sleeping since the attempted kidnapping concerned her, although she wasn't surprised. Gerald had come out of the dark like some looming monster and had invaded Danny's very secure world. Katherine could only imagine what horrors and fears the baby's limited understanding must now attach to that night.

A few days ago Katherine had moved the crib into her bedroom to reassure and soothe Danny, but also for her own peace of mind. Letting Danny out of her sight terrified her as much as his bedroom terrified him.

Quietly she went into the kitchen. Through the locked screen door came a light breeze from the side yard.

Shaded by poplar trees, a lone rabbit headed for a neighbor's newly planted vegetable garden. Katherine watched for a moment, thinking that by the following summer Danny would be old enough for a sandbox. She closed her eyes and took an unsteady breath. God, she hoped that whatever the police had on Gerald they got the evidence to make it stick.

Closing the door, she glanced at the baby. Earlier she'd positioned the playpen so she could see Danny clearly and now she noted that he was fast asleep.

Katherine sighed longingly, aware that the fear—both hers and his—manifested itself the most strongly when she was home. And that created a problem. Should she move to a new apartment? Where wasn't a question as much as whether relocating would keep them safe with Gerald still running around loose or if she stayed here she could hire a bodyguard. Surely the fact that the police had made no attempt to contact Gerald for questioning would make him bold enough to try snatching Danny again.

She fixed herself a glass of iced tea, sat on one of the counter stools and sipped thoughtfully. Since that night, she'd been trying to get in touch with Jennifer for some answers about Gerald. At this point any explanation for his behavior would be welcome.

Deciding to make another attempt, Katherine pushed her glass aside and reached for the receiver. She contacted the overseas operator and gave her the number of Jennifer's hotel in Australia. "I'd like to make a person-to-person call to Jennifer Brewster."

She waited while all the connections were made and the operator spoke to the desk clerk at the hotel.

After the hotel rang Jennifer's room without getting an answer, then paged her with no results, Katherine told the operator, "I'll just speak to the desk clerk."

The desk clerk came on the line. "Ms. Brewster isn't in the hotel. Can we give her a message?"

"This is her sister and I've left numerous messages the past few days. Do you know if she's received them?"

"Just one moment." A minute or so later, he was back on the line. "Yes, she did get the messages and she's left one here for you."

In her earlier attempts to call Jennifer, Katherine hadn't been specific simply because leaving a message that Gerald had tried to kidnap Danny would be terrifying. She did, however, feel that despite Jennifer being half a world away, she should know. Katherine knew if it were her, she'd be on the next plane home. Her hope that her sister would do the same thing wasn't the issue as much as reassuring Jennifer that the police had been called and that Danny and she were fine.

"Ms. Brewster said to tell you that she and a guide have gone to the outback. She mentions photos for her assignment. She expects to be back here at the hotel by the end of next week. She said she'll call you then."

Katherine sighed. At the moment the end of next week was as far away as Australia. "She didn't leave any way for me to get in touch with her, did she?"

"No, ma'am."

She hung up the phone, frustrated. "Damn it, Jennifer, why couldn't you have taken a few minutes and called?"

The phone rang just as she'd lifted her hand away; the shrill bell made her jump. She grabbed for the receiver before the ringing awakened Danny. "Hello?"

No response.

"Hello?" she asked again.

Still no response, but the line was definitely open; she could hear voices in the distance.

Katherine swallowed, stopped herself from saying anything and waited. It seemed like minutes—though she knew it could only be seconds—and then she heard a shuffling noise. The sound was chillingly familiar. Gerald had made a shuffling noise...

Her pulse threatened to leap from her wrist. She gripped the receiver as though squeezing it would produce sound. "Hello!" she said in a near shout.

"Katherine, for God's sake, you almost broke my eardrum." The offhand tone of the male voice that definitely wasn't Gerald's drenched her with relief.

She loosened her hold and frowned. "Who is this?"

"Sloan. I'm on my way over and I wanted to be sure you were home."

Her heart raced and she wasn't sure if it was anger at him for scaring her or disgust at herself for overreacting. At this rate she'd be a basket case. "Damn you!" Katherine snapped. "Why didn't you say something when I answered the phone?"

Her angry question didn't seem to faze him. "Someone came to my office door. I put the phone down to see who it was. I didn't expect you to answer on the first ring."

"I thought..." She could feel tears gather at the corners of her eyes. *A phone call,* just an ordinary phone call and yet her nerves felt more jangled than that night she'd discovered Gerald in her apartment. Was this some harbinger of what was to come? Would she and Danny have to endure this hovering sense of danger until Gerald was locked away?

Sloan's voice was suddenly gentle. "You thought I was Gerald, didn't you?"

"Oh, God," she whispered, her throat strained and raw.

"Katherine, it's all right," he said, using the same soft tone he'd used the day he'd told her Robert had been cheating on her. She could easily picture Sloan—sitting on the corner of his desk, his head bent as though what he had to say was for her ears only. "Your reaction is understandable. You've been through a hellish nightmare. I should have waited until you answered and then gone to the door."

She swallowed. His words soothed, connecting her to him as if he were some cord of safety. "Yes, you should have," she said, still too shaky to just let it pass.

"As I started to say, I'm on my way over. We have some plans to make."

"I'm thinking about not doing this," she said, her earlier misgivings returning. In truth, she'd made no such decision, but talking to Sloan gave her the courage to verbally test the idea. She would simply be honest and confess that the lack of information about Gerald disturbed her. Certainly Sloan would understand her hesitation in simply going to the Cape without knowing any more than just a few vague facts.

At the ensuing silence from Sloan, she realized that a definite refusal might just get her more details about why they would arrest Gerald.

"Sloan?"

"I heard you."

"I thought I could possibly..."

"Forget it."

"You don't even know what I was going to say."

"We'll discuss it when I get there."

"There is nothing to discuss if I decide—" She was talking to a dial tone. "Damn," she muttered. They hadn't spent more than those moments at the police station together and already he was taking over. Peevishly, she wondered if his cavalier attitude was in direct proportion to the money the police were paying him. A hired husband, she thought grimly, had all the appeal of a real ball and chain.

She hooked the receiver none too gently, her spirits sagging. And what, pray tell, would she do? Stay here and endure her goose bumps of fear for God knew how long? And just the fact that Gerald hadn't made another kidnapping attempt, rather than easing her mind, made her nervous. Was he waiting for the right moment? One where she'd be the least suspicious? Or was he setting up some scenario to distract her while someone else snatched Danny?

Stop it, she warned herself. Think about solutions instead of potential problems. She could take some time off from Stems 'n Petals and go to see her parents in Arizona, perhaps leave Danny with them while she came back here and looked for another apartment. But what if Gerald followed her? What if he waited until she'd left Danny and then made his move? Could she risk Danny's life that way? Or, for that matter, bring such problems to her parents' doorstep?

She massaged her fingers into her temples, trying to relieve the growing tension. Her options weren't very reassuring. But then again, until Gerald was out of the picture or decided he didn't want Danny, did it really matter where she went?

Sloan arrived in less than half an hour.

"Looks like a nice day for traveling," he said by way of greeting when she opened her door. He stepped inside, and Katherine, immediately struck by her reaction to him, let her hand drop from the doorknob, moving back a step.

Being close to him here in the coolness of her apartment didn't seem to fit. Unlike any of the men she'd ever known, he exuded laid-back authority, even wearing leather and denim. Since Robert, and her sister's debacle with Gerald, Katherine freely admitted she was less than willing to trust any man who wasn't completely open. She liked to know what to expect and what was expected of her.

The fluttery sensation that now slipped delicately into her womb had to be something other than a too curious reaction to Sloan Calder. The man embodied every reason she could think of to be wary. And trust? If ever a man was more closed off and distant—not exactly attributes that embodied trust—Sloan Calder had perfected them both.

Fluttery, curious sensations indeed! The situation and the events of the past few days were too serious for that kind of silly reaction. Besides, Sloan was a total contrast to the men she felt comfortable with. Men with open smiles and kind eyes who dressed in suits and ties, certainly not a black-haired man in tight faded jeans and a black leather jacket. Not exactly an advertisement for total trust.

She took a deep breath, too aware of the sensation widening from fluttery to disturbing and settling deep. Dispassionately, or so she hoped, she said, "From the way you're dressed, I'm surprised my neighbors didn't call the police."

He gave her the barest of grins. "Us hired-for-cash types have to dress the part."

"You had to remind me, didn't you?"

"Reassurance, Katy. This way we dispel any misgivings you might be having."

"Misgivings about what?" she asked, telling herself that the way he said Katy sounded only friendly. At his steady look, she realized quickly what he meant. "You mean about going away with you? You thought that my comment on the phone about not going was because I might be afraid of you?"

"It crossed my mind."

"I know how professional you are, Sloan. I checked you out thoroughly before I went to you about Robert. And certainly the police hiring you is an excellent reminder of that professionalism. But Gerald has not been arrested and no one seems to think that telling me why, beyond a few vague references to some other investigation, is not reassuring.''

''And the more you've thought about it, the more you've decided you want some answers,'' he said, as if relieved he wasn't the cause of her hesitation.

''Yes.''

A waiting silence fell between them and although Katherine seriously doubted he'd simply tell her everything, she found herself viewing her situation with odd reasoning. Certainly she wanted only professionalism from Sloan, but she couldn't deny that a personal awareness had slipped into her thoughts. However fleeting and illogical, she'd basked in her sensory reaction to Sloan.

From his jacket pocket he drew out a small package and handed it to her. ''This is for Danny. Since there's a beach near the cottage I thought we could take him down there to play.''

Wrapped in the see-through plastic was a deflated red beach ball similar to the one Danny had enjoyed at the police station.

Katherine was somewhat taken aback by the gesture. ''How thoughtful, Sloan. Danny will love the ball.''

''Yeah, I thought he might.'' Sloan had stepped around her and was looking closely at the apartment. She'd moved the sleeping Danny to his crib in her room so as not to disturb him when Sloan arrived.

Katherine clasped her hands together as Sloan examined the windows and went into the kitchen, where she heard him open and close the back door.

He returned and stood for a moment, as if trying to piece together how Gerald had gotten inside. Despite his having said nothing to her, she felt as if she was about to be interrogated. Even the police hadn't made her so tense. No, she realized, it wasn't the potential questions Sloan might ask, it was the man himself.

He motioned toward Danny's empty room and she quickly explained that she'd moved the crib to her room and why.

"Any ideas on how Graham got in here?" His eyes studied hers and she found the probing sensation so unnerving she had to look away.

"None. I didn't find anything broken nor did the police."

"How about the obvious?"

"I don't know what you mean."

"Does he have a key?" he asked matter-of-factly.

Her attempt to relax vanished. "A key!"

He continued to watch her, one eyebrow coolly lifting at her outrage. "I assume that means he doesn't, or at the very least, you don't think he does."

"You have a hell of a lot of nerve," she said, planting her hands on her hips. His comment made her sound like some ditzy female who didn't even know who had keys to her home. "Gerald Graham does not, nor has he ever had, a key to my apartment."

Sloan, however, seemed unaffected by her snappishness. In fact the level of his voice didn't change at all. "Your sister lives here, doesn't she? And Graham *is* Danny's father, isn't he? It's not so off-the-wall that she might have given him a key."

"It's not only off-the-wall, it's preposterous. Jennifer hates Gerald. She wants nothing to do with him and told me explicitly that she doesn't want him near Danny." Katherine turned away, feeling as if she were skating on the edge of hysteria. She hadn't been this overwrought at the police station, nor had she been when the police came after Gerald had fled.

She felt Sloan behind her, though he didn't touch her. She shivered, her reaction coming from the closeness of this man in contrast to the terrifying encounter in this very room with Gerald. Mistrust, she suddenly realized, had many sides. What she felt with Sloan was an entirely different type of danger.

"Katherine, I'm not accusing you of anything or blaming you, but it's hard to believe your sister wouldn't have told you something more concrete about why she ended the relationship with Graham. Hate stems from some strong motives. Since I don't know Jennifer, I have to assume that she knows a lot more about Danny's father than she wants to tell you.''

She turned then, his words bringing out into the open her own doubts about Jennifer's reasons for refusing to talk about Gerald. Doubts and questions she'd wrestled with since the night of the kidnapping. Unnerving and disturbing, for in less than five minutes Sloan had figured out what Katherine had taken weeks to conclude. What she didn't know about Gerald was suddenly ten times more important than what she did know.

''I respect my sister's right to privacy,'' she said, grasping for some defense. ''Just as she respects mine.''

Sloan gave her an incredulous look. ''You mean you never told her about Robert?''

Katherine had, but only the barest of details. At the time she had ended her relationship with Robert, Jennifer had only just met Gerald and Katherine hadn't wanted to dump her own problems on her sister. Sloan was the only one who knew the entire story. Ruefully, she realized the irony in Sloan being the one who'd uncovered Robert's secrets and now here he was again, dealing with even more perplexing and, Katherine feared, more dangerous secrets.

She felt exposed and it made her uncomfortable. ''I told her I broke it off with him.''

''But you didn't give her any details.''

''Some, but most of them were disgusting and humiliating. I didn't want anyone to know how foolish and stupid I'd been.''

That was when he touched her. Just a brush of his fingers across her cheek. She watched his eyes, the gray-green so compellingly honest, she drew a breath.

In a low voice he said, ''Ah, Katy, if we could only undo the foolish and stupid things we do.'' Then, clearing his throat and stepping back, as if his words pointed to some personal self-exposure, he added, ''Perhaps your sister felt stupid, too. Maybe she had a similar humiliating and disgusting experience with Gerald.''

Katherine wanted to ask him what stupid and foolish things he'd done, but reminded herself he wasn't here for that. His observation about Jennifer, though, was revealing.

She'd never thought of Jennifer as being plagued by disgusting details or caught in a humiliating situation; just messy and reckless ones. Her own blindness to what Robert had been up to for so long had just been too horrible to share. Besides, Jennifer had always been the one who needed support or bailing out of those messy and reckless situations. Katherine had simply followed the pattern of habit. She'd been a big sister with a sympathetic ear, while her own difficulties remained private and personal.

She sighed. No doubt, she assured herself, she hadn't pressed Jennifer about Gerald because she had hoped her sister's vagueness was a sign of late-arriving maturity, or of her taking personal responsibility for her actions.

To Sloan, she said, "If I ever get in touch with her, I intend to get some straight answers about Gerald. You know she's in Australia on a photo assignment, don't you?"

"Yeah, Drummond filled me in."

"I wish you'd fill me in on why Gerald can't be arrested."

He shrugged out of his jacket and tossed it onto her couch. Moving back to stand beside her, he slipped an arm around her neck and bent to whisper in her ear. "When we get to the Cape I'll answer your questions."

She was so startled by his sudden closeness and familiarity that she didn't move. He smelled deliciously sexy and she had to clear her throat before she spoke. "Promise me?"

"Yes," he murmured.

The whispery sound of their voices made the exchange seem intimate and fraught with meaning. She should be stepping away from him, she told herself urgently but found herself a little off balance from the sudden change in his attitude, the lazy sensuality in his tone.

Feeling a little bold and more relaxed than she had since before the attempted snatching, Katherine didn't protest when he took her arm and slipped it around his waist.

She wasn't aware of the two figures hovering just outside the slightly open door. The Irwin sisters, both widows in their mid-sixties, smiled with the benevolent certainty that true love does indeed happen at the most unexpected times.

In a hushed voice one said, "How lovely."

In an equally hushed voice, the other agreed, adding, "And how romantic."

Katherine's back was to the door when suddenly Sloan tugged her fully into his arms. When she began to fight the intimacy, he murmured, "Go along with me, Katy. Don't resist." Astonished, she had barely formed her protest when he fit their bodies together and pressed one hand against the small of her back. "Easy, sweets, this won't hurt a bit."

His words sizzled along her spine so that she could scarcely breathe. Her heart had gotten lost somewhere between her breasts and his chest. She felt him comfortably nestled against her stomach. Her instinct to come up on tiptoes so that he could press deep into her was so natural it stunned her. Fighting her response, she tipped her head back to protest his strange actions. Hadn't he just reassured her that she needn't fear any intimacy between them? When his mouth descended, her eyes widened.

"Sloan...?" My God, he really intended to kiss her. But the why and the surprise were swirling away...

"That's it, sweets. Play along with me. Open your mouth just a little more...."

"But you can't kiss me...not that way...we don't know each other..." His mouth consumed her protests. Katherine simply went limp with astonishment. What was so incredible was that he managed to make the kiss both tantalizingly intimate and yet not forced upon her. If she'd shoved him hard enough, he would have released her. Then why wasn't she resisting? Why, instead, were her arms sliding up and around his neck as if this moment, this man, this flawless mastery of her mouth, was all that mattered?

She should at the very least be suspicious. She didn't trust men who said one thing and did another. He'd said no intimacies, yet not only was she allowing him these liberties, she was participating, liking it, wanting it....

She slipped her fingers into the thick hair at his nape, drawing his head closer, his mouth deeper, tasting him, exploring textures with a hunger that had no basis except in the quickening sensation the mating of their tongues produced. Pleasure danced and skimmed, finding a mutual rhythm, a simmering, a tantalizing sweetness.

His hands moved up to her neck, cupping it, and his thumbs stroked her jaw and her chin, easing her mouth away. When she opened her eyes, his were heavy-lidded, aroused and darkened with something else. The taste and the feel of him so rocked her senses she had to grasp at her rambling thoughts. Something else was in his eyes. Regret? Concern? Denial?

And she should be doing something. Pushing him away. Demanding an explanation.

"Maybe this was a bad idea," Sloan muttered even while he drew her close again. She went simply because her knees felt numb and tingly. She agreed, it had been a bad idea. But what she wanted to know was why he'd initiated it in the first place. And she was about to ask him just that when she heard a giggle behind her.

She jumped and Sloan tightened his arms.

"Come in, ladies," he said in a cordial voice. Katherine tried to pull away, but Sloan kept her close.

Marion Irwin gushed with the enthusiasm of a mother of the bride. "Why, I do declare, Mr. Calder, you were right. Isn't it wonderful, Nina?"

Nina, the smaller of the two women and a pure romantic, gave Katherine a hurt look. "Katherine Brewster, why didn't you tell us? Why this is so exciting! At first we didn't believe Mr. Calder, but we know you're much too sensible to take Danny and go away with a man unless it was very serious. Marion and I feel honored to be the first to know."

Katherine paled, confused and annoyed at the embarrassing position Sloan had put her in. She glared at him just long enough to let him know that she'd deal with him when they were once again alone. At the moment, dispelling her neighbors' conclusions—whatever they were—was more important.

Again, she tried to push him away, but he held her fast, his wrist so close to the lobe of her ear that she could hear the ticking of his watch.

"What did you tell them?" she whispered, wishing she'd never let him put her arm around him. It didn't help any that she couldn't lay all the blame on Sloan for their closeness; she hadn't been exactly passive.

"About us, sweets."

Her thoughts dominoed. "About us? What about us?" She was certain her heartbeat was louder than the volume of her voice. Could he hear it?

He eased his hold on her, apparently assuming she would simply do as she was told. He drew her forward, speaking loud enough to include the two women. "I know you wanted to wait until Jennifer got back, but I didn't want Marion and Nina thinking I was another kidnapper."

He kept referring to her neighbors as if he knew them, but then, hadn't they called him by name? "Damn it, Sloan..." she warned.

He quickly bent his head and brushed his mouth across hers, effectively stopping her question. "I told them about us out in the yard when I drove up. They were peering at me very suspiciously."

"I don't doubt it," she said ruefully, recalling her own comment about the neighbors calling the police when he'd arrived.

Marion's eyes sparkled. "Sloan is just the kind of man you need, Katherine. Why if Gerald tried to even get close to that baby..." She shuddered. "We just know Sloan would..." Marion paused and frowned as if unsure what Sloan would do. "Well, whatever he would do, it would be effective."

Katherine rolled her eyes. My God, she thought, one would think Sloan had some secret power. Both Marion and Nina were like mother hens to Jennifer and Katherine. Sloan's charm had to have been extensive and his story convincing for the two of them to be so wholly in favor of him.

"We know you're leaving shortly, but we'd love to celebrate your engagement. We have a bottle of champagne we've been saving for a special occasion...."

"And that lovely cheese," Nina added.

"With the butter crackers. Oh, this is such fun. An engagement party...and your ring, Katherine." Marion's gaze dropped to where Katherine's left hand was trapped and hidden against Sloan's waist. Suddenly she was not only aware of the nonexistent ring, but too conscious of how hard and lean his body felt. Marion continued, "When we come back you'll have to show us your ring...." Her voice trailed off as the two women hurried up the staircase to their own apartment, chattering as they went.

Sloan let go of her so fast she almost lost her balance. "I apologize," he said, dropping all pretense that he'd enjoyed touching her. "I didn't realize the kiss would get so complicated."

She'd been prepared for him to say something cute or even provocative, but his sudden change in manner disarmed her. "Was it necessary to tell them we were engaged?"

He rubbed one hand along the back of his neck as if the muscles were cramped. "It's important that we seem normal and natural not just to our neighbors on the Cape, but here, too. Obviously I couldn't tell them the real reason you were going away with me."

"Why did you feel the need to tell them anything? I'm an adult. I hardly need the neighbors' approval to take Danny and go away for a few weeks."

He glanced at her as if waiting for her to answer her own question. When she didn't, he said, "They're very protective of you and Danny. Outside they asked who I was and what I wanted. Since being married is the plan, I just added the requisite engagement."

"But they've never seen you. Why would they believe you?"

"I don't think they did," he said sagely. "That's why when I heard them at the door I kissed you. I knew they'd believe you. From what they said about you, I figured if they saw us in that intimate an embrace they'd draw their own conclusions."

Katherine scowled. "What did they say about me?"

"Never mind," he said dismissively.

She was in no mood to be coddled. "Look, I've got enough unanswered questions. What did they say?"

He peered at her as if he expected her to withdraw the question. When she lifted her chin and stared back, he turned away and said, "They think you're afraid to trust men and that you spend too much time alone."

Katherine was stunned, not at what Marion and Nina had said, but that they'd told Sloan. "And you've assured them you're going to change all that," she said, feeling as if he knew too much about her. Already he knew more about Robert than anyone, and now this.

He swore succinctly and even a brief glance at his face revealed he wasn't pleased by the direction of the conversation. "I thought I was solving a problem before it became one. My motive wasn't complicated. If you have a reasonable and logical explanation for going away with me, they won't ask questions or get suspicious. Having this temporary arrangement spooked because two well-intentioned old ladies get nosy about you and me would be a disaster."

Whether it was his obvious discomfort at the scenario's complications that prompted her, or her own curiosity as to just how this would all play out, she folded her arms across her chest and gave him an inquiring look. "Well, you certainly were right about things getting complicated." She glanced down at her naked left hand. "I can't wait to hear your explanation for me not having an engagement ring."

"I'll tell them we're still looking," he growled, obviously not having thought of a ring. "The complications I was talking about don't involve the engagement." He dragged a hand through his hair and walked over to stare out the windows.

Suddenly Katherine wasn't sure she wanted to know, nor was she sure she even dared ask.

"The kiss, Katy." He paused, drawing a long breath. "French-kissing was a mistake."

She swallowed, still able to taste him.

He turned slowly, not coming toward her, not giving her any sense of what he was really thinking. "I take full responsibility for it," he said in a low and obviously annoyed-with-himself voice.

She had participated, not even to him could she deny that. "Maybe we both just overreacted. You know, got caught in the moment?"

He arched an eyebrow at that. "Yeah, right," he said succinctly, and she knew he didn't believe her explanation any more than she did. "You kiss too hot, Katy."

She felt her stomach plummet to the floor. "So do you," she whispered with an automatic honesty. Her ears were suddenly acute to sound, her body tense and sensitive. How could she have kissed him so easily, so naturally? A door closed upstairs and she knew Marion and Nina were returning.

"What a helluva mess," Sloan murmured.

She felt a kind of softening toward him. He wasn't making any assumptions, and his obvious annoyance at the impact of the kiss reassured her. He wouldn't take her participation as a sign she wanted more from him. And she didn't, she assured herself fervently. The threat to Danny was enough to deal with.

Feeling more confident, she said, "Sloan, we're adults. We're certainly not so out of control that one too intimate kiss will destroy a prearranged relationship."

He gave her a long, steady look that made her pulse quicken. Coming close to her, he stared at her mouth for a heated moment and then cupped her chin. "Don't deceive yourself, Katy. Prearranged relationship or fake roles as husband and wife, that kiss has the potential for real problems."

Like more kisses, like touching, like making love? She felt suddenly dizzy. To deny the tension between them would be foolish. "So what are we going to do?"

"The only thing we can do," he said in an even voice. "We make damn sure it doesn't happen again."

Chapter 3

Sloan hadn't expected her to return the kiss.

Now, hours later and many miles from Harbor Bay, and despite the champagne, the texture and taste of her tongue lingered. All too deeply, Sloan realized. What should have been an insignificant kiss had raised myriad sensations.

He'd expected resistance, perhaps surprise, even astonishment. Yet he'd been stunned by the heat she'd caused and the gut-deep knowledge that if he wasn't very careful of any future "intimate" gestures, they would have a hell of a lot more to deal with on Cape Cod than hiding from Gerald Graham.

Sloan glanced over to the passenger side where Katherine had curled up and fallen asleep. Danny slept securely strapped in the rear car seat. After the Irwin sisters had returned with champagne and snacks and they'd all toasted the engagement, the two women had insisted on helping Katherine pack. Sloan had kept an eye on Danny, grateful to have the women around, as it spared him from any private and awkward moments.

Not entirely logical, he decided, since he was about to spend weeks playing the role of her husband. Although the fake marriage was Drummond's idea, Sloan had to take full responsibility for the phony engagement. He did take some consolation in the convincing act they'd put on for Marion and Nina Irwin. Too damn convincing, he decided ruefully.

He slowed the car to look for the landmarks Drummond had mentioned. Cape Cod curved like a giant scorpion's tail out into the Atlantic from southeastern Massachusetts. Dotted with resort towns and quaint villages, Sloan knew many of the Cape's back roads wound through wooded areas and twisted through populated locations without benefit of clear signs. He brought the car to a halt just outside a rotary that had five roads spoking off in different directions. Facing Sloan now, erected in the grassy center of the rotary, was an archaic signpost. Each white-painted wooden slat had one end shaved to an arrow point to indicate the direction for more than a dozen towns. Sloan skimmed the names, looking for Chelsea Beach.

Midnight approached. Here off the main roads, the houses were dark and he hadn't seen another car for miles. Of course, if Chelsea Beach had been close to the tourist towns of Hyannisport or Barnstable, getting lost would be almost impossible. Here, however, down narrow roads with few street lamps and obviously an early-to-bed way of life, Sloan knew a wrong turn could have them wandering around for hours. His own fatigue was setting in and he wasn't interested in more hours of driving.

"Sloan . . . ?" Katherine sat up, rubbing her eyes and pushing her fingers through her hair. "Where are we?"

"I hope not about to get lost." He finally located the weather-beaten Chelsea Beach marker painted in faded black letters. "We're about five miles from Chelsea Beach. How are you feeling?"

"Cramped and hungry." She stretched and straightened her clothes. "Butter crackers, cheese and champagne aren't high on my choices for dinner. And you must be starved. You barely ate anything."

"I wanted to get going." Actually, he disliked champagne and his appetite had been nonexistent. He'd felt decidedly uncomfortable over the engagement farce. What had begun as a simple explanation for Katherine and Danny going with him had taken too dangerous a turn the moment he'd kissed her.

She released the catch on her seat belt, and stretched again. "I didn't mean to go to sleep on you, but I didn't realize how tired I was. I have to blame it on not being in the apartment. Danny and I haven't slept well since Gerald..." She visibly drew a long shuddering breath, and Sloan felt a sense of satisfaction that she felt safe with him. He wished he felt as safe with himself, enough so that his determination not to repeat the kiss could be guaranteed.

"How's Danny doing?" Refastening her seat belt, she turned around to check.

"He's been asleep since we crossed the Bourne Bridge." Sloan slowed down, read a sign and took a left turn. Katherine patted Danny and then settled back in the seat. She'd changed from the skirt and blouse she'd worn to jeans and a red flowered knit top that wasn't tight, but Sloan had noted before they left her apartment that the top very definitely defined her breasts. Breasts that he'd felt pressed against him during that kiss...

Damn, he thought in disgust. One lousy kiss shouldn't be that memorable. And never had he felt the need to tell any woman that a kiss wouldn't happen again. Grimly, he wondered if his promise was to reassure her or to deny his own reaction.

He reminded himself that *not* breaking promises was his one virtue in a life of too many vices. For the next few weeks, he would need all the virtue he could muster.

Katherine rubbed her arms and folded them against her body with a shiver. The night air was damp from the ocean breeze. Rather than roll up his window—he needed the air to stay alert—Sloan reached behind him and felt around for his gray fatigue shirt. He'd changed into a lighter-weight one when he was loading the car.

"Here, put this on."

She started to reach for it and then quickly drew her hand back. She looked away and shook her head. "I'm all right."

Sloan frowned. "You're cold. Put it on."

"No, really. I'll be warm in a few minutes."

He told himself that if she was too stubborn to wear his shirt then to hell with it. If she wanted to be arbitrary then fine. He drove for a few more minutes, the shirt in a clump between them on the seat. He knew he could roll up his window and solve the problem, but he didn't. Male ego, perhaps, but he wanted her to accept the shirt because he'd offered it, not shake her head and shiver as if putting it on represented some intimate bond rather than mere temporary warmth.

He waited another few minutes for her to change her mind and when she didn't, he swore under his breath and slowed down. Easing the car onto the road's shoulder, he brought the vehicle to a stop.

Her eyes widened. "What are you doing?"

Instead of answering, he braced his back against the driver's door and hoped his face was sufficiently shadowed by the darkness. The gray shirt lay like a crucial turning point between them. He knew he was making an issue out of a nonissue, but her refusal to accept the obvious warmth the shirt would give her bothered him. He wanted her to feel as at ease about wearing his shirt as she did about going to sleep just a few feet away from him.

Katherine stared at the shirt as if it spelled out their relationship in the coming weeks. "You can't make me wear the shirt, Sloan."

"Yeah, sweets, I can. I can put it on you and you damn well know it."

"Proving what? That you're stronger than I am?"

"I don't have to prove that. I am stronger."

"Then what?"

He watched the way she rubbed her lips together, his mind deliberately skirting what he really wanted to do. He knew that even though she'd said she trusted him, she didn't. And he wanted to prove that he had no intention of reading any complicated meaning into her wearing his shirt. He should have said either or both aloud, but instead he kept his voice as devoid of emotion as he could. "It will prove that if you put it on you'll be warm. Not complex and not difficult."

"I'm not used to men telling me what to do."

"Ah, now we get to the crux of the problem. Given a choice between being cold or doing what a man tells you, you'll choose cold," he said as if suddenly enlightened.

"But my choice, Sloan."

"A classic battle of wills, is that it?"

"Perhaps."

He lowered his voice. "And perhaps not."

In the illumination cast by the dash lights, he could see the quick rise and fall of her breasts. Watching her, the way she leaned against the seat, the way her lap dipped into the snug vee of her thighs, the way her hands clasped and unclasped as if she wasn't sure where to put them, suddenly gave rise to a disturbing curiosity within Sloan. He wondered if she'd ever necked in a car; if a guy had ever taken off her top, unhooked her bra. Had she ever let her fiancé rest his head in her lap and nuzzle his mouth into the secret sweetness of her cleavage? A memory of doing that very thing with Angela one summer night after a fireworks display slid through Sloan's mind. She'd been chilly, but he hadn't offered his shirt, instead he'd coaxed her to open her blouse and he had warmed her, first with his hands and then by deepening the heat with his mouth.

Having Katherine sitting next to him, shivering yet refusing the offered warmth of his shirt shouldn't have tugged out that vivid memory of his wife and so quickly connected Angela to Katherine. He scowled in the darkness, aware of an acute sense of disloyalty.

God, he thought, what made Katherine so different from the other women he'd known? She was less provocative, certainly not as overtly sexual. He couldn't say she wasn't his type for he'd never had a type—until Angela, that is. Sloan had loved her with all the power and commitment of every romantic platitude. Then she'd been killed when it should have been him.

Sloan pushed the painful guilt back into its private place in his soul.

Yet despite his vow of "never again," despite his inner denials of awareness of Katherine, to his astonishment he felt a warm flush against the back of his neck. He was glad for the shadowed interior of the car. His embarrassment would be complete if she became aware of the front of his jeans.

And what the hell was he trying to prove with the shirt? Would her compliance signify she knew who was running this operation? Did he want her in the shirt because it was the safest way to touch her? Or did his motives have to do with some more primitive, basic role of ownership?

Hell, he was being too damn analytical; too much pop psychology, which he had little use for. He didn't want to analyze Katy or the thoughts and feelings that were skidding recklessly into dangerous areas.

Making a quiet decision, Sloan reached for the shirt at the same time she did. Their fingers collided in the folds, backed away and then brushed again. He finally snagged her wrist, ignoring the thumping pulse he felt. He laced their hands together, wanting to reassure her, needing to reassure himself. Her fingers and palm were chilled, and he turned it so that both his own hand and the folds of the shirt warmed her.

She laughed a little, as if wishing she had never gotten caught in the sudden tension. "I can't believe I'm letting your shirt be an issue between us."

Sometimes a straight-on approach to dealing with trouble worked best. He murmured, "Is it the shirt? Or you wearing it?"

A car's headlights swung into view. The white glare starkly revealed the uneasiness in her face. She glanced down at where he held her hand. Sagging back into her side of the seat as the oncoming vehicle passed, she pulled free of his grip. In the darkness, she said softly, "I'm just nervous. I don't want to give off any false signals and after . . ."

"The kiss?"

She nodded. "And even after Marion and Nina returned, they really believed we were engaged. Marion told me in the bedroom that she could tell by our eyes that we were in love. I mean, that is so ridiculous. We barely know each other."

"It was an act, Katy."

"I know that. It's just that wearing your shirt—"

Wouldn't be an act, he realized suddenly, understanding. But it didn't have to be this complicated, either. Sloan pulled the garment from the seat, tugging her closer to him. She was obviously startled by his move for she slipped across the seat on only one token resistance.

"What are you doing?" she asked, but her words were muffled in the heavy cotton as Sloan pulled the shirt over her head. The material bunched around her neck, and Sloan ignored her scowl as she shoved her hair out of her eyes.

"I can't believe you wearing my shirt has turned into such a major deal," Sloan said as he took her right arm and pushed her hand into the sleeve. He repeated the same motion with her other hand.

"Ouch!"

Startled, he froze. "What?"

She winced. "My arm. Just below my shoulder. Gerald twisted it and it's still sore."

Way to go, Calder, rough the lady up a little. That'll surely make her trust you to protect her and her nephew. "You didn't tell me that." His hand moved to below her shoulder, massaging in slow circles. "Has a doctor looked at it?"

"He said it was just a pulled muscle. But after seeing Gerald loom up in Danny's room, and thinking about what Gerald might have done, believe me, the sore arm is a small price to pay for keeping him from taking the baby."

"Is it bruised?" Sloan could feel his rage climb.

She shook her head dismissively. "It's okay, really."

"Hell, no, it's not okay! Nothing excuses a Gerald Graham or any man like him who knocks women around. Don't dismiss him hurting you any more than you've dismissed him scaring Danny."

Katherine's eyes widened at his vehemence.

Working the shirt down, he spoke quickly, distantly, his fury tempered but cold. "When I was a cop I saw too many women get knocked around. Most were convinced that it was their fault that the guy was angry." He closed his mouth, cursing inwardly for saying anything at all. But hearing Katherine's casual acceptance of being hurt by Gerald had been more than he could take.

"Lean forward," he ordered tersely, wanting to get the shirt on the rest of the way so he could back away from her.

This time she did resist. "I can do it."

But he paid no attention. He urged her forward and yanked the shirt down so that the long flap tucked around her hips. She was lost in it, her breasts no longer defined, her body a gray mass of warm cotton.

He let her go and she scrambled back to her side of the car. He drove on down the road. He glanced at her once and noted that she no longer shivered. Despite the foolishness of what had gone on before, the sight pleased him enormously.

A few miles later they passed the Chelsea Beach Plaza. Floodlights glowed down on the empty parking lot. Sloan noted a grocery store, a toy store and a drugstore among the businesses. A police cruiser patroled slowly and then drove off in the opposite direction.

A gas station was across the street, and Sloan reminded himself he had to get the beach ball filled with air for Danny.

Stopping at a red light, he said, "Drummond's directions to the house are in my shirt pocket."

She pulled out the white paper and unfolded it. Sloan switched on the car's inner dome light.

"Take a right at the light after the plaza," she said. As he did, she added, "Didn't the chief say the house was near the beach?" At Sloan's affirmative answer she rolled down her window. "We must be close. I can hear the ocean."

Ten minutes later Sloan turned the car onto a gravel driveway beside a sand-colored cottage. Maybe it was the realization that she and Danny would live here with Sloan, or the nearby darkened houses that meant neighbors would assume they were an ordinary couple with a little boy who'd arrived during the night; or maybe it was the roaring sound of the Atlantic just over the sand dunes, but Katherine suddenly began to realize the enormity of the lie she'd be living because of Gerald Graham.

With that came a sense that in the past few years her life had consisted of too many lies and half-truths. From Robert's unfaithfulness to the silence from Jennifer about Gerald to the vague answers of the police. Even Sloan's faked kiss for the benefit of the neighbors qualified.

And now, here on Cape Cod, she'd be drawn into an even bigger lie, a charade unlike anything in her experience. Was this when she was supposed to take a deep breath and make the best of a difficult situation? Was she supposed to be brave and cooperative? Should she refuse to get into any more battles of will with Sloan and just be a participant?

She sighed, the answers as difficult as the questions. However, one thing was true. The Irwin sisters' comment to Sloan about her being alone too much had been solved. As to their other comment—her being afraid of men, well, that was ridiculous. Wary, yes. Unwilling to be as trusting as she'd been with Robert, of course. Yet her continued awareness and fascination for Sloan, regardless of the fact that he had been *hired* to playact the role of her husband, made Katherine wonder what that said about her sense of reality.

"Katy?"

She masked her concern with a small grin. "I'm sorry. Did you say something?"

He pulled the keys from the ignition. "Just that I'll go inside and get some lights on, then be back for the bags."

Katherine nodded. In the rear seat Danny stirred and sighed, but didn't awaken. She decided to try to get him inside and settled without waking him.

She opened her door and got out, stretching to relieve her cramped muscles. She'd slept with her legs drawn up and though she had deliberately played down the pain in her arm, it was bothering her. No doubt from not having moved it much until Sloan had put the shirt on her.

Standing, she glanced down to where the shirt hung below her hips. The long sleeves, which she recalled Sloan had worn bunched up at his elbows, fell almost to the tips of her fingers. But it was warm, wonderfully so, and with the strong ocean breeze, she was seriously contemplating asking him if she could keep it.

She touched her fingers to her sore arm, a little stunned by Sloan's comment about abused women. He'd said nothing of his personal life, and she'd assumed that was on purpose. After all, their relationship wasn't a chosen one, but arranged and paid for. And yet she felt a thread of trust because of his words. From what she'd sensed about him, she didn't think he shared his past with anyone. Least of all a relative stranger.

Sloan returned, barely glancing at her. "It's small," he said tersely, as if by whatever standard he used to measure house sizes, this cottage failed. He passed her, jammed the key into the trunk and flipped it open.

Katherine peered at the cottage, thinking that after being confined in the car with Sloan, small to him looked enormous to her. "It has a nice yard. From what I can see, whoever was here before planted some flower beds."

"A nice yard and flower beds definitely add to the picture," he said sarcastically. He pulled her bags out and started for the house.

She stopped him before he passed her again. "What picture? What's wrong?"

"Nothing."

"Don't tell me nothing. You're angry about something."

To Katherine's relief, he didn't glare at her, but at the cottage, as if the dwelling had somehow outsmarted him. "Drummond said there would be plenty of room. Plenty of space and privacy. There's not enough room in there for Danny to practice walking, never mind two people who have our kind of problems."

Katherine touched his forearm, the skin warm and tight with muscle. Her uneasiness returned, but this time it wasn't related to how she felt about Sloan but how he felt about her.

He glanced down to where her hand lay on his arm. She raised her eyes to look at his ruffled hair. She found herself studying the blackness, the thickness, the way it layered and cupped his nape. She remembered slipping her fingers deep into its heavy mass during that kiss, enjoying the coarse feel, the denseness and the way the midnight color enveloped her fingers.

How strange, she thought, feeling somehow linked to him. The kiss, the shirt, even his brief words about the roles they would be playing. All these added to a deepening tension between them.

Therein lay the core of their battle of wills. Softly she asked, "You're not talking about Gerald, are you?"

He met her eyes then, his voice too calm. "No, sweets, I sure as hell am not."

Later, after the car had been unpacked and Danny settled, Katherine stepped out onto the deck, absently noting the particulars. A waist-high wood railing enclosed the area attached to the cottage. An umbrella table was to her left. To her right were extra chairs. Her eyes found Sloan where he'd sprawled out on a blue and white cushioned chaise. Beyond were sand dunes and the ocean that rumbled with a haunting timeless rhythm. The crisp breeze blew thick with the scent of salt and seaweed.

At first Katherine thought he'd fallen asleep, but then she saw him lift a glass to his mouth. Whiskey, she was fairly sure. She'd noticed the newly opened bottle on the kitchen counter.

Katherine paused at the sliding screen door, noting how still he stayed, how easily he accommodated the darkness. He'd angled the chaise, and she studied the tightly muscled line of his body. She remembered the squishy feel of Gerald when he'd surprised her in her apartment. And Robert. His body had been flat and smoothly contoured, as though specially designed to sell a line of expensive suits.

Sloan wore boots and jeans, and watching him against the ebony of the night she thought how remarkably he blended in. Not in a sinister way, but with an aura of power. He knows his limits, she decided summarily. He knows when to begin and when to stop, when to hold on and when to let go.

Katherine closed the screen door quietly. Despite his shirt, she was cold and nervous and wondered if she should save her questions for the daylight. Then he'd be rested and holding a mug of coffee, not tense and sipping whiskey.

For a woman who doesn't trust men, she concluded logically, approaching him now seemed reckless at best. Then again, Sloan had been the one avoiding her since they'd arrived.

Walking toward him, she pushed her hands through her tangled hair. His shirt hung in roomy folds over her jeans. Her makeup had long since worn away, leaving only a remnant of blusher. She certainly didn't look enticing or even as marginally "together" as when he'd kissed her so thoroughly at her apartment.

She came to a stop a foot or so from where he was seated. He neither glanced toward her nor gave any acknowledgment that he knew she was there.

Katherine relaxed a little. She liked not being pressed, allowed to feel her way as if she were setting the boundaries. She knew instantly she could retreat to the safety of her bedroom and he would do nothing to stop her. Just that tiny unspoken assurance convinced her to stay.

Licking the dryness from her lips, she asked, "Who should I thank for the crib?" She recalled her astonishment when she'd seen the crib set up in the tiniest of the three small bedrooms. She knew that a police safe house didn't automatically come equipped with baby furniture. Plus someone had done some food shopping. In the kitchen, besides the whiskey, she'd found fresh milk and cream in the refrigerator, an unopened can of coffee and other breakfast items.

"Come and sit down," Sloan said. "I don't like people standing behind me and analyzing me." He didn't look at her, and she shivered at the way he'd guessed what she'd been doing.

"You knew I was there all the time, didn't you?"

"Since before you opened the door."

Still she didn't move closer. "You could have said something."

"And spoil all that inner conflict you were wrestling with on whether you're safe here with me?" He lifted the glass and sipped, seemingly unaffected by how she might interpret his question.

She moved to stand in front of him. "I told you . . ."

Finally he looked at her, his eyes cool, his tone precise. "I'm not talking about your life, sweets, I'm talking about your virtue."

Confronting the sexual tension between them so bluntly disarmed her as much as Sloan himself. He was not only seated, but seated low in the chaise. She stood so that she towered over him, which should have given her at least a sense that she controlled the situation, but she felt rootless, dangling at the whim of the wind.

She stared down at him, thinking she should turn and leave him to his whiskey and the night. They could talk tomorrow, there would be plenty of days ahead to answer questions. Tonight they were tired and tense. Toying with blunt truth or provocative possibilities wasn't wise.

Foolish and reckless, she acknowledged, yet she felt it was important not to be overwhelmed or cowed by him. Tipping her head to the side, she gave him a direct look. "Maybe I'm not as virtuous as you think."

He raised both eyebrows, as if surprised by her boldness. Katherine suddenly didn't feel so brave. Never had she said such a thing to Robert, and to make such a come-on to Sloan . . . God, had she left her good sense at home in Harbor Bay?

Realizing the folly of her words, she tried to move away, but he caught her, fisting a handful of his shirt. Setting his drink aside, and with a smoothness that if she hadn't known better she might have thought he'd practiced, he dragged her down onto the chaise. He spread his legs and settled her between them, her bottom snug in the cove of his thighs, her back against his chest. Katherine's breathing resumed with a rush. He smoothed the tail of his shirt where he'd bunched it with his fingers.

In a low voice, he murmured, "An interesting comment given that I've had just enough whiskey to make me think about retracting my earlier promise about not kissing you."

His hands rested on her stomach, not moving, just burning through the shirt to create hot bubbles inside her. She swallowed, but it did little to relieve the strain on her throat. "That was a stupid thing for me to say."

"But enlightening." She wished she dared to turn around and see his face. Was he teasing her or was he serious? But when he made no move to kiss her or even touch her beyond his hands and where their bodies melted together, she decided he was only teasing her. In an even voice, he said, "You asked about the crib for Danny. Drummond sent someone yesterday to get the place aired, lay in some food items and bring the crib."

She didn't know where to put her own hands. Her choice was his thighs or pressed on top of his fingers. Gingerly she rested them on his thighs. "Yesterday? But yesterday the chief hadn't even told me about this."

With a seemingly unconscious gesture, Sloan moved his hands up to just beneath her breasts. The movement dragged the shirt up and she immediately tugged it back down. "The chief likes to think he knows what's best and acts accordingly."

"No wonder I feel like I'm being manipulated." Surely an understatement given her body's position. Yet he wasn't holding her down. She might not have settled between his thighs of her own volition, but she hadn't tried to leave, either.

"Tomorrow we'll get whatever else we need."

"You said something else earlier, before we came into the cottage."

"I said a lot of things."

"About the flower beds and yard adding to the picture."

She felt a slight stiffening and a change in breathing from steady to quick-paced. "Ah, yes, the picture. What I meant was that the only things missing are the vine coverings and the white picket fence."

This was the time to move, to push herself away and put some distance between them. Still she stayed. "The picture being a happily married couple?" When he didn't deny her observations, she added, "Why do we have to do or say anything? It's no one's business who we are or why we're here."

"If Danny weren't involved, it wouldn't matter, but he is. Babies attract attention and with all the missing kids these days the last thing we need is someone deciding Danny might be one of them."

Katherine sat up, turning to face him. His head was back, his eyes closed, but when she moved to get off the chaise, he pulled her back down. Scowling, she asked, "Isn't that being a little extreme? We certainly don't look like the kind of people who would abduct a child."

Slowly he opened his eyes. "Really? And what do those kind of people look like?"

She thought of Gerald. His boozy, smoky smell, his squishy body, his threatening—

"You're comparing us to Gerald, aren't you?" At her nod, he shook his head. "He's a lousy example. He's a desperate father who resorted to stupidity and got lucky. Lucky in that he got away. Plus, you saw him in the dark after he'd broken into your apartment. No doubt he didn't exactly look like an advertisement promoting the joys of parenthood. If he'd succeeded in snatching Danny—"

"Oh God."

"I said *if*. *If* he did, he would no doubt go away some place, blend into the community as a father raising his son. The least amount of attention he attracted—meaning the more traditional he acted—the less likely the locals would be of looking for Danny's picture on milk cartons or missing children posters."

She had to admit his logic made sense. "So you're saying we should basically do the same thing. Not cause any undue attention."

"Correct."

"Just a family on vacation for a few weeks," she murmured, taken aback by the sudden flash of eagerness at the thought of the possibilities.

Sloan touched the place on her arm that hurt from Gerald's twisting. His fingers kneaded and she closed her eyes at the soothing motion.

"Look at me, Katy."

Her lids felt heavy and she had to force them open.

Sloan slid his hand to her shoulder and then cupped her neck. He pressed and then skimmed his thumb along her bottom lip. "What happened after Marion and Nina came back with the champagne? How did we act?"

His gaze followed the light motion of her mouth as she spoke. "You sat next to me on the couch and put your arm around me. Once, you kissed my temple."

"And what did they think? What did you tell me in the car?"

She swallowed, trying to recall. He stopped moving his thumb, as though he knew touching her robbed her concentration. Caught by the night, the vee of his thighs, the lingering graze from his thumb, Katherine tried to halt her thoughts from tumbling into total recklessness. *She wanted him to kiss her again.*

"Come on, Katy, what did you tell me in the car?"

"Sloan..."

To her astonishment, he urged her up and then he, too, stood. Not to kiss her, or take her into his arms, but to walk to the edge of the deck. Only when there was a certain amount of distance between them did he look at her again. His look told her more than she wanted to know, his look told her he'd read her thoughts.

"You don't want me to kiss you," he murmured, the wind carrying his voice into the night.

She pressed her lips together to stop her reply. *Yes, I do* hovered on her tongue for long thick moments. His words hadn't embarrassed her, but his restraint condemned her. Yet she was grateful that he at least was thinking straight. She might have been floundering in a sea of dwindling control, but Sloan wasn't. In an indirect way, he was reminding her of why they were here.

Katherine folded her arms across her body, the salty wind making her shiver. Sloan remained at a distance.

Dragging her thoughts back to what they'd been discussing, she said, "Uh, Marion and Nina . . . they thought that we . . . we were . . ."

He waited a full five seconds and when she didn't finish the sentence, he asked, "Perfect together?"

Katherine's thoughts instantly drew the most erotic conclusion. "Perfect together" as in gloved intimately, you inside me? She knew her face was flushed, and the chafe of dampness between her breasts made her grateful Sloan wasn't close enough to sense anything. She wished she were alone so she could shed the shirt and turn into the chilly wind, get rid of the heat that prickled her skin and made her pulses race.

Finally Katherine said, "Yes, they said we were perfect together."

"What else?"

She shoved her other hand through her hair, finding her scalp hot, her hair tangled and damp. "What else?"

"Yeah, sweets, what else?"

"They could see in our eyes that we loved each other."

"And do we?"

"Of course not. We barely know each other." Too late, she realized the stupidity of that comment given where her thoughts had mired themselves.

Sloan said, "Then I suggest that since we managed to convince two women who know you as well as they do, repeating the same role for a bunch of neighbors who don't know anything about us shouldn't be too difficult."

"But what about—?" She couldn't finish.

"When we're alone?"

She could only nod.

Finally he came back to where she stood beside the chaise. Picking up his glass, he drained it and then took her arm. Ushering her back inside the cottage, he closed the sliding-glass door and locked it.

Sloan let her go. "The weather will be warm. We can spend a lot of time outside. That will just leave the nights to deal with."

Alone at night. Like tonight. If Sloan had kissed her as she had wanted, they very well might be making love right now.

Instantly she shoved the possibility aside. Katherine Brewster would never have allowed that to happen.

"Good night, Katy," he murmured and went into his own room.

Katherine checked on Danny, then went to her room. "Katy," she murmured with a sense of anticipation. She pushed the feelings aside. Don't expect anything from him but his protection, she reminded herself, then you won't get hurt.

Chapter 4

"We'll say that you lost it on the beach."

"Why can't you just go in and buy one without me?"

"Because, sweets, I don't know what size you wear," Sloan said as he lifted Danny from the shopping cart and handed him to her.

Earlier he'd offered to carry the one-year-old, but Danny had clung relentlessly to Katherine. Given his terrifying experience with Gerald, Sloan understood the child's caution of men. However, Danny's eyes had lit up when Sloan had told him about the yet-to-be inflated beach ball. The boy remembered the one at the police station and had given Sloan a wide-eyed look and said, "Ball."

Katherine had been ecstatic, saying she'd never heard him say the word so clearly. They'd both laughed and Danny had happily repeated himself numerous times as they'd made their way down grocery aisles. Sloan had just finished loading the bags into the car and had promised Danny that they'd get the beach ball blown up before they returned to the cottage.

"Not knowing my size is not a convincing argument," she muttered.

"It will be if the one I buy doesn't fit."

She juggled Danny on her hip while Sloan locked the car. Touching her back, he urged her across the Chelsea Beach parking lot and then headed toward the jewelry store.

He'd deliberately saved this purchase for last, and he knew he'd surprised her. His excuse for her not having a ring in Harbor Bay had worked simply because they weren't going to be around. However, it had struck him earlier this morning, as he'd watched Katherine help Danny with his breakfast, that a wedding ring would be a necessity if this fake marriage was going to appear realistic.

They were almost to the jeweler's door when again she balked. "I have a better idea. There's a dime store across the street. If we went there and bought a ring it would be as fake as what we're doing."

Sloan sighed heavily. He had a knot of tension along the back of his neck. He'd tried to attribute it to the double bed, since he was accustomed to the sprawl of his king-size. Then he'd blamed it on lack of sleep, because despite not kissing her, not touching her the night before, his thoughts had engaged in too much speculation on how her legs would feel wrapped around his hips. But this morning, when he'd gone into the bathroom to shower, he'd found she'd hung his shirt on a hook behind the bathroom door.

Had it been there all night or had she slept in it? Both were irrelevant questions, the second ripe with exactly what he'd told himself in the car would not happen; finding intimate significance in her wearing the garment. Yet seeing it hanging there, filled with her scent, had made the question burn through his usual good sense.

Katherine, on the other hand, had displayed little effect from the tension of the previous night. She'd looked rested and relaxed. Perhaps he'd imagined that wire of tautness, or perhaps he'd been more gripped by the whiskey than he'd realized.

Then again, she might be better at role-playing.

Total relaxation around her might be impossible, but to their neighbors, Sloan didn't want to raise any questions.

As he'd predicted the previous night, a baby attracted attention. Already a few women at the Chelsea Beach plaza had admired Danny. Sloan knew his fake family idea would work because people paid little attention to the obvious; he'd had enough experience as a private investigator to understand that a ring on Katherine's finger would raise zero questions, while the absence of one would raise too many.

Katherine hoisted Danny higher up on her hip. "You agree with me, don't you, Sloan? That's why you're not arguing and not trying to shoot down my suggestion."

"Suggestion about what?"

"That a dime store ring would be best."

Sloan crossed his arms over his chest. "When one of the neighbors asks you why you have a green finger, what will you say?"

Katherine frowned, glancing across the street. A man shooed away a teenager, who tried to snatch an armful of Cape Cod souvenir T-shirts from an outdoor display table. She watched the boy run off and then grinned as if she'd found the most logical explanation. "It's very simple. I can say we were robbed and the ring was an old one that you'd given to me when we went steady as teenagers."

Sloan lifted an eyebrow. "And you treasured it all these years as if it were real gold."

"Yes," she said, smiling as though his idea would make the story more substantial.

"No."

Her smile dissolved. "No? But why?"

"For one, no wife of mine—fake or real—is going to wear a ring that turns her finger green. Two, you would have never gone steady with me. I was the kind of kid fathers warn their daughters about. Your parents would have been apoplectic at the idea of you even talking to me, never mind anything serious. Besides—" he wished it weren't so easy to imagine her at the blossoming threshold of womanhood "—if you'd rebelled against your parents and gotten involved with me, I would have corrupted you thoroughly."

She had tipped her head to the side while he talked, and now he saw a kind of fascination in her amber eyes, very similar to what he'd seen on the deck in the moonlight.

"Corrupted me? Really?"

"Don't look so curious."

"But I am. No one has ever tried, or perhaps I should say, come right out and admitted that he would corrupt me."

All his warning bells told him to leave this right here. *Take her into the store, get her the ring and stay out of any more conversations that take you both into areas you want to avoid.* What annoyed him was his own reluctant but growing curiosity about her. He tried to tell himself his reaction was a simple aberration, for he'd made a point of never viewing a female client in any context beyond the scope of their particular problem. Katherine had come to him once and he'd treated her in a totally professional manner. Why was he having such a hard time doing that now?

He stepped away from the jewelry store door to let a customer go inside. He damned the question even as he asked it, "So you lied to me last night?"

"Lied about what?"

"Your comment about not being as virtuous as I think."

She swallowed and glanced away. He resisted cupping her chin and making her look at him. Perhaps she'd been faking all the upbeat talk and relaxed demeanor. Then, in a composed and breezy voice, she said, "Last night I was merely trying to point out that I'm not some hothouse flower. I don't need to be handled as if a kiss or a comment is going to shock me or make me uncomfortable. Anyway, no one here would know that we didn't know each other when we were kids."

"Sweets, my grandmother used to say that lies are like tangled webs. They become damn difficult to keep straight. Since a fake marriage and a fake family raises the least amount of questions, then we're better off to stick to the truth for all the incidental stuff. No one is going to ask to see a marriage license, or how long we've known each other or..." He glanced at Danny. "Or if I got you pregnant before I married you. But if you have a wedding ring that turns your finger green that could make someone curious."

She watched him, her eyes studying him as he talked. "What did you do? Lay awake all night thinking of all the possible problems we could run into?"

"Among a few I hadn't planned to run into," he murmured.

This time when a customer emerged from the jewelry store, Sloan ushered Katherine inside before she had a chance to find another excuse.

The glass case counters formed a rectangular center in the store. An intricately tooled mahogany grandfather clock filled one corner and a wall of shelves displayed sterling silver serving pieces arranged artfully with delicate china. Sloan and Katherine walked down to the glass case that displayed an assortment of rings for every occasion. A silver-haired woman approached, wearing a serene smile.

Sloan cupped Katherine's neck and to his surprise felt her pulse pounding. He dipped his head and whispered, "You're doing fine, sweets."

"I don't feel fine. It's bad enough that I feel manipulated again, but I feel like such a fake," she muttered.

"Consider this a rehearsal for the next few weeks."

Danny pointed to a red bowl and said, "Ball?"

Sloan ruffled his hair. "In a few minutes, tiger."

"Good morning," the saleswoman said warmly. "How may I help you?" The woman admired Danny. "What a handsome boy. I can see he takes after his father."

"And just as stubborn," Katherine added so naturally that Sloan was startled, but liked the comparison.

To the saleswoman, he said, "We're looking for a wedding ring. My wife lost hers on the beach."

"Oh, dear, how awful," she said automatically. "I'm sure we have something you'll like." She reached behind her and brought out a black velvet mat. "Now, did you want a ring similar to your lost one or did you want something different?"

Sloan and Katherine glanced at each other as if one was waiting for the other to describe the nonexistent first ring.

Finally Sloan pointed to a tray in the locked case. "The yellow-gold band." Glancing at Katherine, he added, "Since this is a new beginning for us, what about a new style?"

To his astonishment, she moved away from him and studied a display a little farther down the counter. Thoughtfully, she said, "I really liked my old ring, Sloan. I'd like to see how close we can get to that."

Sloan frowned, feeling as if he'd missed a signal. "Finding one that looks like the first one is gonna be tough if not impossible."

She gave him a look of beguiling innocence, and he found himself intrigued by her assertive shift. She asked, "You mean because of the way the diamonds were set? I'm sure they have something similar."

At the word diamonds, the saleswoman's face lit up. She nodded and gushed with pleasure. "Oh, I completely understand you wanting a similar ring, Mrs. — ?"

"Calder. Katy Calder," she said easily.

Sloan blinked. *Katy Calder?* He was sure he had heard wrong. Not at what she'd said, but that she'd connected their names as if she'd been doing it for years.

"Oh, yes, Mrs. Calder, some things are best if duplicated. You know, we women are very nostalgic, Mr. Calder," she said confidingly. She peered at Katherine's left hand. "No engagement ring, either. Perhaps — ?"

Katherine shook her head. "Just one ring."

"Of course, diamonds on the wedding band are very popular these days." The woman was taking a set of keys to unlock one of the cases when Sloan took Katherine's arm.

She jumped a little, as if she'd forgotten he was with her. To the saleswoman, he said, "Would you give us a few minutes?"

She beamed, repocketed the keys and said, "Certainly. I'll be just down the counter. Take your time."

Sloan guided Katherine to the end of the counter to make sure they were out of earshot of the saleswoman.

She put Danny down on the carpet and handed him a soft toy she took from her purse.

Studying Katherine, he reminded himself that he didn't like arguments with women. A fierce determination shone in her eyes and Sloan found himself more than fascinated. She very clearly had wrestled control of the ring's purchase from him. He recalled the shopping trip with Angela for her rings. He'd suggested and she'd agreed. Simple and direct.

But Katherine Brewster wasn't Angela. He'd reminded himself of that when he'd watched Katherine from the police station window. Yet, what he thought he'd settled as an unshakable fact suddenly shifted to a more troublesome reality. He didn't want Katherine to be Angela. He wanted Katherine to be Katherine.

In a low voice, Sloan said, "Katy Calder?"

"Well, I could hardly say Katherine Brewster."

"The saleswoman doesn't know our names, sweets. You could have said Brewster."

Her eyes widened, and he knew her mind was scrambling for a reason why she hadn't. "For heaven's sake, Sloan, you've been the one pushing the role-playing. The least we should do is get our names straight."

"And Katy Calder sounds more convincing than Sloan Brewster?"

Her astonishment delighted him. "You would have taken my name?"

"Sweets, on that issue we could have done whatever you wanted."

"You're serious."

He grinned. "But I like your choice. Katy Calder sounds very authentic, certainly more so than the dime store ring."

She narrowed her eyes, realizing he'd boxed her into a corner. If he could cordially go along with her choosing the name, she should accept his choice of a real ring rather than the green finger kind.

He dipped his head and brushed a kiss across her mouth. Her lips were warm, wet and softly responsive. He knew she hadn't expected the impromptu gesture, but then the unexpected seemed to be turning into the norm. For that matter, he hadn't intended any of the past twenty-four hours to be so emotionally strained and complicated. Buying the ring had been part of a realistic facade, but he hadn't counted on her having her own ideas. And he hadn't counted on liking the sound of Katy Calder, either.

Back off, he reminded himself. Get some distance and some objective truth into this mix or you're gonna have trouble. This is business and Gerald Graham is the reason we're here. Liking the way she had so easily attached their names was just a gut reaction; a throwback from his earlier thoughts about her sleeping in his shirt and wondering about her legs around his hips.

He took a step back when she licked her lips. "And diamonds, sweets... I'd say that's pretty upscale from the lady who wanted the cheap ring."

Katherine brushed a straying strand of hair off her cheek. "I was simply letting you know I didn't like you making the decision without asking me."

Sloan refrained from mentioning she'd done exactly the same thing to him when she'd connected their names. Repeating Katy Calder in his mind, he realized what he shouldn't like about it. The rhythm of the name swept into his thoughts; a dark erotic rite of passage that engraved itself so deeply, so securely, the image terrified him.

Hoping she couldn't detect his unease, he said, "Katy, this isn't real. I think we'll work a lot better together if we don't forget that."

"But it's supposed to look real to everyone else. Isn't that what you've been telling me since we kissed in my apartment?"

"Yes, but—"

"Oh, I get it, you want me to be meek and pliable and abide by your every decision. You don't want this even fake marriage to be equal, you want to be the boss."

Exasperated and wishing like hell he'd never gotten embroiled in any of this, he said, "Might I remind you that the Harbor Bay police department is paying me a helluva lot of money to be the boss?"

For a solid few seconds she simply stared at him. Then, in a low whisper as if she was almost afraid to ask, the question seeped out. "Did they pay you to kiss me the way you did?"

The knot in his neck throbbed. "Katy, listen to me..."

"I asked you a question."

"They're paying me to make sure you and Danny stay safe."

"And if that includes kissing me intimately, then that's fair game, is that it?"

He glanced around quickly. "Look, this isn't the place to discuss this."

She was not about to be distracted. "Did they pay you to kiss me?"

"Forget about the damn kiss!"

"I can't!"

Sloan stared at her in disbelief at her bluntness, wanting to extricate himself from the situation. Katherine's hands flew up to her mouth in an obvious hope that she could somehow put the words back into the privacy of her thoughts. He wanted to draw her into his arms, but the very volatility of the exchange made him hesitate. Her eyes told him how embarrassed she was by the slip.

Sloan took a deep breath, deliberately allowing the silence between them to lengthen. Danny happily banged the soft toy on the carpeted floor.

Finally, he lifted her chin so that she had to look at him. He noted the flush on her cheeks. "Sweets . . ."

"Don't pretend you didn't hear what I said." She cast quick glances around the store, looking everywhere but at him. "God, what you must think."

"I think you were saying what you feel," he said softly. He touched her throat, soothing his thumb along her beating pulse, considering how arousing the beat would feel beneath his mouth. "Don't ever be embarrassed about being honest."

She took several deep breaths and he simply waited for her to regather her composure. Finally, in a soft but carefully objective voice, she came back to why they'd come into the jewelry store. "If you were really my husband, I wouldn't want you to make the entire decision as to what kind of ring I'm going to wear for the rest of my life."

The rest of her life? Clearly she hadn't realized what she said this time. Admittedly, if this were real and if they were looking at rings, he'd want her to have diamonds.

Reality, Calder. He needed to get them both back to reality without embroiling them in another heated confrontation. "Katy, we're not dealing with the rest of your life, only a few weeks of it."

By her sigh, he assumed her unawareness of what she'd implied was as honest as her earlier outburst of feelings.

"I guess I should take a few minutes to think before I speak," she muttered, and then added, "Of course, you're right. It's only weeks. I know you're supposed to be in charge, but if I'm going to be realistic in this fake marriage and family, I want some say just as I would if this was all real.''

They stared at each other, and Sloan wondered how they would get through the next few weeks. They'd been in Chelsea Beach less than twenty-four hours and already he felt as if he were stepping through an emotional mine field.

Danny had pulled himself up and was hanging on to Sloan's pantleg. Katherine reached down. ''I'll get him,'' Sloan said as he lifted the toddler. When the boy didn't reach out to Katherine immediately, Sloan decided to carry him.

They made their way back to the ring counter and the saleswoman hurried over.

''A decision?'' the woman asked as she unlocked the case.

''Yes,'' Sloan said. ''The gold band with the diamonds.''

Katherine swung toward him, scowling. She curled her fingers around his wrist and squeezed. When he glanced at her, she shook her head.

''That was your choice, Katy.''

''But I just told you why—''

He dropped a quick kiss on her temple, drawing her close. She sagged wearily against him. Sloan berated himself for not thinking through the whole issue of buying a ring more carefully. It had been a long time since he'd given a damn about a woman and it showed. He'd botched these past few moments badly.

The saleswoman beamed when Sloan indicated a wide band inset with four diamonds. ''An exquisite choice.'' The woman handled the ring so as to best display the dazzle of the gems. ''These are cut diamonds, not chips. Here, let's see how it fits.''

Sloan clasped her hand and despite her trying to pull away, he brought it easily to the counter. For the first time he noticed her fingernails were lightly polished but not long and daggerish. He wondered how they would feel sliding around his bare back.

He slipped the ring on her finger, ignoring the rush of sensation in his own chest that the gesture created. After Angela he'd vowed, never again. But this isn't real, it's all fake. Just a role to keep her safe, to keep Danny safe, he repeated to himself over and over again.

"Sloan..." she managed on a strangled note that could have signified any one of a dozen emotions.

Before she could refuse, he said, "We'll take it."

"No."

The saleswoman glanced at both of them, clearly getting impatient.

"Katy, it fits. It looks stunning on your finger and Danny is getting restless." He winked at the toddler. "Besides we have to get your ball blown up, don't we, tiger?"

The toddler wiggled and grinned. "Ball!" he squealed.

He covered Katherine's hand, ignoring her attempt to pull away. "She'll wear it."

The saleswoman looked vastly relieved. "Will that be cash or charge?"

"Charge." He handed Danny to Katherine, took out his wallet and walked over to the cash register. Katherine gripped Danny, turned around and walked out of the store.

Katherine stood on the deck, staring at the wide gold band. The diamonds gleamed at her from the third finger of her left hand. The events that had unfolded in the jewelry store still stunned her. She'd intended only to challenge his authority by saying she wanted diamonds. In her wildest imagination she wouldn't have believed he would actually have bought the ring.

And the conversation...

She rubbed at her arms, not sure if she was chilly or nervous. My God, telling him that clearly and that boldly that she couldn't forget their kiss was tantamount to admitting she wanted him to do it again.

Sloan must wonder if she had some suppressed urge to turn their roles into reality. Especially given her ridiculous second remark. He'd certainly been correct. They were only going to be together for a few weeks, not the rest of her life.

What had happened to her polished sophistication? Where had her innate caution and lack of trust in men been?

Katherine had always been calm and down-to-earth. Her sister was the one given to flights of fancy, to doing and saying things that were either inappropriate or avenues to trouble.

Gerald and Robert, she mused. Two men who at this moment she felt better able to deal with than Sloan. Gerald wanted Danny, therefore making sure that didn't happen was pretty straightforward. Robert had preferred variety to monogamy and when she'd learned that she'd broken their engagement.

How extraordinary, Katherine thought, that meeting and knowing Sloan had resulted from her distrust of Robert and now Gerald. There'd only been that one other time that she'd had contact with Sloan; when she'd delivered the tulips and jasmine arrangement for his wife's casket. She shivered now in the warm sunlight, recalling all too vividly the distraught and drunken Sloan she'd encountered that rainy afternoon.

Glancing again at the ring Sloan had slipped onto her finger, she wondered about his wife. What had he been thinking when he'd changed his mind from the gold band to the one with the diamonds? Which type had he bought for Angela?

She slid her hands into the pockets of her white slacks, damning the rawness in her throat that hadn't abated in the two hours since they'd been home. She'd been engaged to Robert for real and it had become a farce. Now here she was, involved in a farce that included wearing a very real and very expensive ring. She didn't know a lot about diamonds, but when the saleswoman had said they were cut and not chips, Katherine had immediately added more zeros to the price.

Now she needed to talk to Sloan, but she didn't know quite how to approach him. If she'd been passive and agreeable at the jewelry store, a simple gold band would have been the result. Unfortunately showing her independence with some measure of assertiveness had backfired on her. Not only had forcefulness resulted in her admitting she couldn't forget the kiss, but she now wore this incredible ring.

She sighed. They were here to hide from Gerald. Hadn't Sloan reminded her of that almost as many times as she'd reminded herself? Certainly she bore as much responsibility for keeping that fact in mind.

Then there were those brief moments just before she'd come out here to the deck.

After they'd returned home, Danny had been fed and put down for a nap. While she'd been busy with the toddler, Sloan had carried in the groceries and then gone into his bedroom to change his clothes. Katherine had begun to assemble sandwiches for lunch, when she decided it would be nice to eat on the deck. On her way to wipe the table off, she'd had to pass Sloan's room. He'd left his door open and her glance, she'd told herself, had been unintentional and inadvertent.

The shades in his room must have been pulled because he stood almost in total shadows. His head was bent in concentration while he worked at closing the buttons on his jeans. The peek of white briefs was stark against the faded denim and his hands. He wasn't wearing a shirt. Thick hair matted a lean but muscled chest.

Her entire body had felt weighted down while her head had felt as if it were floating. Softly, quietly, her mind urged her to take the few steps necessary to get out of his view should he glance up. But she stayed, fascinated and at the same time fearful any movement would get his attention.

Just as she'd gathered the fortitude to step away, the phone rang.

Katherine jumped like a voyeur who'd been caught. Sloan's head reared up instantly. His hair was rumpled, his face unreadable, his gray-green eyes seemed to pierce hers as if they were face-to-face.

The second ring jangled and he didn't move.

"Oh God..." she murmured.

His fingers had halted. His legs were slightly apart, his hands still low on his belly, his chest a feast for her fingers. And finally his eyes, they caught hers, stripping her thoughts of any excuse she might invent for watching him.

The third and then the fourth ring.

Neither moved. Neither spoke, neither had to. A silent language, sizzling with intimacy, skittered and flashed between them with the power of a lit fuse.

Katherine finally broke the contact and fled to the deck. A few seconds later she'd heard the phone stop in the midst of the sixth ring.

Katherine took a deep breath as she reentered the kitchen. He was still on the phone. His bare back was to her as he leaned on the counter, writing on a notepad. An open bottle of beer sat nearby.

"I don't want to hear about any delays, Joe. The deal was a few weeks."

Please, she thought, agreeing with Sloan, no delays. She opened the refrigerator and took out a package of ham, then cheese and a jar of pickles. She put them on the counter. The kitchen wasn't large and she had to step around him to get to the sink.

"One other thing," Sloan said to Joe Drummond. "Does the department have any objection if I do some repair work on the house? Nothing major. The deck has a loose railing, a couple of windows need to be tightened, that kind of stuff." He took a sip of his beer. "I had a feeling you'd appreciate the free labor. Yeah, don't worry. I'm keeping track of the expenses. I'll be in touch."

He hung the phone up and concentrated on writing a few more things down on the pad before picking up his beer and turning around. Katherine concentrated on assembling the sandwiches and although she didn't glance at him, she could feel him watching her.

She poised a tomato and began to slice. Still he said nothing, but in her peripheral vision she saw him lift the dark bottle and sip.

Without looking at him, she said, "Lunch will be ready in a few minutes. Why don't you take your beer and that bag of chips and go on out to the deck." And on your way, please stop and put a shirt on, she said to herself as she came close to cutting her finger instead of the tomato.

He straightened, but he didn't leave the kitchen.

Her heart felt as if it would burst from her chest. She turned to get some plates from the cabinet and realized he stood in the way.

"Running away or trying to ignore what's going on between us will only make this worse," he said in a low voice.

She pretended to ignore him and reached up to get the dishes, but he snagged her wrist, bringing it down and gripping her other one. "Sloan, don't . . ."

"I knew you were watching me," he said in such a non-threatening way she was sure she must have misunderstood him.

While his hands held her wrists securely, she didn't feel trapped so much as worried that he could feel her pulse pounding. "I wasn't . . . I mean, I was . . . I just . . ."

He raised an eyebrow at her fumbling for answers. "My fault. I should have closed the door."

She slowly lifted her lashes and met his eyes. She saw rigid restraint there, as if he were deliberately diffusing the tension by meeting it head-on and taking the blame.

His approach to it all made her feel better. "That doesn't excuse me standing there like some pervert."

He chuckled. "Pervert? You? Be serious. How about unexpected curiosity. After all, we are and will be in close quarters for the next few weeks. We're bound to catch each other at odd or uncomfortable moments. I think we're better off if we just acknowledge them and go on from there."

How did he make it sound so easy, so uncomplicated? His agreeable dismissal of those fraught moments made her relax. Sloan released her wrists, reached into the cabinet and handed her the plates. He picked up his beer and the bag of chips.

Katherine went back to finishing the sandwiches. She should have let the entire issue drop, but she wanted to know what he'd been thinking if he'd known she was watching him. She put the sandwiches on the plates and they walked out to the deck.

After they were seated, she posed the question. "If you knew I was watching you, why didn't you glance up or say something?"

Sloan's face closed down as if she'd asked him to reveal his soul. He put his sandwich down and took a sip of beer. "Like what? Come closer and I'll show you more?"

That sense of wired tension that seemed to be growing permanent rather than sporadic swayed between them.

Trying to keep it from getting taut, she said softly, "I can't imagine you saying such a thing."

She felt a gulf of distance where only seconds ago he'd been reassuring and understanding. "You think you know me so well that a crude comment like that wouldn't occur to me?"

She wished she'd never asked the question. "No, I don't think I know you that well...."

"You don't know me at all," he said in a flat voice. "Us being here together is about Danny and Gerald Graham. It's about a fake marriage and a fake family and nothing more."

She stared at him, stunned by his cold withdrawal, by his sudden mood shift. He could kiss her intimately, he could buy her an astronomically expensive ring, he could create roles for them to play, he could even admit to a sexual attraction. But he was right. Unless he allowed her, she'd never know anything about him.

And with a new insight, she realized she wanted to know everything about him.

Chapter 5

"Hi. Welcome to Chelsea Beach."

Katherine glanced up from where she'd kneeled to weed around the rosebushes in front of the cottage. A young couple, both blond-haired, in their mid-twenties, wearing jeans and matching T-shirts, grinned back at her.

Smiling, Katherine got to her feet.

The woman said, "I know this is barging in, but we wanted to say hello. I'm Linda Rowen and this is my husband Hank. We live in one of the houses on the seawall near the beach."

"Yes, of course," Katherine said. "I saw the houses. They're magnificent. But how do you get anything done with that breathtaking view of the ocean?"

Linda laughed. "Sometimes I wonder if the surf will surge in and wash everything away. My parents keep reminding Hank and me that we're thumbing our noses at nature. But then again," she added with a shrug, "I guess when you want to live near the water you have to expect the unexpected."

Katherine could relate to unexpected. In Harbor Bay her apartment hadn't been damaged by nature, but Gerald's invasion had certainly changed the way she viewed her home. Never again would she feel the same sense of safety and coziness.

Realizing she hadn't introduced herself, Katherine pulled off her gardening gloves and offered her hand. "I'm Katy Calder." She nodded toward the cottage. "Sloan is doing some repair work on the deck." And then, in what she was sure sounded like an afterthought, she added, "He's my husband."

Linda nodded. "Hank met him and Danny this morning at the hardware store."

Katherine didn't know how she was supposed to respond to that since Sloan had said nothing about meeting a neighbor. Then again, she thought reasonably, why would he mention Hank? Sloan wasn't really married to her so it wasn't as if they were an average couple new to the area who happily joined into the Saturday morning gossip. No doubt he'd thought nothing more about Hank Rowen than he had about buying her the ring. She gave a momentary glance at the wedding band and reminded herself that the price of the ring was still an unresolved and so far undiscussed issue. No doubt he'd listed the ring along with the hardware items and other purchases for later reimbursement.

However, she did wonder what he'd said about Danny. But then again, Sloan had said people presumed the obvious. Therefore Hank probably thought what he was supposed to think. Danny was Sloan's son.

Katherine had encouraged the blossoming relationship between Sloan and Danny. The red ball had been the beginning. This morning, when Sloan had been getting ready to go to the hardware store, he'd asked Danny if he wanted to ride in the car. The toddler had been so excited he'd forgotten the cookie he'd been eating.

Although Katherine felt Danny spending time with Sloan would help him get over the trauma of Gerald's attempt to snatch him, she'd been surprised at the baby's willingness to go without her. And she'd mentioned that fact to Sloan as she got Danny ready.

"I promised him we'd buy a red truck," Sloan said matter-of-factly.

"I think that's called bribery."

"That's what it's called."

"Really, Sloan, I don't think it's a good idea for him to think that every time you take him somewhere you're going to buy him something."

"Why?"

"Why! Because it will spoil him."

"So what. He'll associate red balls and red trucks and maybe ice cream cones with me instead of being scared of men in general because of Gerald. Besides, one month of spoiling won't turn him into a little monster. After I'm gone you and that paragon of motherhood, your sister, can unspoil him."

The sarcastic jab at Jennifer had left Katherine bristling and naturally defensive, but Sloan and Danny had gone out to the car and Katherine had told herself to let the comment pass. Admittedly, from Sloan's standpoint, Jennifer didn't appear very responsible.

To Linda and Hank, she said, "I know Sloan will enjoy seeing you again, Hank. I was just about to get us something to drink. Will you join us?"

Hank spoke to his wife. "Honey, I told you we should have waited until later this afternoon. The Calders are busy."

"Hank's right, Katy," Linda added. "We don't want to interrupt."

"Nonsense. I'd planned to stop in a few minutes anyway. I'm glad you came," Katherine said, genuinely pleased at the opportunity to be with other people. Since their arrival four days ago, she'd talked to the saleswoman in the jewelry store and the checkout girl at the supermarket. Keeping a low profile was necessary, but she wasn't accustomed to such isolation.

The aloneness seemed to breed a deepening awareness of her attraction to Sloan. She was fascinated by his determined distance, curious about the few glimpses into his past that he'd allowed her and—most dangerous of all—curious about her own body's response to him.

At worst, she could call her reaction lust. At best, an emotional and nerve-racking complication that she simply didn't know how to deal with.

And at her age she should know, she realized grimly as she gathered up her garden tools. Her wariness of men, due primarily to Robert and observing Jennifer's reaction to Gerald, had become automatic. Yet in a thousand ways Sloan behaved differently and that dissimilarity lay at the root of her own floundering emotions.

She put the weeds and winter debris that she'd raked from around the bushes into a plastic bucket. Glancing at the hearty bushes, she realized with a pang of disappointment that if the police investigation was cleared up on schedule she wouldn't be here in July when the roses bloomed.

Linda and Hank followed her around the cottage to the deck where Sloan was installing a gate for Danny's protection. The toddler sat on the floor, happily playing with his new red truck.

Coming up to Sloan, she swallowed quickly, getting a grip on her thoughts. The south side of the cottage was warmer and Sloan wore a sweatband, no shirt and a pair of jeans that defined his hips and thighs with a snug sexy authenticity. Katherine wore a pair of sweats and a blouse. To Linda and Hank, she and Sloan probably looked like a stereotypical married couple puttering around on a late spring morning.

"Sloan?"

Without lifting his head, he gave the final screw a few tightening turns. "I hope Drummond doesn't freak out over the gate. I mentioned repairs, but not additions."

"We have company," she said quickly, so that he didn't reveal too much.

He looked up. His hair, anchored by the band, was almost a blue-black against the bright sun. Katherine saw a rivulet of sweat run down his chest. She managed to follow the drop until it disappeared into the mat of dark hair.

He tossed the screwdriver down and came forward. "Hank, good to see you again. And thanks for the gate idea. It was brilliant." He dropped an arm around Katherine's neck, talking as if he'd come home from the hardware store and filled her in on meeting Hank. She nodded at the appropriate times. "I told him we were on vacation and that we didn't have room for the playpen in the car. He suggested that a gate for the deck might work just as well.''

"It certainly was a good idea," Katherine said. She slipped her arm around Sloan, finding her need to touch him overwhelming. For the past few days they'd been very careful around each other. Either Linda and Hank's presence made her bold or she was naturally at ease playing the role of affectionate wife. She slid her hand up his back, his flesh hot and a little damp from the sun. He went very still at her touch and she wondered if he'd pull away, but he didn't.

Through the exchange of pleasantries, Sloan and Katherine learned that the couple had bought their house on the seawall two summers ago. Hank worked for a local contractor and Linda had recently been hired by the Chelsea Beach Tourist Association. Sloan told them that he and Katherine were just renting for a few weeks.

"We'd been so hoping for ordinary summer-long neighbors," Linda said with a disappointed sigh. "The cottage has had some odd occupants. Three men the first summer. After we bought our house, I told Hank I thought they were all hiding from the cops. I don't think I ever saw them on the beach and one of them was real heavy in the chest, as if he carried a whole arsenal under his coat. And that was another thing, they wore jackets all the time. Can you imagine? Jackets in the summer on Cape Cod?''

Sloan grinned. "Probably those bank examiners Joe mentioned. Remember, Katy?''

Katherine hesitated, amazed at how easily he could come up with a lie. She felt like an actress without a script. "Um, yes, Joe did say something about them.''

Linda frowned. "They sure didn't look like bankers to me.''

"Not bankers, honey, bank examiners." Hank explained, "They're the guys that come in when it looks as if someone cooked the books." Giving Linda a squeeze, he added affectionately, "Don't mind my wife. She watches too much of those tabloid-type programs.''

"Katy likes the garden programs," Sloan said before Katherine had a chance to say anything.

"You mentioned at the hardware store that your wife was into flowers." Hank gestured back toward the front of the cottage. "She sure looked as if she knew what she was doing with those rosebushes."

Katherine started to say something when Sloan added, "Katy always knows what she's doing when it comes to flowers. She's a florist."

Linda smiled. "How interesting. Working with flowers must be a wonderful job. How did you ever get into that?"

Katherine gave Sloan an is-it-okay-if-I-speak-for-myself look. She was peeved at his summarily recreating her as if to suit the image he thought worked best for the circumstances. On the other hand, she was curious as to how he would answer. To her knowledge he knew nothing beyond the fact that she owned a florist business.

She glanced at him, waiting, but he drew her a little tighter against him and said, "Why don't you explain, sweets."

She smiled brightly. "You're doing fine."

"She hates it when I brag about her, but—"

"Never mind," Katherine said with an exasperated roll of her eyes. Sloan was obviously enjoying this and heaven only knew what he'd concoct. Ignoring Sloan's grin, she said to Linda and Hank, "My parents owned a florist business. They retired a few years ago and moved to Arizona. My sister had other interests and I've always loved flowers, so I decided to continue with the shop."

"Is it located around here?" Linda asked. "I'd love to give you my business."

"No, in—"

"Rhode Island," Sloan said quickly.

Hank nodded and added, "What about you, Sloan? What kind of work are you in? You didn't mention it this morning."

For a few seconds the question hung in the air and then Katherine said, "He hates to talk about his work when he's on vacation." She gave Sloan what she hoped was a proper wifely grin. "I offered Hank and Linda a drink. We have beer, soda and iced tea. Why don't you take care of that while I put Danny down for his nap."

"Good idea," Sloan said with a quick squeeze of gratitude for the change of subject. He crossed over and lifted Danny up from where he'd managed to get his red truck caught beneath the chaise.

"Hey, why don't Linda and I run over to Pete's and get a pizza," Hank suggested.

Linda nodded enthusiastically. "That's a great idea."

Katherine and Sloan glanced at each other, their eyes mutually agreeing. Sloan said, "Sounds like fun."

Katherine took Danny from Sloan and carried him inside the house and into her bedroom. She laid him on the bed to change him. She heard Hank and Linda leave, saying they would be back in about twenty minutes.

"No anchovies," she heard Sloan call out.

A few minutes later, after she'd gotten Danny resnapped into his playsuit, Sloan came into the bedroom. His entrance was so casual, so ordinary, that for a moment she forgot that this was the first time he'd been in the room since the night they'd arrived and he'd carried in her bags.

"Everything okay?" he asked in an easy voice, leaving the door ajar. He'd pulled on a faded gray T-shirt that made his eyes more gray than green. He'd taken the sweatband off and had obviously just run his fingers through his hair. Casually, he carried a soda can.

Glancing away and giving Danny's foot a playful tug, she said, "I think so."

"You didn't mind about them getting pizza and bringing it back?"

She shook her head, and told herself to relax. There was absolutely no difference between talking to Sloan in here alone than out on the deck alone.

He said reassuringly, "You're doing fine, Katy. Since Linda is involved with tourist promotion, Hank apparently keeps up with who comes and goes in Chelsea Beach. He approached me at the hardware store and introduced himself. At first I thought he was just a friendly neighbor-to-neighbor type, but when he said he'd seen us eating lunch on the deck, I decided to tell him we were here on vacation and renting the cottage. I know you were trying to play catch-up outside."

He came closer to her. While the bedroom wasn't tiny, Sloan's presence made her senses more acute. She lifted Danny off the bed and the toddler gave Sloan a big smile.

"I think you have a friend forever," Katherine said, glad for the diversion.

He ruffled Danny's hair. "A red truck will do it every time, right, tiger?"

The toddler wiggled and grinned, repeating the word truck, but not quite able to get the *T* sound clear so that it came out sounding like an *F.*

Sloan and Katherine both laughed and Danny joined in.

Katherine hugged her nephew, knowing that if she could sustain these moments of happiness and trust for Danny, she would have Sloan to thank.

She carried Danny to the door, intending to take him to his room.

"Katy?"

She glanced over her shoulder. "Yes?"

"Thanks for changing the subject when Hank asked me what I did for a living. I hadn't decided how specific I wanted to be. I may just tell him I do something bland like sell insurance."

"You don't look like an insurance salesman," she said with no hesitation.

"No? What do you think I look like?"

Too attractive and too dangerous, but she had no intention of saying either. "You're very distant, Sloan. Usually salesmen, at least the ones I come in contact with, are outgoing, gregarious and sometimes even pushy."

He scowled, ignoring her description of a salesman. "Distant, how?"

She considered being vague, but decided against it. Taking a breath, she plunged in. "You do things as if your reasoning is always right and will always be accepted. Setting up our phony engagement in Harbor Bay. Buying such an expensive wedding ring. Meeting Hank at the hardware store and not mentioning it to me. Did you forget or did you just assume I would follow along with whatever you said?"

For a long tense moment, he simply stared at her. Meeting his eyes made her wince inwardly. She had definitely hit a raw nerve.

"I've been out of practice at being a husband," he said grimly. "Besides, I was the one who warned you of the danger of too many lies, wasn't I? If it comes up again, I'll just tell them what I do. Hank won't be all that interested once he knows I don't fit the hard-bitten stereotype. Most of the P.I. work I've done since Angela was killed is security type or white-collar investigations."

"Until Danny and me."

"Yeah." He lifted the soda can, and she couldn't see his eyes.

"Let me go and get Danny settled." While she did so, Katherine decided that Angela's death must have changed his mind about the cases he took. That was followed by wondering why he'd accepted this one.

When she returned, she was about to say they could continue the conversation in the living room, when he said, "I came in here to compliment you. You handled the situation on the deck like a pro."

She might have handled those few moments with Hank and Linda like a pro, but inwardly she'd been nervous. Given a choice, she now wished she hadn't been so anxious to invite Linda and Hank to stay. "I almost slipped up and said Harbor Bay."

"I know. A natural reaction. I don't think they noticed me interrupting you."

"Faking this marriage to the woman at the jewelry store was easy, but here with two neighbors, I feel like such a liar. They're nice people, the kind I'd like to get to know better."

"You know we can't take the chance and tell anyone why we're here."

Katherine's uneasiness about talking in the bedroom grew. "It's just that not being myself feels so awkward. I have to be on guard and watch what I say."

He sighed deeply as if what she'd said was all old ground, old decisions, unchangeable. "You knew that when you agreed to do this."

She whirled around, her self-restraint suddenly feeling as thin as the bedroom walls. She was glad Hank and Linda had gone to get pizza. At least she wouldn't have to worry about being overheard. Forcefully she said, "I didn't like the idea of coming here with you. I didn't even want to agree to it, remember? But since the police chose not to arrest Gerald—" She cut her words off when she felt her temper rising, and turned again to leave the room. There was no point in rehashing the obvious.

Sloan set the can down, and gripped her arm when she tried to leave. "If your sister had checked her brain instead of the stars in her eyes, she would have known what Gerald was."

Katherine had wondered the same thing, but not in such harsh words. Feeling as if she were being too simplistic, she repeated what Jennifer had told her. "She loved him once."

"Obviously her judgment when it comes to men and love isn't that sharp," he muttered.

"And you're making more unfair cracks about my sister," Katherine snapped, recalling the sarcastic paragon-of-motherhood comment of before. She also remembered that at her apartment, Sloan hadn't been critical while Katherine had. "You don't even know her," she finished, even though she, too, had disturbing questions.

"I know one thing. When it comes to being a mother, you're doing a helluva lot better job than she is."

From the deck came a burst of laughter. So intent had Katherine and Sloan been in their discussion that they hadn't heard Hank and Linda return.

Hank hollered, "Hey, you two, come and get it while it's hot."

Sloan attempted to usher her out the door, but she pulled away from him. Her sister might deserve to be criticized but not about being a lousy mother. "Jennifer adores Danny. I volunteered to keep him. You have no right to make her sound thoughtless and neglectful."

He mouthed an obscenity, then yelled "We'll be right out" to Hank and Linda. Turning to Katherine, he gripped her shoulders and brought her up tight against him. She could feel the hammering of his heart and the slight shift of his hips as he settled their bodies together. The provocative angle felt too natural, too inviting and impossible to ignore.

In a gruff voice, he said, "I don't have to make her sound like anything. Her actions speak for her. If your sister had used her head instead of her hormones you and I wouldn't be stuck here together playing this insane role of the happily married couple."

She tossed her head back, knowing the gesture held sexy connotations and found herself staring into his eyes; a gray-green intensity that should have made her blush or cower or back off.

"A role, I might remind you, Sloan Calder, that was not my idea," she said without bothering to whisper.

"For God's sake, keep your voice down."

"Maybe I don't want to. Maybe I don't care. Maybe I want . . ."

"Shut up," he said so evenly and quietly that the words were twice as effective as they would have been if shouted.

Tension tightened between them. He lowered his head, his mouth a breath away from hers. She slipped her hands around his waist, her fingers pressed into his lower back.

But the kiss she'd expected, wanted, and hoped for, didn't happen. Nothing in her experience with Robert, nothing in her dreams of someday finding the ideal man prepared her for Sloan's restraint. For seconds she watched in amazement as his face and eyes took on a guarded and distant expression.

"Are you afraid to kiss me?" she whispered, not at all sure where her temerity for such a question had come from.

"Terrified."

Stunned by his simple admission, she asked, "But why?"

"Because I know where in hell kissing you would lead. And that can't happen. Damn it, I won't let it," he said with such vehemence that she caught her breath. He released her suddenly, as if touching her burned him.

Katherine gripped the door for support and watched him as he walked away. My God, she realized with amazement, this was all wrong. Wasn't *she* supposed to be pushing *him* away? Protesting? Yet she'd neither done or even thought

about any of them. Sloan had freely admitted to being terrified of kissing her, though she knew he'd wanted to.

The tightness in her breasts and the curl of bubbly warmth
deep in her belly couldn't be ignored. Somewhere, sometime, she had embraced the roles they were playing and had
made them a reality in her heart.

Drawing in a shallow breath, she focused her mind on the
only reason she was with Sloan. For Danny's safety. Even
so, she realized how complicated things were getting. She
would have kissed Sloan back, and it wouldn't have been
enough.

The days passed with so much sweet agreeability that
Sloan seriously considered admitting he wanted her just to
break the tension.

On day seven, he walked across the beach to the water's
edge with a small pail to fill for Danny. Katherine and
Danny were building a sand castle on the sheltered side of a
sand dune.

Scowling, he confronted what he'd been trying to deny.

She was getting to him. And not just sexually. What he
was feeling—heart and soul—was much more dangerous.

Not an encouraging conclusion, considering the fact he
prided himself on having perfected his ability to sidetrack
and ignore any situation that vaguely resembled that of a
serious relationship. Which in itself was hellishly damning.
He knew better. He knew how to shut down his feelings, to
walk away from any involvement that went beyond his own
self-imposed boundaries.

After Angela's death, he'd isolated himself and the few
women he'd slept with since knew enough not to expect
anything from him that resembled more than a casual relationship.

He kicked a shell back into the water, glancing across the
expanse of the Atlantic. So why in hell did he feel so exposed by this one woman? "Why is she a problem that's
growing instead of shrinking?" he muttered beneath his
breath.

Katherine had effectively caught him off guard. She'd
masterfully and without warning or pretense touched some

exposed piece of him when he hadn't even realized there was a piece of him left that could feel anything.

Had he really admitted to being terrified of kissing her? God, no wonder she walked around him as if on eggshells, he concluded grimly. She probably thought he was totally weird.

He dipped the pail into the water and filled it. They'd been in Chelsea Beach a little more than a week. With any luck, Drummond would have the evidence to arrest Gerald within another few days and then they could go home and back to their separate lives.

Which suited him just fine, he assured himself. He'd made a clear vow after his wife's death. Involvement carried a price that he couldn't afford to pay ever again. Nothing had changed since then.

Pretty straightforward. Now all he had to do was stick to it. Lifting the pail, he walked back up the beach. The weather had turned hotter than usual for late May and Sloan had suggested they go down to the beach. The tiny confines of the cottage had made him edgy. And given how close he'd come to kissing her the other day, space and breathing room were a necessity.

Katherine apparently understood that, and with a graciousness he knew he didn't deserve, she'd left him alone. Unfortunately that both disturbed and fascinated him. He didn't want her getting into his head, but on the other hand, he enjoyed being with her.

Sloan grimaced at his own mixed messages.

Since that almost kiss, he'd decided the best course of action was to be open about, and only about, the impersonal issues, such as the questions she'd raised in Harbor Bay about Gerald. Those were a hell of a lot easier to answer than questions about what was going on between them.

Katherine grinned as he approached the sand dune where they'd laid out the blanket. "I was beginning to think you'd decided to take a walk down the beach."

"Just doing some thinking."

He liked the freshness and wholeheartedness of her smile. Not like the women he'd known, who got off on pouty and

*provocative or worse gave nothing but shallow smiles that
never reached their eyes.*

"About what?" she asked, hesitantly curious.

*She wore a pair of cutoffs and a I'm A Chelsea Beach
Tourist T-shirt that Linda had given her as part of a local
promotion.*

Danny wore more sand than he did clothes, but Katherine had him well protected from the sun. Sloan wedged the pail of water into the sand beside the toddler.

Sloan studied Danny's creation, which looked like a collapsed moat. "Quite a castle, tiger."

"You're trying to avoid answering me, aren't you?"

Danny clapped his hands, giggling and spraying loose sand across Sloan's thigh.

"Look, I know I've been moody and not very good company the past few days, but I don't want to get into an argument with you." He pulled his shirt off and tossed it aside.

"Sometimes an argument can clear the air," she said, as if any response from him was better than the tension between them. Then, in what he was sure was an unconscious gesture, she reached over and brushed the sand from his thigh. He wore cutoffs, too, and the touch of her fingers against his bare skin had his thoughts taking her fingers higher, beneath the denim's frayed edges. Carefully, he moved so that she couldn't reach him.

"I don't like to argue with women."

She dusted her hands together. "Real married people argue and disagree. As well as answer each other's questions."

Sloan gave her a measured look. "What questions?"

She busied herself with Danny's castle. "About Gerald. About what is going on with the other investigation. I don't like the strain between us, Sloan. Maybe some answers will help to relieve it."

He refrained from correcting her with a more primitive problem—the need to get into each other's pants. Feeling the sensual wire between them stretching too taut, he muttered, "Strain is a nice homogenized word."

Her cheeks and nose were pink from the sun and her once neat ponytail had loosened, sending strands of hair against her cheeks and down her neck.

If Danny were asleep, he would kneel in front of her and kiss her. A terrifying kiss that was wet, hot and deep. And the hellish thing was, he knew she'd respond. Not tentatively, but eagerly.

And eagerness from Katherine would be damned hard to back away from. A hell of a lot harder than turning the conversation to less volatile areas.

"What did you pack for lunch?" he asked in an attempt to change the topic. He settled himself as far away on the blanket as he could get without being obvious, then opened the basket and peered inside.

If she was startled by the shift in subject matter, she didn't let on. "You just ate breakfast two hours ago!"

"Danny's starved. Aren't you, tiger? Look at the way he's been eating sand."

"Sweetheart, no, it's yukky." She tried to brush the sand off his hands and face. "Too bad the water's so cold or we could take you down and rinse you off."

Sloan dug a bag of potato chips and some foil-wrapped fried chicken—left over from dinner the previous night—out of the basket.

"You're a good cook," he commented as he broke off some white meat for Danny.

"You told me that last night."

"Worth repeating. See, Danny agrees."

The toddler was indeed eating enthusiastically. Katherine took out a container of fruit and lifted the lid off. Sampling the melon, she offered a piece to Danny. He pushed it away and reached toward the chicken.

Sloan gave him another piece and then took a bite from a drumstick. He gazed across the sand dunes. A few beachgoers were scattered about, but the lifeguard stands were empty. "Just think, in another month this beach will be packed."

"Yes, aren't we lucky? We'll miss the crowds."

"I bet you're looking forward to getting home and getting your life back to normal."

"Yes, I am."

"And getting back to work."

"Yes, that, too. Although I'm fortunate to have competent people working for me. When I called my manager to tell her I'd be away a few weeks, she was delighted I was taking a vacation. Sometimes I think they could manage for years without me. What about your business? You don't work with a partner, do you?"

"Not at the moment. Working alone keeps things simple. I just lock the doors."

Sloan threw some food scraps out for the sea gulls, thinking how much less complicated this kind of conversation was. Cocktail party stuff, but safe, and God, he needed safe.

He cast a quick glance at Katherine, who had busied herself cleaning up Danny. She tucked the toddler against her, rubbing his back and urging him to sleep.

He was about to ask her a few more safe, boring questions when without looking in his direction, she asked, "Why are we having this pointless conversation?"

He chuckled at her directness. "Because a pointless conversation is a lot safer."

"Than what?" She glanced up then, her eyes wide with interest.

He debated with himself all of five seconds. "Than getting into figuring out how I've managed to keep from kissing you," he said, knowing the one comment answered a thousand other questions.

She fussed with making sure Danny was comfortable. "I don't know how you can toss off a remark like that with such blandness. It's as if you disconnect yourself."

Sloan frowned. Yeah, maybe that was what he did. Maybe disconnected meant safe and uninvolved. Danny's eyes drifted closed and Katherine rocked him slowly, until he was asleep. She then eased him down onto an unsandy section of the blanket. The only place left for her to sit was beside Sloan. She did so without hesitation.

"Ask your questions," he said gruffly, reminding himself of the trade-off. Questions about the investigation were safe territory.

She sat cross-legged, one of her knees just brushing his ribs. "What kind of investigation are the police doing that they couldn't arrest Gerald?"

He forced himself to concentrate, all too aware of the slight nudge into his ribs. "The investigation's within the department. Gerald is being paid by the mob to prey on inexperienced police recruits. He invites the newly graduated from the police academy to his restaurant for a free dinner and some friendly conversation. Eventually Gerald gets to know them well enough so that he can spot the odd one."

"Odd?"

"Different. Vulnerable is a better word. Anyway, he befriends that odd one over a period of time so that the cop feels comfortable enough with him and starts spilling his guts about being broke or in debt, or reveals a problem with a girlfriend."

Katherine grimaced. "It was that charm and smoothness that attracted Jennifer."

"Yeah. Once he has their confidence, he invites them on a trip down to Atlantic City to gamble and party."

Katherine looked startled. "Did you say Atlantic City?"

"Yeah. Does that mean something to you?"

"Atlantic City is where Jennifer met Gerald. She was down there for a piece she was doing on women who gamble. Gerald owns a video camera and he told her he was one of those amateur news hounds who roams around waiting for a disaster to happen."

"Did she know he was from Harbor Bay?"

"Apparently they'd been on the same plane. Gerald had flown down with some businessmen for a weekend, which made sense since he owned a restaurant in Harbor Bay."

Not wanting to examine his motives, Sloan slipped his arm around her and urged her down so that she was lying full against him. He heard her sigh.

"Better?"

"Yes. I was getting cramped trying not to touch you."

"Behave yourself," he said gruffly.

She snuggled in closer, her arm around his waist, her hair brushing his shoulder. "I'll be on my best behavior."

He ignored the amusement he heard in her voice, reminding himself that not one damn thing could happen if he didn't cooperate. "You want to hear the rest of this?"

"Mmm," she murmured. Her breasts pressed against the side of his chest and with a start he realized how easily he could lift her on top of him. He could roll on top of her, or slide his hand over her bottom.... When she wiggled a little closer, Sloan slipped one of his legs between hers, and ignored the warning messages his senses were sending him.

"Where was I?"

"Gerald in A.C. with his video camera and a new cop."

"Oh yeah. Gerald sets things up by introducing the recruit to a few friends and some women. Then when the recruit is relaxed, Gerald videotapes the scenes where the cop is gambling with mobsters or..." Sloan frowned, finding his own stomach turning slightly at what he was about to say.

Katherine had been lacing her fingers through the hair on his chest. At his pause, she propped her head up on her hand and stared down at him. "Or what?"

."Or he taped the cop having sex with one of the women."

Instead of a blush, which he would have expected, she got angry. "That's horrible."

"Yeah, well, Gerald isn't exactly a choirboy. He then takes the video back to his mob friends, who makes copies. They send one to the recruit, along with what they want from him by way of inside information."

"Blackmail?"

"Nice, huh," Sloan said sarcastically. "The threat of exposure to the department, to the cop's friends and family, guarantee the recruit's cooperation. That's when he begins alerting the mob about internal police operations, such as planned raids and arrests. It worked for too damn long."

"Sounds like the police have stopped it."

"They have, but they need airtight evidence for convictions, so they're being supermethodical about putting the case together before it goes to a grand jury. That's what they were in the midst of doing when Gerald tried to snatch Danny."

She nodded in understanding. "So what happened that the police were able to catch on to the blackmail?"

"One of the victims committed suicide. He left a note identifying Gerald and the videotape."

She went very still and then dropped back down toward him, tucking her head into his neck. "Oh God."

Sloan anchored her tighter against him. "What is it?"

"I heard gossip and rumors from some of my customers. Speculation because the cop was so young. Stems 'n Petals also did many of the spiritual bouquets for the funeral." Sloan thought he felt some tears against his neck. Suddenly she pulled away and sat up, her voice fiercely angry. "Gerald killed that recruit, Sloan. Maybe not directly, but he surely drove him to it. He's not only a child snatcher, but a murderer."

Chapter 6

"Come on, Danny, you can do it. Just a few more steps," Katherine coaxed, softly reassuring the year-old toddler.

His giggle was a little shaky as his bare feet tested the damp sand suspiciously. The beach didn't have the dry, familiar solidity of the cottage deck, nor was the sand soft like the carpet in her Harbor Bay apartment.

Down on her knees a few inches in front of him, Katherine held out her hands. "You're such a big boy," she said encouragingly. She knew he was trying to figure out how he could reach her without letting go of the high wooden chair next to him. But just as he loosened his small grip, a sudden ocean breeze made him grab for the lifeguard stand.

She inched herself closer. Danny squinted in the late afternoon sun as if to say she hadn't come close enough. She laughed, wishing that Sloan was with them. No doubt he'd offer some irresistible bribe like ice cream and Danny would march away from the wooden support without a protest.

She glanced back toward the sand dune where she'd left Sloan sleeping. After their conversation about Gerald, Katherine had sensed a withdrawal. Not so much closing her out as closing himself in. She wasn't sure if there was a significant difference between the two, but she'd had the impression he'd pulled away from her emotionally, even as his arm had gripped her against his body more firmly. She hadn't objected and had, in fact, curled tightly against him. They'd stayed that way, neither speaking, both occupied with their own thoughts.

Katherine had been rethinking and reevaluating her own fury at Gerald. Her unceasing anger at him had wedged itself even deeper after Sloan's account of the young police recruit's suicide. She also had a new list of questions for her sister. Had Jennifer known about Gerald's illegal activities? Had she been aware that he so cavalierly toyed with people's reputations and their lives? Or had she been so deeply involved she'd simply ignored any signal or clue to Gerald's true character and looked the other way? Of course, Jennifer had eventually broken it off and refused to see him. In fairness Katherine had to credit her sister with that bit of wisdom, however late she'd found it.

As in the past, and now more so after Sloan's revelation, her sister's attraction to, and affair with, Gerald baffled her. But then Katherine had remembered Jennifer's gag-me-with-a-spoon gesture when Katherine had become engaged to Robert. Jennifer had informed her Robert had all the sex appeal of the Irwin sisters' poodle. Katherine ruefully concluded that when it came to men, she and Jennifer could give lessons on poor and painful choices.

At some point in her musings, Katherine had found herself wondering what Jennifer would think of Sloan. Certainly, when it came to sex appeal, a prolonged look at Sloan Calder would convince any woman to rewrite her list of top ten male attributes. Perhaps because he was so obviously unaware of his appeal, of how his naked chest, worn-white denim cutoffs and black hair could make Katherine's heart pound and her mouth go dry.

Lulled by the warmth of the sun and the security of being tucked close to Sloan, she'd drifted off to sleep, her thoughts wandering into some very pleasurable dreams.

A while later, she'd been awakened by Danny dumping sand on the blanket and in her hair. Regretfully she'd rolled away from Sloan and sat up. He'd slept on, his breathing even and deep. Since they'd arrived at the cottage, Sloan hadn't been sleeping too well. That conclusion had come thanks to the thin walls of the bedroom that allowed her to hear him either up and prowling around or tossing in bed.

Sprawled across the sandy blanket, Katherine had decided not to disturb him. She had, however, indulged herself in a few luxurious moments of appreciative staring.

His black hair was wind-ruffled, his face lean and his body tight with corded muscle. Not the bodybuilder type bulges or the pump and press pectorals, either, but muscle that suited him as naturally as the inviting hair on his chest and the intriguing way his cutoffs banded his hips.

He'd stirred slightly, one hand sliding across his belly, his fingers disappearing beneath the button of the cutoffs. He'd scowled a little, as though the encounter with clothes felt strange. Katherine had turned away quickly, recalling her voyeuristic look at him that afternoon when he'd stood in his bedroom. She'd tried to shake out her thoughts, telling herself that she was being outrageously bold. She was also somewhat amazed at the path Sloan could seduce her thoughts into traveling. One would think she'd been sequestered in a nunnery for most of her life. She wondered if that was how Sloan viewed her.

Not once had Sloan given her a once-over, stripping-her-with-his-eyes glance, or whistled at her, or flirted with her. In the past she'd experienced each of those from men to varying degrees, and she'd found the attention at worst annoying, at best harmless.

Yet she'd barely known Sloan when he'd kissed her with such deep intimacy. A kiss, she'd reminded herself, that she not only had allowed, but hadn't found annoying. He'd made her ache in hidden places with feelings that were far from harmless. But he'd reminded her constantly why they were in Chelsea Beach. She knew the folly of letting her heart run ahead of her head. She'd learned that from her own experience with Robert. And yet with Sloan the caution seemed to be mutual.

His wariness had been most evident when he'd flat out refused to kiss her, saying he was terrified because of where it would lead. Since she was fairly certain he wasn't talking long-term relationship, she'd concluded he'd meant a sexual relationship. Yet in some strange way his refusal to kiss her had made her less mistrustful and less questioning of her own desire. And certainly more bold. Hadn't she fallen asleep in his arms on the blanket without a qualm? Could a woman trust a man physically yet still be afraid of trusting him for a committed, monogamous relationship? Perhaps in essence that was what Sloan was saying to her. "You can trust me not to seduce you into having sex, and you can count on me being gone when this is all over."

A professional doing the job he was hired to do.

As he should be. As she wanted him to be. She did, she'd told herself firmly. Damn it, she did.

She'd repeated that vow to herself a few more times as she'd scooped up Danny and crossed the sand dunes to walk down to the shore.

Now, fifteen minutes later, Danny took a tentative barefoot step forward and then again grabbed for the white wooden support.

Katherine extended her hand again, coaxing, but Danny shook his head. "I bet if Sloan were here, he'd bribe you with ice cream and sprinkles, wouldn't he?"

He let go long enough to clap his hands. "Slo-an . . ." He grinned in excitement.

"You little monkey. When did you learn to say Sloan?"

"Ball!" he said triumphantly.

Katherine laughed. "You're getting quite a vocabulary. Ball and Sloan and truck . . ."

His two new front teeth touched his bottom lip and he tipped his head to the side. Katherine saw the F word coming, fully dressed in a child's innocence.

She clapped her hands quickly to distract him. He closed his mouth instantly, his brown eyes wide with confusion. No wonder, she thought with a grimace. Both she and Sloan had laughed the first time he'd mispronounced truck. She scooted close to him and gave him a kiss and a hug. "Let's call it a car, Danny. Can you say car?"

Now he looked thoroughly perplexed. Then he grinned. "Ride? Slo-an?"

"Yes, you love to go for rides with Sloan, don't you, sweetheart?" The rides had become a morning ritual to get the newspaper and any items Katherine needed. She'd marveled at how Danny had become less high-strung and more outgoing. Her concerns that the toddler might fear men in the future were slowly fading thanks to Sloan.

Having watched Danny since their arrival and now, as he tested the sand and his bravery, she'd noted his eyes were once again wide with a child's wonder and curiosity. No longer did he cling so tenaciously to her, as he had those first few days after the break-in. She knew she had Sloan to thank for the spoiling he'd so generously given the baby. She realized, with a rush of affection for Sloan, that caring about Danny beyond his physical safety wasn't a job requirement. Yet he'd been unfailingly patient, spoiling Danny perhaps, but never in a negative way. From Sloan she'd sensed that he wanted to make sure Danny's world, as a child at least, was inviolate, filled and brimming over with good things and secure memories.

She took Danny's hand. His bravery on the hard sand took a quantum leap now that his hand was firmly in Katherine's.

"Why don't we give Sloan a few more minutes of peaceful sleep. Let's walk down the beach. Maybe we can find some shells or a starfish."

Katherine walked west rather than east, where a bank of rocks separated the public beach from privately owned land and homes. Homes that included Linda and Hank Rowen's weathered contemporary house.

Katherine adjusted her stride to Danny's baby steps as they slowly made their way down the beach. They stopped to watch a sand crab scurry along the water line. She showed Danny a stone and had him feel how it had been washed smooth by the water.

They walked on. Katherine picked up a shell and held it to Danny's ear. "Listen, sweetheart, you can hear the ocean roar." Danny stilled, his face a picture of fierce concentration. She asked him, "Can you say roar?"

After two tries, he said, "Row?"

"Pretty close." She let him listen again. "We'll take it back and show Sloan."

Sea gulls dipped and soared. A few yards beyond her three teenage girls working on early summer tans lay stretched out on towels. An elderly couple passed, smiling and nodding, the man carrying a bamboo walking stick.

Katherine alternately carried Danny and let him walk on his own. She held the shell with the "row," but put some smaller, more delicate ones in her pocket. They would make decorative additions to her florist shop's occasional orders for rock garden arrangements. She made a mental note to check into buying loose shells.

Katherine didn't find any starfish, and after half an hour, she swung Danny up and into her arms. "I think we better get back. Sloan will be looking for us."

She turned around to return the way they'd come, a little surprised that they'd walked almost the entire length of the beach. The sand dunes all blended and for a moment she frowned. She knew they'd come down to the shore, in an almost straight line, to one of the lifeguard stands. Except now, glancing toward the distant bank of rocks, she realized she'd paid no attention to the number of lifeguard stands.

They started back. After a few minutes Katherine halted to ponder whether the lifeguard stand that Danny had clung to was the third or fourth. A figure came toward them, walking with shoulders hunched, and she gave no more than a passing glance.

She got a firmer grip on Danny while her eyes scanned the dunes, hoping Sloan might have awakened, assumed she and the baby were down by the water and come looking for them.

For a brief moment she scowled, walking onward. Her annoyance wavered between anger at herself for walking so far and at Sloan for sleeping so long. Not fair to him, she knew, since she was the one who'd been so careful not to awaken him. However she didn't feel very fair right now, just uneasy.

She shifted Danny to her other hip. The toddler mumbled something, his body heavy against her. The shells she'd tucked in her pocket began to feel more like lead weights. Danny rested his head on her shoulder and he rubbed one fist in his eyes. Her arms were getting tired and with the sun behind the clouds, she felt the chill of the wind. The tide rolled in and she moved higher onto the beach to avoid the splash of water.

The figure she'd seen walking toward her was close enough now that she could see it was a man. She reached the fourth lifeguard stand and hesitated. The man had cut up onto the dryer sand, a few hundred feet away.

Katherine paused to stare and then blinked. A tiny stir of recognition fanned inside her. He didn't have the smooth prowl of Sloan, nor the hesitant step of Hank Rowen. The man walked with a shuffling trudge.

Again she shifted Danny, realizing she had subconsciously been trying to shield and hide him.

As the stranger edged nearer, she made out chino-colored pants and a dark-colored shirt that looked out of place on the beach. Similarities rushed at her. Chinos and a burgundy shirt had looked out of place in her Harbor Bay apartment, too.

In Danny's room.

Katherine froze. The sand gripped her feet like cement. Gerald! His name exploded in her mind with the force of a blow to the head. It can't be him. He couldn't just appear on the beach like some aberration that a demon had sent to terrify her.

But the clothes were the same.

Her draining and instinctive fear was the same.

His shuffling walk . . . coming closer and closer. . . .

Danny began to squirm and fuss, and she realized he'd picked up her apprehension.

"Easy, sweetheart," she murmured, sliding her hand around the back of the toddler's head to keep him tight against her. She cursed herself for walking so far, and for not paying close enough attention to any landmarks that would identify where she'd come down to the beach.

She cursed Sloan, too. Why wasn't he looking for them? Inside her, the tiny beginnings of trust she'd precariously allowed herself to feel for Sloan died.

She glanced behind her to where she'd been, but the tide was coming in fast now. The teenagers she'd seen sunbathing had gone. She cast a furtive glance back at Gerald. He was just a few yards away, his head down as if he was watching his footing.

While still in Harbor Bay she'd wondered whether Gerald had some other plan to snatch Danny; something devious and unexpected. For all she knew he could have followed them here a week ago. Had he just been waiting for a time when she and Danny were alone?

He walked steadily, a bill cap pulled low over his face. Then he stopped just above the fourth lifeguard stand, peered directly at her for a moment and then, as if making a decision, he again started toward her.

Katherine bolted, gripping Danny so hard she felt him gulp for air. The dry, deep sand slowed her down. The wind tore at her eyes and made them water, the wetness icy on her cheeks. She wiped at them with the hand that still clutched the shell. The sharp edge cut her cheek, but she barely noticed.

She topped the sand dune. A new shot of adrenaline blanked out her sore arms, Danny's wailing and Gerald behind her. Her anticipation of safety, of Sloan being there, had stubbornly and desperately prevailed.

"Slo—?" She halted, his name dying on her lips, her eyes blinking in stark astonishment. Danny's crying fell to a whimper. Where she'd expected to see the remains of their picnic, Danny's pail and the collapsed sand castle—where she knew she'd find Sloan...

She found nothing.

No one. Not even a trace that anyone had been there. Just the snakelike sway of tall reedy beach grass. No sound but the returned panting of her own terror.

"Sloan?" she whispered in a broken croak, now believing that she must be in the middle of a nightmare. They hadn't come to the beach for a picnic. She hadn't heard all those details about Gerald and concluded he was a murderer. She hadn't slept beside Sloan as if he represented a new sense of security.

In a moment she would awaken in her room at the cottage, sweaty with relief.

Any moment, she would awaken. *Oh God please, wake me now....*

Danny began to cry again and feeling his body's trembling, her own terror came back, so alive it licked down her spine like a forked tongue. She tightened her arms around the toddler and faced the numbness of cold reality. She would have to escape from Gerald without help. Just like before.

She whirled at the shuffling sound. He stood only a few feet away.

The nightmare was real.

She screamed.

Sloan had just come out from behind the bank of rocks that separated the public beach from the private land. He thought he heard a yell and halted, listening, knowing the wind could carry sounds in deceptive ways. Sweat poured off him despite the chilling wind and cooling temperatures. He'd tried unsuccessfully to get a mental handle on the fear that had been thickening since he'd awakened and found Katherine and Danny gone.

Since then he'd been gripped with a combination of fury at himself for carelessly going to sleep, and anger at her for not telling him where she was going. Time enough later to lecture her, he reminded himself. Now all he wanted was to find her and Danny. Find them safe. His gaze swept the nearly deserted beach, but there was no sign of them.

High tide pushed the water higher onto the beach, tossing a small piece of driftwood onto the sand while the late afternoon sun bled through the clouds, leaving the skyline a crimson red. Then he heard the sound again, this time a keening wail. A man came down from the rise of one of the sand dunes and hurried toward the more level and harder packed sand.

"Hey! Wait a minute," Sloan yelled, thinking the man might have seen Katherine and Danny. The man neither acknowledged his shout nor hesitated, but hurried farther and farther down the beach.

Sloan worked his way across the dunes. Over the rise of one dune, a good distance from where they'd had their picnic, he stopped and stared. Ahead of him he saw Katherine running through the tall beach grass.

Sloan planted his hands on his hips, wondering where in hell she was going. "Katy!"

But she didn't turn or even slow down. She ran wildly, clutching Danny, tripping in the deep sand, falling once and dragging herself up to her feet and running again.

He started after her, cupped his hands around his mouth and shouted again. "Katy!"

Again, she didn't stop. What in hell was going on? If he didn't know better he'd think she was deliberately running away.

He yelled a third time, then cut across the sand at a shorter angle so as to get in front of her. She zigzagged, circling, losing whatever energy she'd drawn on, but obviously determined she wasn't going to stop. Just as he was within a few feet of reaching her, she fell again.

On her knees now, she clutched Danny so tightly, the boy was red in the face. Whatever remaining anger he'd had at her for going off without telling him died when he knelt down in front of her.

"What happened—" But he never finished the sentence.

She jerked back, her body trembling, her eyes terror-stricken, her hold on Danny rigid.

Sloan stared. "My God."

Her hair was damp from the ocean air and tangled with sand, her face a frightening white, her cheek cut raggedly and bleeding, her eyes wild and desperate. Her tourist T-shirt was plastered against her and wet with sweat. She had Danny so locked in her arms Sloan was afraid she would hurt him.

"Katy," he said gently, trying to loosen her arms.

She shrank back, shaking her head vigorously. "No! Don't touch him. You weren't here. You were supposed to be here. You were supposed to protect us." She swallowed hard, tears glistening. A fresh trickle of blood slipped from the cut on her cheek. She maintained her iron hold on Danny.

The boy squirmed restively and finally found enough breath to scream. Katherine seemed to sink at the boy's screech. She loosened her arms, but she wouldn't release him. In a low, shallow voice, she murmured to Danny, "I won't let him have you, sweetheart. I promise, he won't. Gerald won't get you."

In the process of trying to decide whether she could walk to the cottage or he should carry her, the mention of Danny's father caught Sloan off guard. "Gerald?"

She swung on him with vehemence. "Yes, Gerald. You do remember Gerald Graham?"

Sloan felt as if he'd come in on the tail end of some horror movie. Her breathing sounded more like gulps. He wanted to draw her into his arms, but he knew that was the last thing she'd allow. "Never mind Gerald. I'm more interested in what happened to you."

She glared at him as if he was a little slow. "He was on the beach. He was a few feet away from me, Sloan. Coming after us."

"Who?"

"Gerald! For God's sake who did you think I meant?"

Sloan plowed his hands through his hair. He'd never seen such fierce resolve in anyone's eyes. Or such cold fury. He knew that his only hope of finding out what had happened was by staying calm. Rather than give credence to Gerald having somehow escaped Drummond, Sloan said in a low voice, "Gerald isn't in Chelsea Beach."

"What's the matter with you?" she shouted as though he were a thousand miles away. "Aren't you listening to me? Didn't you see him? He wore chinos, a dark shirt and a hat...."

"Take it easy. I saw a guy running down the beach. You mean him?"

"Yes, that was Gerald."

Sloan stared at her. He didn't know who the guy was, but he was damn sure it wasn't Gerald Graham. "Katy, Gerald is in Harbor Bay being watched by an undercover investigation team. You know that."

"I don't know any such thing. You say that. But why should I believe you when I saw him just a few minutes ago? He came after me to take Danny."

Sloan took a deep breath. No way would he convince her by talking. Although he realized she was distraught, he knew she didn't hallucinate. Was there a chance she was right and the man running down the beach *had* been Gerald? Ridiculous. Then again, the guy on the beach had been hurrying away, his back to Sloan. And at that particular moment his mind had been focused on finding Katherine and Danny, not pursuing some stranger who might have suddenly realized the beach was too cold for walking.

But... Yeah, those damn buts, he thought grimly. If somehow Gerald had eluded the undercover team, how in hell would he have known they were here? And if he had disappeared from Harbor Bay, surely Drummond would have called.

Sloan closed his eyes briefly and faced a basic fact. He'd screwed up royally. What in hell good would it have done if Drummond *had* called? They'd been at the beach. And if that wasn't enough, he'd gone so sound asleep that she'd taken Danny, walked away and he hadn't even heard a goddamn thing.

You're doin' one hell of a job, Calder, he concluded heavily, considering the potentially disastrous scenario that could have taken place. The one time she needed you, you weren't there.

"All right, sweets. Let's go back to the cottage and I'll call Joe." Sloan got to his feet and extended his hand to help her up.

She didn't move, still clutching Danny.

Sloan frowned. "What is it?"

"Why did you leave us alone?"

The whispered question was a disappointed plea and Sloan again cursed himself for going to sleep. He hunkered down in front of her and brushed his fingers across her wet cheeks. She flinched and he let his hand fall away.

"I didn't leave you. When I woke up and you were gone, I thought you might have gone back to the cottage. After checking there and not finding you, I couldn't figure out what in hell had happened to you or where you'd gone."

In a guarded voice she said flatly, "If you'd come back down to the beach I would have seen you."

He shook his head. "I cut from the cottage over to Linda and Hank's house, thinking you might have gone there. They weren't home, so I came back down to the beach from that direction."

She stared off in the direction of the nearest sand dune. "Our blanket, the sand castle..."

"Are a couple hundred feet in that direction," he added, gesturing further to the right.

She swallowed. "It was the third and not the fourth," she muttered to Danny.

"What are you talking about?"

"The lifeguard stands. I couldn't remember..."

Danny shivered, burrowing closer to her. Sloan was shirtless and now that his immediate fear that something had happened passed, he, too, shivered in the chilly wind.

He gripped her arm. "Come on, we'll finish the explanations where it's warm."

She got to her feet, juggling Danny, and then just sagged against Sloan.

Sloan waited. He knew she couldn't carry the toddler any longer. Her cheeks were pale with the strain of just holding him. Yet with an instinct that surprised him, he knew that she needed to relinquish Danny rather than have Sloan take him from her.

Valiantly she tried to manage. Sloan allowed it, walking close to her, but after a dozen steps her knees buckled. She bowed her head over the toddler's and wept.

Sloan touched her hair and to his relief she didn't jerk away or flinch. He was freezing from the wind, and it took all his concentration not to scoop her up and carry her, baby and all. Huddled here on the sand, he sensed an almost desperate aloneness in her, as if those she'd counted on had failed her.

"Sloan?"

He hunkered down in front of her. "I'm right here."

She gulped. "I don't think I can carry Danny."

Sloan brushed the boy's hair off his cheek, but said nothing.

"Would you?"

His heart lifted at this small gesture that a few moments ago would never have entered her mind. "Sure. What do you say, tiger? I don't know about you two, but I'm ready for a hot shower and some warm clothes."

After stopping to retrieve the blanket and the basket, they returned to the cottage. They'd barely gotten in the door when Katherine said, "Are you going to call Joe?"

Sloan glanced at the clock, and handed Danny to Katherine. "Yeah, I'll take care of it," he said. "You go ahead and get Danny into the bathtub."

Later, while the toddler splashed in the warm water, she heard Sloan on the telephone. She sat down on the lid of the commode. Her shoulders and her arms ached, and her knees were scraped from all the falls into the sand. She'd caught a glimpse of herself in the medicine cabinet mirror, and had shuddered. Her hair was tangled and sandy, her face pale and smeared with streaks of dried blood, her eyes a feverishly bright brown, as though still tinged with the terror that had never happened.

She stared down at her hands and then lifted them, trying to hold them steady. The wedding ring made her blink, reminding her that despite it being real gold and genuine diamonds, it summed up all that was phony and wrong about her earlier feelings for Sloan.

She'd been a fool to try to make real what was inherently false; the family facade, the mock marriage, the temptation to trust. Reality had existed out there on the beach. Gerald had been after Danny and she hadn't been able to find Sloan.

Her hands trembled slightly and she curled her fingers into tight fists.

No matter what Sloan said, she knew she'd seen Gerald. Certainly if the man had been just a stranger walking on the beach, he wouldn't have come toward her, attempted to...

She'd been the one who'd seen him in Danny's bedroom, not Sloan. And he'd admitted to only seeing the man running away. She'd seen him up close, too close and although the hat had been pulled low, the clothes, the walk...

Danny splashed some water on her legs in an attempt to get a bobbing rubber duck. She quickly retrieved it, then squeezed it. Danny clapped his hands at the squeak. She grinned, squeezing again before giving the toy to him. She drank the sight of him in; wet and chubby, pink and clean. But most of all, safe and unhurt.

She'd examined him closely before putting him into the tub, fearful that she might have hurt him squeezing him so hard in her rush to escape Gerald. After a thorough inspection where she pressed his ribs watching for just the slightest wince, she'd searched for any bruises he might have gotten when she'd fallen. When she'd found none, she'd gone weak with relief.

A tap on the bathroom door startled her. "Come in," she called to Sloan, then took a shallow breath.

He had pulled on jeans and a T-shirt, and carried a mug of coffee and a tube of antiseptic cream. Seeing him here in the fluorescent light alarmed her. He looked somehow older, tired and emotionally drained. His hair had been many times finger combed, and his eyes were dark and troubled, the lines on his cheeks deeper, made more stark by the shadows of whiskers.

He lifted the mug to his mouth and sipped before putting it down on the bathroom counter. For an odd moment the motion and the man seemed like a snapshot from the past.

"My God," she whispered and quickly pressed her fingers to her mouth.

Sloan glanced at her, warily. "What's wrong?"

She blinked. Yes, she'd seen him this way. Once. When she'd delivered the jasmine and tulips he'd ordered for his wife's casket. Then he'd been drunk, but she recalled her astonishment that he didn't slur his words or stumble about. He'd reacted as if the tragedy that had robbed him of his wife had been so profound, no amount of alcohol could blur the pain.

"Why are you looking at me that way?"

She glanced down. "For a moment you reminded me..." She shook her head. No, her eyes and mind were simply imagining things. They were both tired and wrung out. No way could the Sloan of today bare any resemblance to the Sloan she'd seen after his wife died.

"Reminded you that you wanted me to leave you alone?" he asked in a weary voice.

She recalled how she'd cowered from his touch on the sand dunes. "You must think you got stuck here with a wild woman."

He put the antiseptic cream down on the sink. The bathroom suddenly seemed too crowded. Danny happily splashed in the tub. She reached down and pushed a couple of his water toys closer to him. Sloan stood inches from her. If she moved her head just slightly she could have rested it on his thigh. She stood, with every intention of getting Danny's towel, but Sloan shook his head.

"Give him another few minutes. You need to get that cut cleaned." He cupped her chin, then hesitated, as if waiting for her to pull away. They stood very close as he slowly turned her face toward the light. His thumb lightly brushed over the cut to check how deep it was. "How did you get this?" he asked, reaching for a facecloth and turning on the hot water.

"Danny and I found a shell with the roar of the ocean in it. We wanted to bring it back to show you. I must have rubbed it across my face."

"When you were running from Gerald," he said in such a smooth way she wondered if he was afraid she'd freak out again. He'd added soap to the hot cloth and she winced when he touched her.

He rinsed and patted her cheek dry.

She brushed his arm and found it tight and tense. "Sloan?"

He uncapped the tube of cream and applied a thin layer to the cut. "Yeah."

Their faces were very close and whether it was his gentleness with the cream or her own need to find out what he was thinking, she asked, "You still don't believe me, do you?"

He whisked some sand from her earlobe. "Why don't you let me get Danny dry and into his pajamas while you take a shower."

She ignored his offer. "You don't, do you?"

He sighed. "Let's put it this way. I don't disbelieve you."

She wasn't sure if it was her own weariness or her mind beginning to rationalize her actions, but she needed his reassurance. "Do you think I'm crazy or some lunatic who sees things that aren't there?"

He tossed the tube of cream into the sink and drew her into his arms. She went willingly, gratefully. He slid his fingers into her hair. "No, sweets, I don't think you're crazy or seeing things that aren't there."

"But you don't believe that I saw Gerald?"

"Obviously you were terrified. I want to believe it wasn't Gerald, but I'm not ruling out the possibility that it could have been. I called Harbor Bay and left a message for Joe to call me."

"But what if—?"

He kissed her then, but she was sure it was only to stop her from speculating. Then he let her go and in a rough voice said, "Let me handle this part of it, okay? Nothing is going to happen to you and Danny. I promise."

She stared down at her hands once more. The trembling had stopped, but Gerald was still out there. Out there, waiting for his next chance.

Chapter 7

Very close to ten o'clock, the phone rang. Sloan managed to grab the receiver on the second ring.

"Where in hell have you been?" he snapped when he heard Drummond's greeting. Sloan kept his voice low so as not to awaken Katherine. She'd fallen asleep on the couch.

Earlier, she'd gotten Danny settled and then taken her shower. Just when Sloan had decided she'd gone on to bed, she'd joined him in the living room to wait for Joe's call.

Sloan had fixed her a mug of hot chocolate and poured a double whiskey for himself. He'd sat down beside her, but neither had touched the other. Even their conversation had been guarded and awkward from the tenseness and the anxiety involved in waiting to hear about Gerald's whereabouts. Finally Katherine had drifted off to sleep. Sloan had no such inclinations. Since the frightening episode that afternoon, just the thought of sleeping made him sick.

Now, noting Katherine's stillness, Sloan was satisfied that the phone hadn't disturbed her. He turned back to concentrate on the call.

Drummond said apologetically, "I just got your message. I was in Boston. What's going on?"

Sloan got right to the point. "Gerald Graham. Where is he?"

After just the slightest hesitation, Drummond asked, "Is this some kind of joke? You know where Graham is."

"I know where I thought he was. Katherine claims she saw him on the beach—"

"What!"

Sloan finished, "Making an attempt to snatch Danny."

"That's impossible." But Sloan didn't miss the alarm in Drummond's voice. "Graham's here."

"That's what I told her, but God Himself couldn't convince her after what she believes she saw."

"Sloan, look, it's late," he said in a soothing voice that Sloan had heard often whenever Drummond suspected an overblown story. "Why don't we wait until morning to discuss this? You have another talk with her after she's rested and she's thought over what she thinks happened."

"She hasn't flipped out, Joe."

"How do you know? For that matter, what in hell do you really know about her? Maybe she has delusions or PMS or she spooks easily."

"That's a helluva thing to say," Sloan fired back, feeling the strain on his usually controlled temper. He recalled her desperate concern for Danny. "Don't try to turn her into some weirdo because you can't answer my question."

"Hey, don't get so defensive." Drummond paused, then in an astonished voice asked, "Good God, Sloan, you haven't let the marriage bit get to you personally, have you?"

Sloan had no intention of pretending he didn't know what Drummond was getting at, but he also resented the question. In a chillingly calm voice, he said, "Are you asking me if I'm sleeping with her?"

Drummond cleared his throat. "Look, I know you'd never intend for that to happen, but good intentions can be forgotten. Hell, she's not bad looking. You're in close quarters. Supposed to be married. Hormones being what they are... Hey, it's understandable."

Sloan bit down on the expletive. Part of his anger rose not from Drummond hitting upon a potential truth, but because in that precise instant, Sloan faced a new truth about his attraction to Katherine. It was more than sexual.

What Drummond called hormones and "understandable" translated into let's-do-it-because-it-feels-good sex. But Sloan knew instinctively that sex with Katherine would be making love. Perhaps by cold definition the two meant the same, but realistically and emotionally there was a wide difference between them. Sex satisfied the gut. Making love fed the soul.

How much simpler to blow off Drummond's comments, but they nagged at him because they skirted another truth. His deep gut concern couldn't ignore that making love to Katherine would probably open some of those sealed doors to his soul.

"It's a damn good thing you're not here or I'd be very tempted to loosen a few of your teeth." Sloan waited a few seconds, then said, "I want to know where in hell Graham is. Your theory that he'd hang around Harbor Bay until he could get his son is blown away if he was who Katy saw today."

Drummond let the sensitive topic drop and answered Sloan's question instead. "The last report I had was before I left for Boston. Trust me, Graham wasn't anywhere near where you are."

"You saw him or you heard secondhand?"

"What are you getting at?"

"I'm getting at some positive proof that Graham is where you say he is." Both men had been automatically careful about not naming Chelsea Beach; a precautionary measure against the possibility of tapped phone lines. When he heard Drummond swear, Sloan knew he'd made his point. As the chief of police, Drummond took final responsibility for every investigation; kudos and plaques for a success, or head-on-the-platter censure for a failure.

Drummond growled, "You always did have a knack for the jugular."

"No throat-slicing, Joe. Just some answers about Gerald that you can personally verify. I'm sure you don't want to order an after-the-crime investigation to determine how Gerald gave the department the slip. You had to do that af-

ter Angela's death, remember?'' Sloan leaned against the
wall and tried to ignore the comparison he'd been making
since he'd listened to Katherine's terror.

In one way he'd found drenching relief that she was alive
and unhurt and able to get angry and be scared. In another
way he'd had all those premonitions about history repeating itself. No matter how often he'd reminded himself that
these were different circumstances, a different woman, he
couldn't shake the comparisons. In both instances Sloan
hadn't protected them from danger.

Earlier, at the beach, Sloan's own responsibility for
Katherine and Danny had leaped far beyond that of a job
or even the assuagement of personal guilt left over about
Angela's death. Now he felt as if he were reliving the entire
nightmare of Angela's death, but this time with Katherine. . . .

''Are you equating what happened to Angela with this?''
Drummond asked, and then started to defend his officers
and the efficient way his department handled cases.

Sloan listened, but he noted Drummond deftly side-
stepped the one case Sloan knew they hadn't handled so ef-
ficiently. ''How about the way the department stalled
around in finding Angela's killers? You've stonewalled on
arresting Gerald because of the department's own internal
investigation, but I wonder if you aren't being deliberately
blind. Aren't you hoping that your decision to hire me was
enough? Aren't you refusing to believe that Katy might have
seen Graham on the beach because you're not ready to arrest him?''

''Damn it, Sloan—''

''And as far as a comparison with my wife, if I recall
correctly, your department couldn't locate the bastard who
killed Angela. The excuses ranged from lack of men to cir-
cumstantial evidence. If I'd waited around for the detective
you assigned to wear out some shoe leather instead of the
seat of his pants, Suggs Mello and his sleazy cronies would
have been long gone.''

''All right, damn it, all right.'' Drummond sighed heavily. ''I'll admit that if you hadn't been like a pit bull on your

wife's case the attorney general's office might not have gotten Suggs convicted."

"Thank you," he said with just a tinge of sarcasm.

"And you broke a lot of department rules in the process."

"Stretched, Joe. But since I wasn't a cop that was a moot point."

Alarmed, Drummond said, "Now wait just a damn minute, Sloan. The rules this time say you stay with the woman and the kid. Period. The last thing I need is you going off like some loose cannon."

"Relax. I'm doing what I was hired to do. But I'm not about to let what happened to Angela happen to Katy and Danny. Understand me?"

"I could say something about taking this too personally or the dangers of not being objective."

"Don't."

"Yeah, I value my teeth," Drummond replied sagely. "Okay, let's have what you've got. From the beginning."

Sloan reconstructed the afternoon, admitting that he'd fallen asleep, but emphasizing the convincing state of terror he'd found Katherine in.

"If you'd been with her and the kid instead of sleeping, this entire episode might have been avoided," Drummond interjected.

"Condemnation noted," Sloan said gruffly.

Drummond's voice softened. "I've got to hand it to you, Sloan, you can be a hard-ass, but you don't duck and hide when you think you've screwed up. How many hours have you been beating yourself up about going to sleep?"

"Not enough," he said bluntly. "Can you get me some positive proof as to Gerald's whereabouts? Roughly around four this afternoon?"

"Alibi the guy, huh?"

"Yeah."

Drummond was silent for a few seconds. "I'll get back to you."

"Don't worry about the time."

"I'll call you as soon as I can confirm something. And, Sloan, ease up on yourself," Drummond added before hanging up.

Sloan hooked the receiver, leaned against the counter and told himself repeatedly that Gerald had to be in Harbor Bay. He wanted to believe that the man Katherine had seen on the beach, the description she'd given Sloan, her underlying fear that Gerald would succeed and get Danny had just been the right mix of ingredients to create a terrifyingly realistic illusion.

Yet despite his earlier skepticism, he couldn't dismiss the possibility that Gerald may have found them. Sloan dragged his hands through his hair, and hoped like hell he was wrong.

He snapped off the kitchen light and went into the living room, where Katherine still slept on the couch.

He stared at her for a few moments, struck again by her tenacity and her gutsiness. He thought of the Irwin sisters' comment about her being alone and unable to trust men. No damn wonder, he thought ruefully. First Robert had betrayed her, then she'd watched her sister get involved with Graham.

Now because Katherine had done Jennifer a favor and offered to care for Danny, she'd been plunged into another hellish situation.

When he'd watched her from the Harbor Bay police station window, something had shifted and creaked open inside him. Resisting the feeling or passing the reaction off as simply sexual hadn't worked.

Initially he'd taken this particular case as an attempt and hope to make up for his own guilt about Angela, but now, searching back through the past few days and examining his actions, he wondered ...

Sloan shivered, his mind searching for the familiar dark shade of denial, but none existed. The exposed truth stayed stubbornly clear. He closed his eyes for a moment as total comprehension gripped him.

He'd wanted to prove to Katherine that she could trust him.

So many of his actions and responses toward her weren't because he had a job to do, nor were they because Gerald had roughed her up and scared the hell out of her and Danny.

God, he thought grimly, how easy this case would be if he could just pinpoint his motives with simplistic objectivity. But at some point his purpose had become personal and subjective. Wanting her to trust him, he now knew, hadn't just happened. Since he'd told the Irwin sisters of the engagement, his actions had revealed too damn much. And with annoying regularity.

That too hot, tongue-deep kiss that he'd promised her wouldn't happen again.

Admitting his terror that afternoon in her room because kissing her would lead to more—namely her in his bed.

Answering her questions about the police investigation of Gerald because he'd found them less complicated than talking about the growing attraction between them.

And the most puzzling one of all; the wedding ring that he'd bought for her. Not a move or action he could easily dismiss, yet one that wreaked havoc with his logic. Pure impulse, he told himself now, for any other explanation would strain reasonable bounds of credibility. And what in hell did a ring for a fake marriage have to do with her trusting him anyway?

Don't think about this one, Calder. Just chalk it up to impulse and her being spared a green finger from a five-and-dime ring.

Distance, he reminded himself. Focus on her as if she was an ordinary client. Concentrate on the days ahead when she would be out of his life. He could relax then, maybe take a vacation, indulge in a shallow, no-strings relationship where his contribution was only his body. No passing beyond the boundaries of passion and satisfaction. No open doors to his soul, no temptation to get serious, no reminders about the high price of falling in love.

Falling in love? The phrase snagged at his thoughts as if it needed to be translated. No way, he told himself emphatically. Not a chance.

He stood close to her now, pushing aside any nonsense about love, and watched her sleep. He tapped into his more sexual thoughts; in an odd way they were a hell of a lot safer than thinking about falling in love. Prudently, though, he ignored his urge to touch her.

She'd curled into the corner of the couch and tucked her legs beneath the long mocha-colored robe she wore. The fabric was some satiny material that Sloan didn't have to touch to know the garment wouldn't be as soft as her skin. Her hair was brushed and loose, falling just over the collar of the robe. Apart from the cut on her cheek, her face showed no stress from the previous hours.

Perhaps it was the deepness of the night, Katherine's ease in falling asleep with him nearby, or just the safety of knowing she couldn't question or corner him into revealing himself, but whatever the reasons, Sloan didn't fight his musings. He lazily mapped out a fantasy of her standing beside his bed, opening the robe, letting her nudity pleasure his senses, then allowing the garment to slip to the floor.

"You're exquisite," he would whisper.

"I want you," she would murmur.

"Show me."

Coming to him then, erotically bathed in the surreal shadows of moonlight and the satin cream of desire, he would draw her to himself. Indulgence would be sliding his hands up her thighs, skimming his mouth across the dampness of her tangled curls, grazing her belly, feasting on the sweet heat of her breasts. The pulse at her throat would quicken, her lips apart and welcoming, her tongue tasting of passion and impatience. Lifting her onto him, he would know the tantalizing grip of her thighs around his hips, watch her toss her head back and feel her sleek secret closure eagerly glove him.

The erotic whispers, the provocative panting of restraint. He would hold her hips, beginning the ancient rhythm of mating, the promise of a scorching release at their fingertips. Lifting, arching, reaching for the consummation...

"My God," Sloan murmured, so captured by the fantasy he had to squeeze his eyes closed just to black out the images. Beads of sweat broke out along his forehead. The low pounding in his groin made even his ribs ache. What in hell was he doing? Trying to go totally nuts? He took quick shallow breaths to break his breathing pattern. Fantasies, for cris' sakes. And not the hump and grind of a carnal rush, but a hot, jean-tightening hardness that had a hell of a lot more substance.

He dragged a hand down his face, annoyed that he'd invited such evocative yearnings. These were not the kind of thoughts he should be having; not the kind of thoughts he should be wanting.

Sloan backed away from her and went to the door that opened onto the deck. Sucking in gulps of salty-cool air, he made himself stay there until the wind had chilled his body and calmed his arousal.

After some length of time, he turned once again and glanced at her. She hadn't moved. He briefly debated on whether he should wake her and send her off to bed, but decided to leave well enough alone. With a stark honesty, he knew he didn't trust himself to touch her. Besides, she seemed comfortable. Her breathing was even and deep and God knows she needed the sleep.

He relocked the door leading out to the deck and was about to fix himself another drink when he heard Danny cry out.

Sloan jumped at the sudden noise and then hurried into the toddler's room. Danny stood in the crib, a blanket clutched in his hands, his eyes wide and his mouth about to tremble with louder cries.

Sloan brushed the boy's hair back. "Hey, tiger, you're supposed to be asleep."

"Ma-n. Ba-d man..." He hiccuped, reaching his arms out to Sloan.

Sloan lifted him up and out, holding him close. "Just a bad dream, tiger."

Danny tried to say "Katy" but it came out "Kitty."

"She's sound asleep. I think we shouldn't wake her, what do you think?" Danny just stared at him, his eyes a little less frightened. Sloan said softly, "How about you and I chase the bad man away?"

Danny sniffled, his small arms hugging Sloan so tight, he felt a lump form in his throat.

He walked for a bit, soothing the boy, but when he tried to put him back in the crib, Danny gripped him and started to cry again.

"Shh, all right," he whispered, not wanting Danny to disturb Katherine. But he didn't want to leave the baby alone to return to his nightmare, either. "How about if you and I find a nice comfy place and I'll tell you a story." Sloan recalled that his grandmother had used make-believe stories when he'd been about six years old. He'd had a bout with bad dreams when he'd gone to live with her after his parents had been killed in a bus accident.

Danny tightened his hold, and Sloan checked on Katherine.

She slept on, having barely moved. Since she was on the couch and his own bed was littered with clothes and daily reports he would have to file later for Drummond, Sloan took Danny into Katherine's room.

In her bedroom he didn't stop to turn on the light, nor did he completely pull back the covers on the neatly made bed. He simply bunched the pillows up, stretched out and cradled Danny next to him.

Keeping his voice low, he said, "I bet you don't know the story of *The Little Engine That Could*."

Danny burrowed closer, his small hands clutching Sloan's shirt. Sloan wasn't sure how a story about perseverance would be of much help, but since it was the only story he knew by heart it would have to do. However, since the purpose was to lull Danny back into a safe and secure sleep, Sloan figured he could probably rattle off the filing system he used in his P.I. office and still get the same effect.

He tucked his arm snugly around Danny and began. The children's story that he'd memorized from listening to his grandmother came back as clearly as if he'd reread it moments before. And with the story came some other memories. She'd told him more than once that being a child should be a wonderful world of make-believe. "When you have your own children, Sloan, tell them lots of make-believe stories."

His own children. Sloan tried to ignore the slow forming image in his mind's eye. Having children was included in the too-high-a-price-to-pay vow he'd made years ago.

Just another fantasy, he decided. An illusion of the night because he was in Katherine's bed holding a child who'd been forced into too much reality and desperately needed some make-believe in his world.

He glanced down at Danny, absorbing the child's trust and contentment. Then the possibility of his own child took on a new shape. The picture shattered the fantasy, erased the illusion and framed for him a powerful visual. He squeezed his eyes closed, but the scene remained.

Katherine stood at the closed chamber to his soul. Katherine had broken one of the scarred seals. Katherine was heavy with his child.

Midnight had long since passed when Katherine stood in the doorway of her room, blinking at the sight before her. Sloan and Danny asleep in her bed? She felt a little like Goldilocks, except the friendly bears had come to *her* house.

She moved into the room, debating how to extricate Danny from under Sloan's arm without waking either one of them. Pausing a moment and looking at the two of them, a glisten of dampness came to her eyes.

Although Sloan had certainly been attentive to Danny since they'd arrived at Chelsea Beach, the scene before her took a firm grip on her heart.

Danny had cuddled in against Sloan as if he were a barrier against all the bad things in the world. And Sloan held him as if being a fortress was as natural as breathing. Not rigidly tight, but securely. Anyone, Gerald included, who tried to touch Danny would have to get by Sloan.

She recalled Danny's reaction on the beach when she'd seen Gerald. The child had sensed her fear and immediately become apprehensive. Not once had Danny ever acted apprehensive with Sloan. Perhaps a little unsure in the beginning, the kind of natural wariness any child had toward a stranger, but nothing resembling the fear Gerald created in him. But then, Sloan had never rushed at him, or startled him, or frightened him. In fact, now that she thought about it, Sloan had treated her in much the same way. Another reason she wanted to talk to him, she realized.

Just moments ago she'd awakened on the couch with the beginnings of a headache. Her body had been cramped and chilly. Sitting up, she'd worked the stiffness from her legs while her thoughts considered what she wanted to say to him.

However, before she approached him, she'd wanted to get some aspirin for her headache. She'd cited at least two sources for the dull throb in her temples. The last lingering reminder of the traumatic afternoon. Or Sloan.

But both the aspirin and the headache had fled her mind the moment she'd seen Sloan and Danny.

Now she made her way silently to the edge of the bed. She wondered if Joe Drummond had called, and she puzzled on why Danny and Sloan were sleeping in her bed.

She glanced at her left hand. Though the ring was real, what it represented was not. She and Sloan appeared to be married, the three of them appeared to be a happy, vacationing family, but except for Gerald and the diamond and gold ring, everything else was make-believe. Pretend. Fake.

Then why, she asked herself, didn't the part she was playing feel false? Why did the scene before her—Sloan and Danny—seem so obviously right? Why had her anger at Sloan that afternoon been more frightening to her than seeing Gerald?

She searched around on the night table for the bottle of aspirin. Finding it, she slipped the container into her robe pocket.

Glancing once again at Sloan and Danny, she decided to finish the night on the couch and reached down beside the bed for the quilt that Sloan had kicked to the floor.

"Katy?" His voice was drowsy, husky. He stirred and reached toward her. His fingers brushed her robe and his hand slid up the back of her thigh.

She went still at the sudden gesture, but she was sure his touch was a chance one rather than deliberate. He was probably half-asleep.

"I'm sorry," she whispered, not moving away. "I didn't want to awaken you."

"Danny had a nightmare. Didn't want you to get upset. You okay?" His hand brushed the swell of her bottom before slipping around to cup her hip when she straightened. The quilt hung in her hand but the majority of it trailed to the floor. For a fleeting moment she wished she could curl up next to him as Danny had.

She cleared her throat. "I'm fine, just a little headache. We can talk in the morning."

"I'll get out of here so you can go to bed."

"I can sleep on the couch."

"Don't be ridiculous." Then in a low even voice he added, "Sleeping in here had me dreaming about you." His tone sounded slightly disturbed. She wondered if his dream had been of how much longer he'd have to be stuck with her. He peered down at Danny. "Do you think one of us could get him back to his crib without waking him?"

Still caught in the implication of his dreaming about her, she hesitated. His hand hadn't moved from her hip, further distracting her.

"Katy? Are you fully awake?"

"Oh. Yes, of course. I was just trying to figure out the best way to do this."

"Come around to the other side and I'll try to slide in this direction so you can get a hold on him."

She did as he suggested. Sloan tried to work himself up into a sitting position and ease his arm away from Danny. Katherine sat down on the edge of the bed and leaned toward them. Slowly she worked one hand beneath Danny's body and tried to slide her other hand between the child's chest and Sloan's ribs.

"Careful," Sloan whispered. "I think his fingers are still gripping my shirt."

"Can you move a little?" He did, and she dipped her hand down, searching for where Danny's fingers had caught Sloan's shirt. Instead she came in direct contact with Sloan's bare stomach. She froze. Almost immediately, she knew that was the wrong reaction. She should have ignored it and pretended that she didn't know her fingers were below his navel.

He drew in a long breath that pulled at his stomach muscles. The shift slid her hand lower.

"Don't move," he said in a clipped voice.

"I didn't do this on purpose."

"Thank God."

She stared at him, thinking she'd never seen him look so grim. At the same time she felt him trying to slide down so that her hand would move up. Whether she'd miscalculated because of not being able to see where her hand was trapped, or because she just couldn't think over the pounding of her heart, she moved her hand in the wrong direction. All she encountered was the open button of his jeans...

"Hell, Katy, what are you trying to do." It definitely wasn't a question.

"I was just trying to pull it out."

For a long moment he seemed to quit breathing.

Then the implication of what she'd said hit her. "I didn't mean that the way—"

"Tell my body that. God..." He took a breath as if his lungs had caved in. Then in a swift motion, he reached between her and Danny, snagged her wrist and held it. With his other hand he eased Danny's fingers open and released his shirt.

She scooped up Danny, cradling him and soothing him. He stirred awake, but then his eyes drifted closed again.

Sloan swung his legs off the bed and stood. His jeans were indeed unbuttoned, as was his shirt. Instead of looking at her, he fished around the floor for his shoes.

She didn't want to end things tonight with him angry. And then there was that other issue she'd wanted to talk to him about.

"Don't leave," she whispered.

He jerked his head up, staring at her, and she knew her request was the last thing he'd expected to hear.

"Let me get Danny settled and I'll be right back."

Moments later she returned, ignoring the fragments of hesitation that said talking to him in her bedroom wasn't too wise. But then again, simply being with Sloan had a tendency to unnerve her.

She found him sprawled in a chair far away from the bed. He'd switched on the bedside lamp, but the light didn't subdue his mood.

He looked disgruntled and rumpled and wary. His shirt still hung open and she found her gaze slipping to the now closed button of his jeans. A heady feeling, she realized, that Sloan Calder would feel the need to be cautious around her. It puzzled her, but also gave her courage.

"I didn't touch you, uh, almost touch you, deliberately, you know."

He hauled himself out of the chair. "I'm going to bed."

"No, please, not yet." She rubbed her hands down the folds of her robe, surprised at the slickness of her palms. "You don't believe me."

"I believe you."

"No, you don't. You thought I was being a tease or that I was pretending I didn't know what was going on."

"Katy, for God's sake..."

"Isn't that why you're angry?" She moved a step closer to him.

He drew in a long breath. Then in a low voice he said, "You're not the coy type. You're too open with your emotions."

"A discovery you no doubt made at the beach today during my hysteria," she said grimly as she lowered her head. *Tell him,* she told herself. *Just tell him what you wanted to say and be done with it.*

Sloan cupped her chin and made her look at him. "You aren't about to cut yourself some slack, are you? I didn't make the discovery on the beach. I knew it when I kissed you in Harbor Bay."

"Oh."

Looking deep into her eyes, he said softly, "Hasn't it occurred to you that I *liked* where your hand was? That I wanted like hell for you to touch me? Hasn't it occurred to you that the fault was mine and not yours? I'd been dreaming about you and your hand going a few inches lower would have—" He stopped his words. "Never mind. I'm sure you've got the general idea."

He let her go, but she reached for his hand and laced their fingers together. "Thank you," she whispered.

"For what?"

"For being so honest with me. Most men wouldn't have, you know."

"Just what I need," he muttered. "Accolades for being horny."

He seemed to loom over her. His hair was sleep-mussed, his cheeks whisker-shadowed. In his open shirt and low-slung jeans, he was devastatingly sexy and male. She found herself wanting to pursue his admission of being aroused. She felt torn and confused, as if she were two people. The cautious Katherine Brewster and a too-curious Katy Calder. The second one didn't exist, yet the second one fascinated her. Wisdom said let him go. Wisdom said tomorrow was soon enough to talk to him. But Katherine Brewster was the wise one, careful, wary. Katy Calder was the woman in Chelsea Beach. Katy Calder wore an obscenely expensive ring from a man she barely knew, she kissed too hot and she was definitely more daring.

Katy Calder took his hand to lead him over to her bed.

Immediately he balked. "What in hell are you doing?"

"What I've wanted to do since I awakened on the couch."

"Listen—"

"No, that's what I want you to do."

"Hold it." He stepped between her and the bed.

She gave him an amused smile. Never had she seen him quite so rattled. "I want to talk to you."

"Talk? You gotta be kidding. Men and women don't get in bed to talk."

She tipped her head to the side. "Sometimes they do. Just as men and women make love in lots of places beside a bedroom, men and women do other things in bed besides have sex."

"I don't," he said succinctly.

"Then this will be a brand new experience. After all, what would life be like if we always did the same old thing in the same old places?"

For a moment he simply gave her a blank look, then rolled his eyes. "Why do I feel like I'm going to gladly walk into some trap?"

She came up on tiptoes and whispered, "I promise not to make you horny."

He threw up his hands in a frustrated gesture. "Oh, well, in that case then let's climb right in."

A few moments later they lay side by side. Sloan stacked his hands behind his head and stared at the ceiling. Katherine stretched out next to him, her heart pounding, her fingers fiddling with the quilt.

"Talk," he muttered in a tight voice.

She swallowed now, pushing aside those few moments of amusing banter. "I'm sorry." But before he could react, she continued, the words coming quickly. "I'm sorry I acted so irrationally with you this afternoon. Screeching and shrinking away from you as though you were trying to attack me. I know you think you must have taken on some weird female, and I wouldn't blame you if you decided to tell Joe you'd had enough."

"Sweets..."

She felt him relax for the first time since they'd lain down. "You don't have to be nice or polite about this, Sloan. I acted terribly. In fact my hysteria is probably what scared Danny into having his nightmare. I had no reason to assume you had just left us except my own panic. I was the one who miscounted the lifeguard stands."

"Come here—"

"I don't want you to find an excuse for me or comfort me, either."

"You want me to get mad and chew you out and call you the hysterical woman who invented every man's nightmare?"

"Please don't joke about this."

"Then stop blaming yourself for a perfectly normal reaction. You thought you saw Gerald—"

"I'm not talking about running from Gerald. I'm talking about wanting to run from you."

Chapter 8

Wanting to run, Sloan thought grimly. God, he understood that. He knew how it tasted, how it hurt, how it blotted out all rationality. But escaping had taught him something, too. Running away had been his salvation.

If he'd stayed in Harbor Bay after Angela's funeral, he would have killed Suggs Mello. No gun, no knife, no sneaking up on him with a planned strategy. Just his bare hands. Clean, quick and simple. He'd have broken through Mello's flunkies, gone into that plush condo where Suggs issued orders and maintained his polluted respectability, hauled him out of his cushy chair and strangled the son of a bitch.

Without a doubt, Sloan knew that wanting to run and then doing just that had saved him from a probable prison term. Those months away and alone had given time to sink to the bottom. And for a while, he'd mired himself in whiskey and self-pity, but eventually the stagnation had begun to strangle him and he'd known that it was time to go home, time to legally take care of Angela's killer.

After he'd returned to Harbor Bay, he'd made getting Mello arrested, tried and convicted an obsessive priority. The alternative, Sloan had decided during the trial, was a bona fide gift. He had generously spared the SOB from an early acquaintance with hell.

Now he tightened his arm around Katherine. He couldn't fault her for that sense of desperation; he understood exactly how she felt.

"Sloan?"

"What, sweets?"

"I think my reaction of pushing you away and wanting to run was because I've always had to count on myself. Being with you, I'd sort of relaxed and let down my guard. Knowing that the police had hired you gave me this kind of built-in safety factor. And you seemed to do it all so expertly. Even though we've only been here a short time, you've maintained this nearly perfect front of a married couple. All those factors made it easy to shift the responsibility from myself to you. I just expected you to be there when I ran over the sand dune. Then when you weren't, I felt as if—"

"You shouldn't have trusted me?"

"Yes." Her amber eyes held him for an endless moment.

He touched her cheek where the shell had scratched her. "You had every right to expect me to at least be close by. If I'd gone down to the beach first instead of coming here and then stopping at Linda's and Hank's, I would have seen you."

"And Gerald."

"Yeah."

They were quiet for a few moments. From the open bedroom window came the far-off sound of the ocean. Sloan moved his arm and his hand brushed the side of her breast. She didn't pull back or shrink away. Compliance or encouragement, he wasn't sure, but lying in bed with her rekindled the lingering effects from the fantasy he'd had earlier. He should definitely get out of here before all this friendliness took a different turn.

"I concede that you're right," he murmured, trying to extricate himself from her even as staying and doing more than just talking was quickly absorbing his thoughts. "A man and a woman can do something in bed besides have sex. Like come to some new understandings." He wasn't sure what the hell he meant by that, but he did feel they'd reached at least a partial understanding from the mistakes of that afternoon.

"You're going to leave, aren't you?"

She made it sound as if he were walking out of her life forever, instead of just going to his own room. He shifted enough so that he could see her. "Do you read minds?" At her grin, he added, "You're not supposed to say that as if I was deserting you."

"But I'm not finished."

He decided not to ask. He knew his idea of finished and hers wouldn't be found in the same dictionary. With a sigh he decided to stay for a few moments more and simply drew her against him. The silky feel of her robe rubbed against his chest. As he had surmised earlier, the fabric couldn't compare to the softness of her skin.

She curled into him willingly, and then cautiously slipped her arm around his chest. Her breasts pressed into his ribs. He tried not to imagine how she would feel if she were naked. He rubbed his hand down her back, thinking he could get very accustomed to having all their conversations in bed. Sloan felt a deep sense of contentment, but also the beginnings of a very discontented arousal.

"I really should get out of here, sweets."

"No. Please."

"Despite your earlier logic, where we are and you being wrapped around me like this is going to get very difficult in a few minutes."

"I promise not to put my hands anywhere they shouldn't be," she said as if that solved the problem. "And we could change the subject. Like I could ask you if you'd heard from Joe Drummond?"

"Yeah, he called." To Sloan it seemed like a millenium ago. "He's going to find out where Gerald was this afternoon and call me back."

"When?"

"Now would be an appropriate time."

She tipped her head back and searched his eyes, as if confirming whether he was serious or teasing her. Then she turned enough to rest her chin on his chest. "If I kissed you, would you take it wrong?"

He raised an eyebrow in amusement. "Probably."

"No, I didn't mean that. I meant because you said the other afternoon that you were afraid to kiss me."

"I said I was terrified of kissing you. For the reason I gave you in Harbor Bay about kissing too hot. I was trying to avoid being exactly where I am. In bed with you."

To Sloan's amazement, her expression was puzzled, as if kissing and being in bed were everyday topics. Tucking herself in against him once more, she said in a subdued tone, "Robert told me once I didn't know how to do it the way a man likes it."

Sloan hesitated. Need won out. He wanted her to know exactly how she affected him and he wanted her to know that Robert's opinion didn't matter, but more than that, he wanted to see her reaction. "Robert was a bigger fool than I thought. You know how to move your mouth and stroke your tongue better than most women."

Her eyes lit up, and her mouth was suddenly too inviting. "Really?"

Sloan stared at her. "God, I expected a blush and I get curiosity."

She sat up on her haunches and watched him intently. "You've kissed a lot of women, haven't you?"

Somewhere he'd lost control of this conversation. "How in hell did we get on this subject?"

"But you have, haven't you? Kissed a lot of women. I don't mean while you were married. I know you loved your wife very much." Katherine ducked her head when she realized what she'd said. It hadn't been intentional, but then again perhaps it had. She knew so little about him and he'd shared almost nothing of himself with her. Admittedly, they'd both been sketchy about their personal lives, as if details should be avoided given the professional circumstances of their being together. Yet she wanted to know more about him; to get beyond the surface gossip that she'd heard in Harbor Bay.

To her astonishment he didn't get angry, push her away or get up and storm out of the room.

"You're a piece of work, sweets," he said with a chuckle, pulling her down beside him. "No one I know ever mentions Angela, never mind asking whether I kissed other women before and after I was married to her."

"No one ever mentions her? But why?"

"Because they know better. Angela is an off-limits subject."

She wondered if he intended to enforce that now. When he said nothing, she paused, not knowing how to continue, but determined not to utter some platitude. She decided to simply express her true feelings. "I can't even imagine the pain and horror you must have experienced."

Warily, he asked, "You heard the local gossips or you read about the hit-and-run in the newspapers?"

She was familiar with both, but she wasn't talking about the actual incident. She meant the emotional upheaval Sloan must have gone through. Stems 'n Petals had made the casket's floral arrangement and she'd personally delivered the blanket of jasmine and tulips Sloan had wanted for Angela's casket. She'd intended to leave the flowers at the funeral home, but Sloan had insisted on final approval. At his office, he'd barely glanced at her, intent only on a careful examination of the out-of-season blossoms. He'd been drunk, yet so icily in control that if she hadn't known him from when she'd hired him to follow Robert, she would have fled. Sloan had been dressed in black, his steps rigid, his face hollow and haggard. To Katherine he'd looked as if he'd walked out of the bowels of Hell. Since he'd never mentioned that time to her, she was sure he didn't remember her being there, didn't remember what she'd witnessed. Perhaps that was just as well. She doubted Sloan would have wanted anyone to have seen him that vulnerable.

"Yes, I'd seen the news coverage, but everyone in Harbor Bay had an opinion."

"I'm sure," he said grimly.

Sloan lay still, thinking back to his need for Katherine to trust him. Certainly spilling his guts about failing Angela wasn't going to go a long way toward instilling confidence in Katherine. He couldn't be absolutely sure she'd recovered from his not being there for her and Danny that afternoon. Telling her of those dark November days after Angela had died would simply confirm his failure.

Yet Katherine hadn't tried to dig into his past, nor had she offered automatic words of sympathy. In fact the entire conversation had come naturally, easily. Perhaps he had things backward. Instead of avoiding the subject, he should face it directly. Perhaps he needed to tell her, to trust her to listen, to open himself to her.

Holding her close so that he could feel the slightest indication of withdrawal, he said, "It should have been me who died."

The hand resting on his chest suddenly tightened as if to hold on to him, to keep him with her. "You?"

"I was supposed to be driving the car that day, not Angela." He stopped as if reconsidering, but then continued. "She'd been doing some shopping. She called me because her car wouldn't start, so I went to pick her up. I got her car started, but she didn't want to take any chances on it stalling so she took mine and I followed her."

His second pause seemed to last for numerous heartbeats. Katherine wondered if he would swing off the bed and leave the room, after all. Only the almost painful grip he had on her assured her he wasn't going to move.

When he spoke again it was in an unemotional monotone, as though, by some tremendous will, he had disconnected himself from the events he was about to relate. "I followed her," he said again. "She'd stopped at an intersection near my office, and that's when it happened. A black car with tinted windows came right at her. I knew with a gut-deep instinct that it was deliberate. I swung out from behind Angela to try and cut off the collision, but the forward speed of the other driver was too fast, too precise. I watched them broadside her with that kind of slow-motion reaction that the brain falls into when the horror is too much to take."

Katherine felt a chill so deep she was almost numb. She swallowed, her insides nauseous. She reached for his hand where it was braced against her hip and laced her fingers with his. Softly she asked, "You said you should have—"

She couldn't say *died*. "You think they thought it was you?"

"I know it. I'd been threatened by a guy that I helped send to prison when I was still a cop. I'd had a few warnings about pay-back time, but threats go with the territory. I didn't just blow them off, but having been a cop I knew what to do. Or at least I thought I did," he said in painful retrospect. "Anyway, I watched my back, stayed in touch with a police cruiser in the area and didn't venture down dead-end alleys without a weapon. I always checked my car for any explosive devices before I turned on the ignition. I even did that the day I went to pick up Angela."

My God, she thought, hit-and-run, killers, bombs. It all sounded like something out of a movie. She wanted to ask him how Angela had dealt with the continual fear of losing him. How ironic that he'd lost her. Katherine acknowledged a near-reverent respect for Angela Calder. To have lived with and loved a man, knowing he checked for bombs in his car before he got in, meant she'd been an incredibly strong woman.

In that instant Katherine realized a new truth. Angela would have acted differently on the beach with Gerald. She would have been brave, certainly not hysterical. No doubt she would have sent Sloan after Gerald instead of crumbling like some looney woman.

But a comparison didn't matter. She wasn't really married to Sloan, she wasn't anything like Angela. But then in Sloan's eyes, she thought with a twisting regret, she never could be.

Keeping her voice even, she asked, "But how did they know you'd be at that particular intersection at that time?"

"I learned later they'd been watching my office, and waiting for the right moment. Obviously they saw me leave. If they'd moved then, Angela would—" She felt the shudder in his chest and tightened her arm around him. "She'd still be alive." He took a breath. "I found out from a newspaper vendor that a police cruiser had been doing speed-checks in the area. My guess is that the driver saw the cops and just decided to wait until I came back."

She slipped her arms up and around his neck. "You must have been consumed with guilt and—"

Immediately she knew she'd hit a raw nerve. He stiffened and tugged her hands down. "I'm gonna go and call Drummond again." He pulled away from her, swinging himself up and off the bed in one continuous motion.

Katherine scrambled to the other side of the bed. "Sloan, wait."

"There's no more to be said. You know the story now. Don't try to find an excuse for what happened."

"But you couldn't have known."

"I should have known," he snapped, his eyes as hot and furious as she'd ever seen them. "Surviving in my line of work depends on me knowing, not on some goddamned excuse. That's why I always checked my car and watched my back, but that's just basic precaution. Putting someone else at risk, seeing them pay the price, watching Angela destroyed..." He plowed his hands through his hair while Katherine sat frozen.

She wanted to repeat that he couldn't have known, but she made no attempt to say anything. Prudently, she didn't get off the bed to try to comfort him. She'd had some experience with the tentacles of guilt, although not caused by anything of Sloan's magnitude. She'd blamed herself when Robert cheated on her, feeling as though she'd failed. She'd blamed herself for not demanding from Jennifer the truth about Gerald. Danny in danger was certainly a price both women had paid for not being more alert to the kind of man Gerald was.

But for Sloan... My God, those guilt tentacles had to be so entwined that he couldn't escape them in any facet of his life. They'd wound into him and become a part of who he was, just as Angela would always be a part of him.

Sloan had halted a few feet from the door, the moonlight casting him in stripes and shadows. He reached down and picked up Danny's red truck and put it out of the way.

Then in a low voice, he said, "She was pregnant with my baby."

For an incredibly long instant Katherine forgot how to breathe. Of all the accounts of Angela Calder's death that she'd read and heard, her being pregnant had never been mentioned.

"My God, Sloan..." She simply had no words. "My God."

He took another step toward the door and this time she was sure he would leave, but he didn't.

She had no idea what to say or what to do, so she did nothing, allowing the silence of the night to cover them. She wouldn't pry or ask meaningless questions. He'd said this much and now she held her breath. How much more horrible could it get?

He swore.

Finally, and only to let him know she wouldn't push him, she quickly said, "You don't have to say any more."

But as if he hadn't heard her, as though he had to get it out, get it said, he continued. "I didn't know about the baby. I didn't know until days later when I found an appointment card in her purse. She'd seen a gynecologist that same day she'd gone shopping. She never said a word when I picked her up, but later when the car was towed and I went to get her things, I found champagne and candles. She must have been planning to surprise me that night."

This time she knew she had to touch him, had to hold him. She left the bed, crossing the few feet to where he stood, and slid her arms around his waist. His body felt chilled, and as her ear pressed against his heart, the thump felt hollow and sad.

He didn't push her away and in fact gripped her tight against him. Her tears dampened his chest, and her throat felt raw and painful.

"I've never told anyone about the baby. I've never been able to," he whispered.

Her heart swelled with honor that he'd felt comfortable enough to share it with her. She lifted her head, twined her arms around his neck and came up on tiptoe. With her mouth close to his, she said, "I don't know what to say to you. I have no words that have enough meaning."

He touched the cut on her cheek, then slid one hand into her hair. "There are no words. There is only loss."

They stood clenched together as if separating their bodies would hurt, as if not cleaving meant a profound loss. Neither wanted to undo the new bonds they'd formed through the sharing of pain, or by Sloan breaking his vow of privacy. Katherine pressed her mouth against his throat. Sloan closed his eyes to absorb all that she was, all that he needed.

Finally, he lifted her chin and kissed her. Lightly, a fleeting touch, just a brushing of mouths, an acquaintance of textures. She rested against him and he welcomed her, feeling an almost tangible lifting of an old burden.

Maybe this wasn't complicated, he thought.

Maybe this closeness and where it could lead was what they both needed, she thought.

"You feel good against me." He backed against the wall and tugged her against him, then nestled and settled her into the cove of his thighs. She leaned back enough so that he could trace the lapels of her robe. "What are you wearing under this?"

"What do you think?"

"There wouldn't be a chance that I'll get lucky and you're naked?"

She tossed her head back and grinned, liking the sensual teasing, knowing how important the mood change was, how much Sloan needed to put space between himself and his bad memories.

"Not naked," she said.

The phone in the kitchen rang. Neither paid any attention.

"Something lacy and see-through that would go well in a centerfold?"

"Me?" Her eyes widened in disbelief. She might concede she was attractive, but sultry, sexy and seductive she was not. "I'm hardly the centerfold type."

The phone continued to ring.

"Better."

The phone rang again.

"Better?" She shook her head.

He cupped her chin to stop the motion. "Yes. Better as in hot and dangerous and dazzling." At her astonishment he grinned. "That's probably Drummond." He dropped a quick, burning kiss on her mouth. "I'll be right back."

Katherine stood rooted to the spot, her senses spinning. Dazzling? No one had ever said she was hot and dangerous, never mind dazzling. She'd never heard any man use such a wonderful word to describe a woman.

She wrapped her arms around herself and considered her options. And she did have them, for Sloan had made it clear from the beginning that he was uncomfortable with the sexual feelings between them. He might tease her, or even let down his guard enough to kiss her, but she knew he'd carefully avoid rather than aggressively pursue any deep intimacy. He was and would continue to be exactly the kind of man she'd hired to follow Robert. Professional, but honorable.

And yet today—tonight—these past moments had altered their relationship. She had no illusions about anything permanent between them; she wasn't even all that sure about anything temporary, but something new definitely existed between them. Something—an interlude perhaps, a fragmented moment that came rarely and often escaped before being captured—had taken place tonight. Her own self-imposed restraints—necessary to prevent being hurt emotionally—had been on automatic with Sloan. But those controls, meant to keep herself from getting involved, from getting hurt and from trusting Sloan implicitly, had loosened considerably.

A shiver skittered down her spine and her cheeks and neck flushed warmly. She wondered briefly what Jennifer would say if she could see her usually cautious sister. No doubt Jennifer would be shocked. Katherine was the sister who rescued, the sister who was responsible, the sister who'd said after Robert that no man was worth the humiliation of being betrayed.

But then Sloan hadn't made any promises so betrayal wasn't an issue. No, right now the issue was impulse and excitement. Whatever happened between them in Chelsea Beach wouldn't leave here. Any intimacies would be left behind as surely as the house, the rosebushes she'd nurtured and the gate Sloan had installed on the deck to protect Danny.

And despite the expensive ring she wore for the role they played out publicly, privately she could indulge in an interlude. For this wasn't about commitment or falling in love or planning for the future. This was about right now, this trapped moment of no yesterdays and no tomorrows. If she could remember that then she wouldn't get hurt. She wouldn't have to trust him, or plan her life around him, or worry that he might betray her as Robert had.

A practical solution, she decided firmly. If she expected nothing but these few precious moments—moments to be dazzling for him—if she took and enjoyed and closed her mind to anything more, then she'd be fine.

She made her way to the kitchen, pausing in the doorway. Her pulse raced and what had felt impulsively right suddenly loomed with uneasy questions. What if he'd been only teasing her about being dazzling? What if he reminded her that he didn't get involved with clients? What if he compared her with Angela? She swallowed the implications of that last question because she knew if that was the case, she was beaten before she began.

No yesterdays, no tomorrows. Just a firm resolve to enjoy now. She pressed her hands against her breasts. Even through her robe she could feel that her nipples were tight and sensitive; she could still taste his kiss. For a fleeting minute, desire wrestled with restraint. Then she lifted her chin. She would do this because she wanted to. She didn't have to find an excuse or justify a thing.

He hadn't turned on the light, and she didn't, either. He stood with his back to her, the tails of his shirt hanging rumpled and loose. He needed a haircut, but her fingers itched to slide into the thick black texture. She took slow steps toward him. Apart from what he was saying on the phone, the only sounds she was conscious of were her own erratic breathing and the rustle of her satin robe.

She stopped behind him, standing silent, bolstering her courage. Then, before she could analyze her motives beyond the tactile need to shed all barriers and touch him, she undid the robe and let it slide to the floor. Coming closer to him, she slid her hands up beneath his shirt. He stiffened, but he didn't push her away.

Katherine thought again about what he'd said to her. Better than a centerfold. Dazzling. She wanted to dazzle him. Before she considered the ramifications, she silently slipped her hands around to the front of his jeans.

He jumped, swearing. At which time she deftly pushed the button on his waistband from its closure.

He froze, then covered the mouthpiece with his hand. He swung his head around. "For God's sake, Katy..."

She grinned and rested her cheek against his back. She'd only touched the button, but she loved his reaction. She hooked her thumbs into the waistband of his jeans on either side of the opening. She folded her other fingers inward, grasping the material underneath them, as if getting a grip to tear open the zipper.

He glanced down, then turned his head again, "What the hell do you think you're doing?"

She wiggled closer. "Coming on to you," she half whispered, loving the boldness of her own words, feeling a sense of power, the confidence of being Katy Calder.

Sloan scowled as if he'd missed something, but there was no mistaking her fingers hooked into his jeans or her body pressed against his back. Despite knowing he should ignore her, his body tightened; he broke out in a cold sweat. She lightly scraped her nails low on his stomach. No lower, he decided grimly; yet couldn't help imagining the softness of her hands against him. He tucked the phone between his ear and his shoulder and tried to pull her hands away.

To Drummond he said, "Yeah, sorry. Katy came in and wanted something."

She grinned, feeling reckless.

The more he tugged at her hands, the harder she gripped the denim. She stretched up and kissed him very wetly on the back of the neck. The phone slipped from his shoulder and clattered to the counter. His control was also fast slipping beyond any boundaries of restraint. He snatched it up and gave up trying to get her thumbs out from under the waistband.

He spoke quickly. "And Prescott was on his tail all day? Gerald is and was definitely in Harbor Bay? Terrific. Tell Prescott he redeemed himself for sitting on his ass on the Mello investigation. Yep. I'll tell her. A few days and the investigation will be finished. Great. And, Joe? Thanks. I appreciate it and I know Katy will."

He hung up the phone. Without moving or trying to pull her hands away, he said, "Gerald spent the afternoon in Harbor Bay cleaning out his apartment. Cal Prescott, the detective who's assigned to tail him, watched Gerald from an apartment across the street from where Gerald lives. He never left the place until 7:00 p.m."

Katherine felt a kind of draining relief. The man wasn't Gerald. He might have been weird and up to God knows what, but he wasn't Gerald. Then, aware of the denim and warm skin her fingers touched, she realized something substantially more revealing than learning that Gerald was nowhere near Chelsea Beach.

She'd made the decision to come into the kitchen before she knew Gerald's whereabouts. Had she somehow known she was safe from him? Or safe with Sloan? Had the intervening hours with Sloan spawned a new sense of security, an instinctive trust? Had trust rooted in her heart when she'd walked into her bedroom and seen Sloan protecting Danny from a nightmare? Hadn't she seen Sloan as a barrier for Danny that Gerald couldn't get through? Had she simply transferred that blanket of security to include herself?

She closed her eyes and pressed her cheek against his back. *No yesterdays, no tomorrows, just these moments.* She slowly opened her fingers and spread them wide, splaying them on either side of his zipper.

Sloan sucked in his breath. "Katy...no more..."

"You said earlier that you were dreaming about me, that you wanted me to touch you, that I made you horny."

Like no other woman, he thought desperately. Not even Angela. But he couldn't tell Katy that.

Again he tried to move her hands, but to no avail.

"Sweets, you don't want to do this."

"Yes I do. Are you saying you don't?"

"I'm saying that nothing will be the same afterward."

A rather sweeping statement, she thought. "What will be different?"

"We'll be doing this again and again for one thing."

Katherine hesitated. She honestly hadn't thought about "again and again." Maybe because she didn't have enough confidence in her ability to dazzle him so that he would want her over and over again. "Maybe you wouldn't . . . I mean, it might not be that great . . . that dazzling."

He took a deep breath, feeling a rush of anticipation not unlike those timeless seconds before a sexual climax. "For a man the most incredible turn-on is for a woman to come on to him, to be hot for him. I don't mean like a hooker or some sultry female who has all the moves choreographed, but a woman who is careful and responsible and responds because it's natural."

She frowned. The words sounded good, but was he saying something more? Something he couldn't say directly? Was he saying that she wanted him more than he wanted her? Certainly he hadn't swept her up in some burst of passion and taken her to bed. Maybe she'd misread the signals. Maybe he had been teasing her about being dazzling.

Katherine felt her self-doubt creep back, her impulsiveness skitter away. She'd been a fool.

She loosened her grip and Sloan took advantage of it by hauling her around in front of him and lifting her onto the counter. Her legs were bare to the top of her thighs. He stared at what he had hoped would be a sexy nightie and realized that what she wore transcended sexy and seductive. It tore into him, mocked his vow of distance and clutched at the edges of his heart.

He stared at the gray familiar cotton, the open placket, the swell of her breasts pushing at the fabric. His good sense warred with his arousal, tearing his self-control into tiny pieces. "You're wearing my shirt."

"Yes."

"Why?"

"I was cold." She had her knees primly together and her hands folded in her lap. "I've worn it every night since you gave it to me." She watched him as if waiting for him to make the next move.

''And should I say something appropriately obvious like I could warm you up better than my shirt?''

She scooted forward a little, her knees bumping his stomach. She parted her knees and glanced down at his partially opened jeans. ''You've already decided to be noble and say no,'' she said as though resolved to the inevitable. There was no mistaking the disappointment in her voice. Then she brought her gaze up.

He stared for a long moment, allowing himself to sink into her spectacular amber eyes. His resolve not to touch her was collapsing. He decided to be blunt. ''How long has it been for you?''

''Since Robert.''

''Three years! My, God, you're practically a virgin.''

''I'm sorry,'' she snapped, embarrassed and on the defensive.

Sloan realized immediately how he'd sounded. Insulting and unfeeling. He softened his voice. ''Ah, sweets, it's nothing to be sorry about, but three years is a long time. I'd probably be too big and could hurt you.'' At her shiver, he cursed his explicitness. ''Your next experience should be with someone you love.'' He wouldn't think about how much he wanted to be the one she loved.

She only glared at him.

Sloan had some experience with the cycle of female emotions, certainly he had more than a nodding acquaintance with Katherine's after what had happened on the beach. But on the beach had been out of the ordinary. Danny had been involved. Right here, right now, was basic male-female reactions. He'd assumed she would react like other women who hadn't had sex for three years. She'd agree with his reasoning, perhaps blush a little . . .

Just as he was about to help her off the counter, she pushed at his chest and he stepped back, caught off guard.

Her eyes now brimmed with moisture, but they weren't tears of embarrassment. She was furious. ''You don't want this, do you? Why don't you just say so. Why don't you be honest instead of looking for excuses? You don't want me, Sloan.''

"Katherine, listen to what I'm saying to you...." He tried to grip her arms, but she flung them up.

"I am, damn you! I am! You've been very clear and concise." She took a deep breath. "Well, I don't want you, either!"

Then, before he could stop her, she gripped the hem of the shirt and pulled it up and over her head.

"Good God," he muttered, closing his eyes briefly at the exquisite sight before him.

Her skin shimmered like ivory, her breasts rising and falling, the nipples pink and peaked. His gaze skimmed her waist to her tummy to the softness between her thighs. He absorbed it as though he'd just discovered thirst and hunger. His body didn't need the visual, or the scent of her, his groin filled as if searching for a lost satisfaction no woman but Katherine could provide. No wonder he was fighting making love. No wonder he was fighting her.

She balled the shirt up and flung it at him. "And I don't want your damn shirt, either!"

Sloan batted it away. She tried to slide off the counter but he gripped her thighs and pulled them around his hips. The contact of her softness, a damp warm softness, against his belly shot his own restraint to hell.

They stared at each other. Her hair was tangled, her eyes glistening with a dying anger. His hands roamed up her thighs and cupped her breasts. He watched her intensely for any sign of refusal. He pressed his thumbs on her nipples. She closed her eyes, arched up against him and tossed her head back.

His sex pounded with a primitive mating heat. Then she was against him, her hands clawing through his hair. Her whisper, hoarse and raw, fanned his mouth. "I want to kiss you hot again... and again... and..."

"Do it... Katy, come dazzle me..."

Their mouths exploded together. No gentle explorations. No careful touching of tongues. No slow seducing sounds and sighs.

He lifted her from the counter, her thighs gripping his hips, her hands clutching greedily at his hair. Turning, he braced himself against the wall. She made tiny desperate sounds that rocked through him when he kissed her chin and neck.

Somehow his jeans went down enough to release him. She relaxed her body enough to slip down his belly, leaving a trail of satin cream wetness, then gloved him greedily.

"Baby...baby..." He shuddered at the burning straddle of her body, thinking he was capable of nothing but hanging on to her.

He hauled gulps of air into his lungs. Finesse and polish never existed. Frenetic passion did. Her mouth was swollen and red, his hot and hungry. Her face moist, his body sleek with sweat. Her sweetness moved on him in layers of liquid, his sex drinking deep like an opiate wantonly hooked.

"I can make you..." she whispered, sliding up and then gliding down.

"God, yes." He gripped her hips, felt her back arch and then came down for one final plunge. The climax shattered through him, hers following and leaving them both drained, panting and weak. How they remained standing Sloan didn't know, but he did know that he'd been right.

From now on nothing would be the same.

Moments passed, long heated minutes when neither spoke. Sloan held her body tightly, solidly against him, wanting to keep her there permanently. Her neck was damp, her hands still clutched him. Her breathing swept against his cheek, warm and sweet and just a little breathless.

Awkwardness fell between them and Sloan could almost count the beats of apprehension. He grappled with how to tell her just how dazzling she'd been. And yet he couldn't. Not now; not with all their emotions sharply attuned, their bodies luxuriating in the wonderful afterglow of satiation.

He'd promised himself that making love to her wouldn't happen and yet it had. Sloan realized that his terror of getting involved with one Katherine Brewster had nothing to do with breaching a professional relationship. And enclosing himself inside of her so satisfactorily had nothing to do with good sex. All of this had happened because he wanted her for himself. Deeply and forever.

Back away, he reminded himself. Create distance. Throw up those handy barriers. Don't pay any attention to that tiny voice in your heart that says making love to her is unlike anything you've ever experienced.

How simple it would be if the sum of all those hot touches were only sex.

"Sloan..." She lifted her head and he was instantly thankful for the darkness. He didn't want her to make any assumptions or draw any conclusions from his expression.

He slowly lowered her to the floor, while still keeping her against him. She shivered and he spanned his hands against her back. Her skin felt cool and soft and he wanted to warm her. He lifted the shirt off the floor. "Here, Katy, let me put this on you," he muttered, surprised at the huskiness of his own voice.

She backed up and shook her head, pushing the shirt away. "I'm sorry... I never should have..."

He knew she wanted reassurance, and he damned himself for not offering it. Too many seconds had passed, the moment for words of affection lost in the silence.

Sloan adjusted his jeans and tugged up the zipper. Trying to keep his voice even, he said, "I shouldn't have let this happen. I'm not some kid with out-of-control hormones." He watched her, keeping to the shadows, knowing he'd hurt her, knowing he should gather her up and hold her and take her to bed with him.

"It doesn't matter," she said on a gulp.

He locked his jaw to stop himself from saying anything. *It matters, sweets. Damn it, it matters too much.* That's what's so terribly wrong. But all he said was, "Sure. We'll just forget about it."

Sloan deliberately didn't move until she had snatched up her robe and fled the kitchen.

Left there in the dark empty kitchen, Sloan swore savagely. Now he knew the root of his terror. Sometime in the past few days, he'd allowed himself to believe in this fantasy they'd created. He'd allowed himself to believe in the high price of love and marriage and forever after.

Katherine Brewster had done what no woman, including Angela, had ever done.

She'd buried herself in his heart.

Chapter 9

"When Hank and I heard the weather forecast I had to invite you and Sloan over to watch the surf," Linda Rowen said enthusiastically as she closed her front door against the dropping temperature and blowing rain.

Katherine ran her fingers through her damp wind-blown hair after she handed Danny to Sloan. He took the toddler, muttering something about "When you've seen one storm you've seen them all" and walked into the kitchen where Hank was stirring a pot of chili.

Katherine pretended indifference. She had no intention of acknowledging his dark mood nor did she want to risk raising questions from Linda.

Linda rolled her eyes in exasperation. To Katherine she said, "Hank's the same way. Totally bored. He always says it's just a lot of water and wind and cleaning debris out of the yard. Leave it up to a man to ignore nature's grandeur for the more mundane clean-up." She grinned, her eyes sparkling with excitement. "But you come with me, Katy. You've got to see this."

Linda crossed the thick biscuit-colored carpet to a massive wall of glass hidden by azure-blue curtains. Katherine noted the room's furnishings had a nautical theme; one

particular table was inlaid with tiny seashells. On one wall
hung a large oblong painting of nineteenth-century fishermen fighting to save their boats from being swamped by the
huge sea swells.

With the flourish of a magician who knows the audience
will be awestruck, Linda pulled a drapery cord. The storm
seemed to burst into the living room.

Katherine took a step back.

"Isn't it magnificent?" Linda asked, her voice reverent.

"Breathtaking." Katherine instantly decided she was very
glad for the protective glass.

The Rowens' dual level contemporary had been built on
a seawall, but from this vantage point the water barrier below couldn't be seen. This gave the house the effect of being suspended in haughty superiority over the ocean, yet one
glance at the growing fury outside raised the question of
who lorded control over who. The churn and surging power
of the Atlantic gave Katherine a sudden sense of how those
fishermen in the painting must have felt. Awed, respectful
and definitely fearful.

Earlier that morning Katherine had heard a weather
commentator issue small craft warnings and predict that the
Cape would be "caught in the teeth of a howling ocean
storm." Howling was an apt description, Katherine now
decided. The Atlantic had arrayed herself in a cold shore-
battering gray that warned of danger instead of the calm
blue waters that drew swimmers and boaters on a clear
warm day. She watched choppy whitecaps rise up and re-
volt all the way to the horizon rather than gently lap in soft
waves on the shoreline, as they had the afternoon when
Katherine and Danny had walked along the beach.

This morning she'd paid little attention to the ominous
clouds beyond dressing Danny warmly against the chill that
penetrated the cottage. Sloan had gone to get the newspaper alone today. When he'd returned he'd told her a Chelsea Beach local had said they were in for one of New
England's famous nor'easters.

By the time Linda had called with her come-watch-the-
surf invitation, the sky had become dark and brooding; the

clouds had thickened and grown heavy with the predicted rain.

Linda had wooed Katherine by mentioning a fire in the fireplace, a pot of homemade chili and this incredible view of nature showing her mastery of the elements. Katherine knew exactly why she'd accepted the offer so quickly. It had nothing to do with enjoying the Rowens' company or watching nature flex her muscles. It had everything to do with Sloan.

Quite a few hours had passed since the early morning hours of lovemaking in the kitchen. And in the intervening time Katherine's sense of what had gone wrong and why had been mostly her own conclusions. She'd reminded herself of her thoughts before they'd made love. Now if she really believed there were no yesterdays and no tomorrows, then she could leave her feelings for Sloan in Chelsea Beach. If what had happened between them had only been a pleasurable interlude...

Ifs, she thought ruefully. All those damned ifs. And added painfully to them was Sloan's obvious indifference. He'd been so distantly polite, so maddeningly calm and reserved around her that had it not been for a lingering tenderness between her thighs she might have wondered if they had made love at all.

Katherine would have welcomed a fight; a screeching no-win battle that cleared the air and allowed her to vent her feelings. Despite his morning-after grimness, she'd refused to appear shy or embarrassed by her own aggressiveness in their lovemaking. She knew she'd been dazzled by the man and the night and her own rationale. She'd reasoned that she could make love with him and keep her heart and her trust safely tucked in the more objective part of her mind.

Perhaps an oversimplification, but she refused to wring her hands with regrets. She'd done that when Robert had cheated on her, chastising herself for being blind to his betrayals. Ironically, Sloan had been the one who'd urged her to see Robert for the cheat that he was.

Katherine had simply applied Sloan's advice—of seeing herself for who she'd been—to her actions in the kitchen. She'd merely stepped fully into the role of Katy Calder and it had been dazzling. And damn it, she had no intention of viewing her behavior in any other light.

Perhaps his effort to avoid personal entanglements had been right. Since he'd made it clear that his feelings for her wouldn't go beyond the professional ones, he probably had a valid reason to be annoyed that she'd wrestled control from him. But for those few moments he'd wanted her. She might not have his sexual expertise, but the kind of passion that had exploded between them had been real and powerful and wonderfully satisfying.

Yet in the mind-clearing daylight, he'd been the one who avoided her. She'd recalled his comment about being terrified of where kissing her would lead and how if they made love nothing would be the same.

Well, that was certainly true, she thought ruefully. She'd assumed he'd meant their relationship would change, but not to this extent. Now they were barely speaking. Even the pretense of being married tugged with unnatural strain. She knew that deep in her heart lay a flicker of longing; a hope that he would at least act as if he cared for her. Yet even here, at Linda's and Hank's, Sloan seemed to want distance and silence.

Katherine sighed. Of one thing she could be grateful. She'd never hoped to replace his wife. Thank God, for she knew without question that she could never have Sloan as Angela had. Only Angela had owned his heart. And despite those few moments of passion, Katherine believed that if she'd given him a choice he would have chosen to avoid her in that way, also.

As he'd been doing and continued to do, she decided now. She was in the Rowens' living room and he'd immediately escaped to the kitchen to talk to Hank. Or perhaps his comment about having seen one storm had been a not-so-veiled reference to the stormy incident between them a short while ago back at the cottage.

"Kind of leaves you speechless, doesn't it?" Linda asked, obviously concluding that Katherine's silence had been awe from watching the rough Atlantic.

"Why, yes, it's quite incredible."

With a concerned frown, Linda asked, "Hey, are you all right?"

Katherine cleared her throat, and made herself smile. "Yes, I'm fine."

"You look as if you're carrying the weight of the world."

Only Sloan's determination to avoid me, Katherine answered silently, but now that she thought about it, the weight of the world wasn't a bad analogy. She damned herself for dwelling on Sloan, for continuing to hold him in her heart as if she could find some thread of hope. "Just some personal things I'm working through," she said, then added, "That chili is beginning to smell real good."

Linda laughed. "And I better go check on it. Hank tends to get carried away with the chili powder. Can I get you some hot tea, or would you like something stronger?"

"Tea would be wonderful."

"Great. You stay here and enjoy the view. I'll be right back."

Katherine walked to the huge window. The wind and driving rain were relentless against the glass. A familiar feeling of uneasiness gripped her, not unlike the one she'd felt a few years ago, when she and Jennifer had visited a shark aquarium. Now, as then, Katherine hoped that whoever had installed the thick glass knew what they were doing. She pressed her hand against the picture window, the chilly hardness making her shiver. She looked out at the fierce Atlantic and then down to the crashing surf.

My God, she thought, had the water risen or was she just imagining it? She watched for a few moments. Of course she was. The waves were so choppy the height would be illusionary.

Still she backed away from the glass and sat down in a nearby chair, glancing again at the picture of the fishermen fighting to save their boats and their lives. Conversation drifted in from the kitchen and she heard Danny giggle. It reminded her that she was beginning to worry about Danny getting too attached to Sloan, but she didn't know how to keep them separate without being unbearably cruel. No question that the toddler having Sloan as a positive male figure in his life right now was important, but what about later? What about when Sloan was no longer around?

Despite another nightmare in the early morning hours, the baby had gone back to sleep quickly, thanks to Sloan. Katherine had slept little; when she approached Danny's room, she heard Sloan telling him a story as he'd held Danny and walked with him. Just another adjustment Danny would have to make later, she thought sadly. Not having Sloan to hold him and make the bad man go away.

Katherine smoothed her hands along the low band of the heavy oyster-white, fisherman-knit sweater she wore over old jeans. The sweater was new, an unexpected purchase just hours ago by Sloan. His giving it to her had none of the light, sexy banter that had taken place when he'd bought the ring.

She glanced down at her hand, staring at her ring finger. She thought about caring and commitment, and then she thought about their confrontation.

At the cottage, she'd finished dressing and had been fussing with her hair when he'd knocked on her bedroom door. She'd been so startled she'd dropped her hairbrush. She winced now as she recalled her squeaky and too high-pitched "Yes, come in."

He'd stalked in wearing snug jeans, his gray shirt that she'd flung at him in the kitchen and his unzipped leather jacket. His gray-green eyes were as dark and threatening as the storm outside.

In a clipped monotone he'd told her what he'd heard from one of the Chelsea Beach locals about the weather and then had tossed a bag onto the bed. "Here. It's gonna get cold. Wear this."

She dragged her eyes away from him and stared at the lemon-yellow bag. "What is it?"

"A sweater."

She knew now she should have just said thank-you and he would have left. That would have been that. But she hadn't. Since he'd actually approached her and begun a conversation, she'd no intention of ending it.

She picked her brush up off the floor and put it on the dresser. He was almost out of the room when she said, "I brought my own sweaters."

In that tiny millisecond something came back to life between them. Katherine knew it intuitively. Otherwise he would have said fine and continued out the door. But he didn't.

He didn't face her, but turned only slightly. "None of your sweaters are as warm as this one."

Since she knew he hadn't been looking in her drawers, she couldn't possibly know how warm her sweaters were, therefore she had to assume another motive. Perhaps he wanted an excuse for a confrontation, which she welcomed more than this endless strain of silence.

Despite his deliberate coolness, despite what she knew would sound unreasonable, she clung to that tiny flicker of hope. "I don't want the sweater. I'll wear two of my own."

He gave her a direct look that left no doubt he thought her suggestion was ridiculous. "Don't be so damned stubborn."

"Nothing in this agreement between us says I have to wear what you say."

"You're wearing a ring I bought you, one lousy sweater hardly seems a major obstacle."

"Well, then, you can have your ring and the sweater." She pulled the ring from her finger and started toward him.

He glared at her, but he didn't move. She came up so close to him she saw a tiny shaving nick on his chin.

"Back off, Katy."

"Or what? You might lose that cold distant attitude you're so determined to hold on to?"

For a few racing seconds she thought he might pull her close and kiss her. She could almost feel the sway of her own body and she definitely felt the quick rush of heat up her spine.

He drew in a long shuddering breath of control. "I'm not going to fight with you," he said evenly, not touching her in any direct way. He tried to change the subject. "The Rowens are going to think we're not coming."

She persisted. "You said you bought the sweater because it's warm. Why did you buy the ring?"

He stepped away and moved toward the door. In a low voice he said, "You know why."

She shook her head. "It's too expensive for that reason. They had a lot of plain gold bands if you wanted realism."

He swore and shoved one hand through his hair. "What in hell are you doing? Trying to use the ring as some deep vow of symbolic commitment that you think I've buried?"

"I have no illusions about you ever committing to me," she said with unfazed dismissal. At least she hoped she sounded as if she didn't care. "But I do think there's more to this ring than the green finger or the realism reason you've given me or yourself."

His eyes closed for a moment. "God, just what I need. A pop psychologist." He walked over to the door. "Do whatever the hell you want with the ring, but wear the sweater. I don't want you getting sick."

Katherine had stared long after he stalked out and closed the door. The ring had been worth less to him than her getting sick. That was what he'd said, wasn't it?

Yes, she concluded now as she turned the ring on her finger. That was exactly what he'd said. Admittedly she'd taken some solace in the comment even though she knew she was clinging to some overly romantic notion.

She heard the phone ring in the kitchen and a few minutes later Linda returned with a mug of tea and a worried look on her face.

Katherine took the mug and thanked her. Taking a sip, she asked, "Is everything okay?"

Linda pressed her lips together and began to walk around the room. Her gaze seemed to absorb every item as though she wanted to memorize them, especially the painting of the fishermen.

Katherine put her tea down and stood. Finally Linda stopped in front of the window, where the rain lashed unrelentingly.

"What's going on?" Katherine asked warily.

"Hank just heard that the brunt of the storm might hit at high tide."

Katherine had lived in New England long enough to know that high tide combined with an ocean storm can cause inland flooding and devastating shore damage. She recalled thinking a few moments ago that the water looked as if it had risen.

Hank appeared in the doorway. "Linda, for God's sake, what did I tell you?"

"I know what you told me, but I can't," she said as she turned away, but not before Katherine saw her tears.

Sloan came into the room carrying Danny, and Katherine hurried to them. Sloan took her arm and propelled her to the door. "The police just called and are urging residents on the seawall to evacuate. Flooding and massive erosion is expected."

Hank had his arms around Linda, who was crying softly. Sloan nodded toward them, keeping his voice low. "Hank told me this is the first storm where they've had to evacuate. Linda is afraid to leave. She thinks that when she comes back her house will be gone."

Katherine's eyes widened. "Gone! Like in washed out to sea?" The implications of that horrifying disaster settled over her, but then an even greater disaster occurred to her. If the house went and Linda was in it . . . "They can't stay here. They could drown."

"That's what Hank has been telling her."

At that moment Linda pushed away from Hank. "No! I won't leave," she cried. "This is my home, this is what I've always wanted. It's built up high. It's strong. It will get through the storm." She spoke desperately, as if saying the words was all that was needed to make them true. Then, as if she was abandoning her child, she said, "I'm not going to sit in some shelter and not know if my house will survive." Her face paled. "I can't leave!"

Katherine hurried over to her. "Linda, listen to me . . ."

She turned wild eyes to Katherine. "Katy, you understand, don't you? You couldn't just leave your home and not know what would be here when you came back, could you?" Katherine almost wept at the terrified look on Linda's face. She did understand, but she also knew that agreeing would be the worst thing she could do.

"But if you leave then you know you'll be able to come back. If you stay..." She let her words trail off, the implication clear. If she stayed, she might not be alive to rebuild if there was massive damage.

Again Linda's gaze paused on the picture. Katherine looked at the struggling fishermen; first at the men trying to save their boats, and then to the men in the water trying only to save themselves. Katherine suddenly wished her sister was here. Jennifer was so good at looking for the story behind her photos. She believed that a photographer, like a painter, should strive to capture the emotions behind their subjects so that a photo or a piece of art appeared to have multiple meanings.

Often Linda's eyes had strayed back to the struggling fishermen. It had to mean something to her, a something that might help the current situation. But what? In Katherine's opinion the artist had captured the very human emotion of those fishermen struggling to survive.

Quietly Katherine asked, "Don't you think those fishermen in the painting cared as much for their boats as you do for your house?" Linda wiped at the tears on her cheeks. Katherine continued. "But don't you think that when they had to watch their friends washed into the sea that they would have given anything for the choice of escaping the storm over trying to save their boats?"

Now Linda looked at her. "My parents gave us that painting when we moved into the house. I've always loved the determined look on the men's faces. Their expressions have always assured me that they got their boats to safety, that they survived and conquered the storm."

Katherine pointed to three of the fishermen who were in the water, their hands reaching for oars, their eyes wild with the fear of drowning. "Maybe a few were able to ride out the storm, but some didn't." Linda studied the painting, but said nothing. Katherine added, "Those that did survive may have lost their boats, but boats can be replaced. Their friends, the fishermen who did drown, were gone forever."

Linda sniffled, then walked close to the huge picture window. "My house is safer than those boats."

Katherine heard Hank mutter, "She's leaving if I have to carry her out."

Sloan said quietly, "Give Katy a few more minutes."

Katherine felt like one of those floundering fishermen. She took a deep breath, arranged her thoughts and then went to stand beside Linda.

The fury out in the Atlantic roared as if nature had a very thin leash. Speaking slowly and softly, she said, "This is a nasty storm, Linda. Perhaps ten times more powerful than the one depicted in the painting. Don't you think that nature is warning you by its winds and rising water that leaving isn't an option but a necessity?"

For long agonizing seconds Linda stared out the window. In the reflection on the glass Katherine could see a new trickle of tears on her cheeks, but she didn't try to soothe Linda.

Danny began to fuss, followed by Sloan saying, "Shh, tiger..."

Finally Linda lowered her head and nodded.

"Thank God," Hank muttered. Then to Sloan he said, "Now we just have to find a shelter that isn't jam-packed."

Katherine made her own decision instantly, partially out of common neighborly kindness, but also out of friendship. Staying in a barrack-type shelter with strangers and unrelenting noise was all right if there were no other options, but there was one.

She put an arm around Linda's shoulder. "Instead of going to a shelter, why don't you and Hank come and stay with us? We don't have a fireplace, but we have wine and beer. Hank could bring that wonderful-smelling chili. Come on, it'll be fun. When the storm's over, I'll come back and help you clean the debris out of the yard."

Linda looked at her with a hopefulness that said she prayed that debris in the yard would be the only damage. Finally she added, "Yes, I'd like that."

The two women hugged.

At the sound of the doorbell, Hank answered the door only to be greeted by the Chelsea Beach police. "Yeah," Hank said. "We'll be out of here in the next fifteen minutes. Thanks." He closed the door and called to Linda.

"I'm coming," she said. "I just have to get a few things from the bedroom."

Katherine walked over to Sloan, who was trying to get Danny into his jacket. "Here, let me do that."

Sloan slipped a hand around her neck and tipped her face up. Before she had a chance to say anything he lowered his head and kissed her warmly, lingering a moment to gather in the taste of her. Then he regarded her with a deeply felt admiration. "You're pretty incredible, do you know that?"

She was so taken aback by the impromptu kiss and compliment that she didn't know what to say.

"I retract my comment about you being a pop psychologist. That was as professional a job of changing the way someone viewed their circumstances as I've ever seen. Very impressive."

Katherine felt a flush of pleasure at his pride in her. "I can't take total credit. A few years ago my sister explained photography analysis. Basically it means finding the emotion and the story behind the picture. When I saw the painting of the struggling fishermen and combined it with Linda's obvious love of the sea and her house, I couldn't help but draw an analogy. The difference here was that Linda could see the futility of fighting the sea in that picture. She still had the option of escape to safety, whereas the fishermen were trapped."

"Photography analysis, huh? Well, whatever it's called, you did a helluva job convincing Linda." He paused when Danny began to squirm and then added, "I apologize for some of my less than noble comments about your sister."

Katherine grinned and in a spontaneous gesture threw her arms around both Sloan and Danny; the baby squealed. Not in a hundred years would she have guessed that Jennifer, clear off in Australia, would be the one who broke through Sloan's cold distant attitude.

"Take it easy, sweets."

Katherine took Danny, glad for the distraction of cuddling the toddler. Her eyes glistened. "You haven't called me that since—"

They both stared at each other, both remembering. The words, the arousal, the high moment of bursting pleasure.

"Don't do this to me, Katy," Sloan murmured.

"Do what?"

"I don't want this to happen again. It can't. It just can't."

"But you weren't entirely to blame. I was the one who approached you. You didn't want me, remember?"

He cupped her chin just as Linda and Hank returned with the clothes they intended to take. Sloan whispered, "There hasn't been a single moment since I kissed you in Harbor Bay that I haven't wanted you."

Katherine blinked at his not-to-be-misunderstood comment. Sloan let her go and went to open the door for Linda. Katherine shifted Danny to her hips, but her eyes followed Sloan, her thoughts tumbling in new directions. Not a single moment, he'd said. Not even the past hours when he'd been so obviously unaffected by anything she did or said?

She felt a warm sensation inside her and wondered if it was only pleasure at the discovery that she could attract him, or if her feelings were deeper.

Deeper, as in falling in love with him?

He was wrong for her. All wrong. Angela would always own his heart, she reminded herself. How could she possibly overcome a perfect memory? Then the truth hit her. *Love.* How could she have allowed herself to once again love a man she couldn't trust to love her in return?

Katherine wasn't prepared for Sloan's reaction when she opened the door of the cottage half an hour later to welcome Hank and Linda. His stare at Katherine was so hard, so furious, she had to look away.

After the chili was put on the stove to reheat and Linda and Hank had taken their things into the living room, Sloan said, "Katy and I were about to run into town for some extra batteries. Danny's asleep. Would you mind?"

Sloan slung his arm around her neck and although to Linda and Hank it probably looked like a perfectly normal gesture, Katherine knew better. He was saying "Don't argue with me."

Just as Katherine knew there were batteries in the kitchen, she knew that because of the thinness of the walls an argument between them in one of the other rooms would easily be overheard. And unlike the afternoon that Hank and Linda had come and introduced themselves, the weather wasn't conducive to anyone going out to the deck.

Linda smiled. "Of course we don't mind staying with Danny, but I don't know about finding batteries. The stores usually sell out quickly when a bad storm is predicted."

"Yeah, well, we might get lucky." Sloan tossed Katherine's jacket to her and opened the door. "Let's go," he growled.

She shoved her arms into the sleeves but before she got the front zipped, Sloan had ushered her outside into the howling wind and rain and into the car. She scowled as he slammed the door and stalked around to the driver's side.

Once inside Sloan slumped in the seat for a long moment, watching the rain pour onto the windshield. Katherine sat stiffly, her entire body tense. She shoved her wet hair back and tried to relax.

Sloan swore once, a succinct graphic phrase that Katherine deliberately ignored. He jammed the key into the ignition, drove to the next block so as to be out of sight of the cottage and stopped.

Turning to her, he asked in a too-calm voice, "Just what in hell did you think you were doing?"

Katherine didn't pretend ignorance. She knew he meant Hank and Linda coming to stay with them instead of going to the shelter. "I'm sorry. I wasn't thinking. I was just being a good neighbor."

"Yeah, well, your soft spot of friendship and generosity has us in a real mess, Ms. Brewster."

His formality only underscored the distance he obviously wanted. Well, that was just fine with her. At the moment she wasn't exactly feeling close and cozy, either. "And God forbid, Mr. Calder, that I might think about a friend needing support rather than Gerald and his twisted objective."

"Have you been thinking about him? I haven't heard you mention him lately."

The tension she'd felt all day suddenly escaped. "Of course you haven't, you've been avoiding me, remember? Besides I have the Harbor Bay police and Sloan Calder to keep me in this cocoon of safety. Gerald is fast becoming nothing more than a bad memory," she snapped, hoping she at least sounded coolly indifferent.

"Cut the sarcasm," he said in a cryptic tone. "And never mind about Gerald. At the moment he's the least of our problems."

"The problem being that I acted like a friend." She pressed her lips together, suddenly feeling a rush of tears that she didn't want.

"Hell, I'm not angry about you being a friend. But asking them to stay with us presents a major problem. Such as putting us in the same bed since Hank and Linda would wonder why we had separate bedrooms." He shoved a hand through his hair. "Damn it, Katy, why didn't you think of that?"

"Because I didn't! I was concerned about Linda. For heaven's sake, making her leave her home is bad enough, but for her to have to stay in some shelter while she waits to find out if her house is going to survive the storm ... I just couldn't let her do it. I never even thought about sleeping arrangements or about you being upset, but then you haven't exactly been sweet and friendly lately, so perhaps I wasn't expecting any more of a mood change than I've already been seeing."

He glanced away; answering her charge would be more difficult for him than ignoring it. She was right. He hadn't been sweet and friendly. He'd been deliberately cold and, hopefully, indifferent. And yet here he was, now embroiled in an impossible situation. Going to the Rowens', he'd thought, would avoid any reoccurrence of the previous night. Now this. He felt like one of those fishermen in Linda's painting, struggling to survive. "What would they have done if we weren't here? If we'd never met them?" Then he shook his head, he could have avoided all of this. "God, if only we hadn't gone over there this morning."

Ifs, she thought, more of those damned ifs. "But we did go, and I did what I felt should be done."

"Yeah, like taking care of your sister's kid while she tours Australia."

Katherine glared at him. "She is not touring. And you're being nasty about Jennifer again."

He slipped his hand around her neck; reluctantly, she thought. Nevertheless she saw a flare of remorse in his eyes. He spoke in a husky whisper. "Katy, you know what you are? You're too good, too nice, too worried about everyone else but yourself."

She didn't want to tell him that what he said sounded a lot like her own thoughts on bailing her sister out of her problems. "And what's wrong with that? You make it sound like some cardinal sin."

"What about you? Who worries about you? Who takes you in and puts themself out for you?"

She stopped herself before she said Sloan Calder. For indeed he had done all those things since they'd left Harbor Bay. But given his mood, if he didn't deny it outright, he would merely say that what he did for her was his job, a case that would be forgotten within days of its conclusion.

And right now, especially after the direction her thoughts had been taking about being in love with him, she didn't want to hear that she was just a client.

Her long pause had him nodding. "I thought so. There's never been anyone, right? Not that fiancé of yours, not your sister. And I'll bet your parents are blissfully ignorant of this situation with Gerald. And why shouldn't they be? You've been bailing Jennifer out of her mistakes for so many years, you probably decided you'd be expected to handle this one, too."

Katherine lowered her eyes, remembering her decision not to go to her parents in Arizona. She'd told herself that they, too, could have been hurt by Gerald, but listening to Sloan made her realize her reasoning wasn't that simple. Her parents had been upset when Jennifer got pregnant and refused to marry Danny's father, but much of their disappointment had been aimed at Katherine. In subtle ways rather than blatant ones.

She could hear her mother's soft, careful voice. "Jenny always listened to you, honey. What happened this time? We know you young women do things differently these days, but an unwed mother is still not easy to accept. And if you'd married Robert, honey, you would have set a good example for Jenny. Then she would have seen how important it was for poor little Danny to know his daddy.''

Of course her parents hadn't known Robert was a cheat and Gerald a potential child-snatcher. Katherine sighed. She'd always come out of these mother-daughter conversations feeling blame-ridden and guilty. She wasn't entirely sure that was her mother's intent, it was more of a habit. For when she and Jennifer had been growing up, it *had* been Katherine who set the example. Katherine who took care of the problems when their parents weren't around.

As she'd done in Harbor Bay when she'd made the decision to keep Gerald from taking Danny by going with Sloan.

Now she jumped when Sloan tugged her closer. His grip was firm and hot, and her pulse leaped in response. In a totally illogical comparison, she wondered what kind of example her mother would think Katherine had set by having sex on a kitchen counter. Inwardly Katherine grinned. With an inner whoop of joy, she knew she didn't care. She didn't give one single damn what her mother, or Jennifer, or anyone thought. And even knowing there would never be anything between herself and Sloan, those moments of pleasure, of no inhibition, of being Katy Calder and not the carefully wary and uptight Katherine Brewster had been, well, extraordinary.

She turned to Sloan, so lost in her own thoughts she'd forgotten the gist of their conversation. ''I'm sorry, what were you saying?''

Sloan scowled, then grumbled, ''Linda Rowen. Remember? She's the one who wanted her house perched over the Atlantic as if it were a duck pond. And when her pond produces a sea monster, she's wringing her hands saying incredibly stupid things like her house is stronger than the same ocean that eats ships.'' He shook his head in disgust. ''And now that she's come to her senses we're stuck with the two of them for God knows how long.''

''All right,'' she said, not even annoyed with his anger. ''I'll talk to Linda about arrangements tomorrow.''

''Tomorrow, hell. Talk to her about leaving before tonight.''

"Sloan, I can't—"

"Then you're not listening to what I'm saying. In the same bed. You and me. In the dark. All night, sweets. And don't give me that scenario about people doing other things in bed besides have sex."

"Of course they do other things," she said, giving his cheek a pat. "They sleep."

"Katy, for God's sake, be reasonable."

"This will give you a new way to try out your cold distant attitude toward me," she said breezily as she settled herself back on her side of the car. Smoothing her hands down her jeans she realized how good she suddenly felt, how in control of her feelings. "I have absolutely no intention of seducing you, coming on to you or even touching you. But Linda and Hank are staying. And if you find me too intolerable, you can go to one of the shelters."

"Me! Go to a shelter? Good God," he muttered. Sloan knew she meant it. Certainly she didn't believe they could just *sleep* in the same bed. But he also knew that when she decided to do something, she did it. Proof positive was in her determination that the Rowens were staying. Going to a shelter indeed! Face facts, Calder. The only shelter you want are the arms of Katherine Brewster. "Just in case I forget that sleeping is all we're supposed to be doing, I'm going to buy some insurance."

By the time he'd slammed the car door, Katherine was fighting a dizzying hot flash. Not from embarrassment or shock, or even from the realization that if he bought condoms they very likely would make love. None of those caused a sinking sensation in the pit of her stomach. How could she have been such an ignorant fool? Not once had she thought about birth control before, during, or after they'd made love in the kitchen. She blinked in astonishment at her own mental blindness.

Dear God, she could be pregnant.

Chapter 10

By six o'clock the storm had made the sky so black it seemed more like midnight. Amid the whistling wind and distant howling of a very angry Atlantic, the electricity went off.

Katherine had just finished serving up the chili at a table Sloan and Hank had set up in the living room.

"Terrific," Sloan muttered. He put his beer bottle down and shoved his chair aside. "I'll get the candles so we can at least see what we're eating." He went out to the kitchen, and Katherine could hear him pulling open the drawers.

"Oh, God, why doesn't this storm end?" Linda shivered as she felt her way from the deck doors back to the table.

For most of the afternoon Linda had been watching the storm. Whenever the rain had lessened she'd gone outside to check on the severity of the damage. Katherine was thankful the cottage was protected by sand dunes and the shoreline located a good distance away. Now Hank tried to tell Linda, for what seemed to Katherine like the millionth time, that their house was in a more precarious position than homes that were built further inland. As Katherine listened to the back and forth talk, she knew that Linda was looking for any reason to convince herself that her house would still be on the seawall after the storm.

"First thing in the morning we'll go and see how she weathered," Hank said reassuringly.

Linda laughed nervously. "Everything will be all right. I know it. All those people who built on the seawall couldn't be wrong. I mean, that is the most expensive section of real estate in Chelsea Beach," she said as if the ocean would consider monetary cost when twenty-foot waves pounded the coastline. Then almost immediately following her determined rationale, she clutched Hank's arm and began to wail about all her possessions that would be gone forever.

Katherine sighed. She felt badly for Linda, and understood her concern for her belongings, but she was finding her whining and nonstop need for encouragement irritating. Of course Katherine's preoccupation with Sloan and the now realized possibility that she might be pregnant hadn't helped her own attitude any.

She stood, glad that the darkened room hid her annoyance. "I'm going to check on Danny." She'd fed him shortly after she and Sloan had returned from the drugstore. Then Sloan had sprawled on the floor by the couch while Danny courageously walked with no help. Katherine had only put him to bed moments before, so she knew that checking on him was just an excuse.

What she really wanted was a few minutes alone, so she didn't have to smile and converse and be sympathetic. Her insides churned with a distressing ache that simply wouldn't go away.

Stress, she decided, or plain old fear.

In Danny's room she tucked the quilt around him and checked the window that faced the side yard. The wind rattled the frame, and she found water seeping in under the casing. She tried to work the catch that locked the double-hung glass, but after a few tries, and a broken fingernail, she decided that the wood must be swollen from the dampness. She made a mental note to mention it to Sloan.

Katherine stood for a moment and watched Danny drift off to sleep. She adored her nephew, yet looking at him and knowing the circumstances of his conception just reminded her that she could be another Brewster daughter with a child and no husband.

Scowling in the darkened room, she wondered if there was some good sense gene that both she and Jennifer lacked. First Katherine had fallen for Robert the cheat, then she'd watched her sister fall for Gerald the potential child-snatcher, and now she'd foolishly made love to Sloan with nary a thought for the consequences. Should she be pregnant and have his child, she would be forever linked to Sloan. A link she had no doubt he wouldn't want any more than he wanted her.

Sloan's wife loomed into Katherine's mind, followed quickly by her memory of Sloan the night before the funeral when she'd delivered the jasmine and tulips. Angela. Perfect, ideal and adored by Sloan. Even her name came from the word angel. She would forever be the standard by which Sloan judged every woman. None had, or ever would, measure up. Not only had Sloan lost Angela, but their baby, as well. The ideal American family had become an American tragedy.

The countless contrasts between herself and Angela made Katherine cringe with defeat. Angela wouldn't have screeched like a wild woman on the beach. Angela would have been dressed in satin and lace when she'd seduced Sloan, not in his gray cotton shirt because she'd been cold. Katherine doubted centerfold types like Angela—and surely she must have been one—ever got cold. And Angela would have had the seduction scene set with candles and music and romance, not in a kitchen on a counter with passion so hot Katherine hadn't until a few hours ago remembered they'd used no birth control.

"Hardly the actions of a perfect, ideal woman," she muttered to herself. Perhaps Sloan's distance wasn't a bad thing. Maybe he wanted her to understand that just because they'd had good sex, Katherine needn't think there was more; she needn't think she could ever be another Angela.

And what better way to do it? After all, if he'd been all loving and tender afterward, she would have probably assumed that he cared, or even worse, she might have gotten the idea that she could actually replace Angela.

No chance of that, Katherine concluded shortly. What she and Sloan had had were a few moments of hot, hot passion. That had been Jennifer's excuse with Gerald—she hadn't planned to make love, one thing had led to another and then it had been too late. At the time Katherine had thought Jennifer had sounded like a fifteen-year-old held captive by raging hormones in the back seat of a car.

Katherine now settled on at least one certainty about her own actions: blazing, spontaneous lovemaking and a resulting pregnancy weren't limited to impassioned younger sisters.

She closed Danny's door halfway and returned to the living room.

"Katy, where in hell are the candles?" Sloan yelled from the kitchen.

Linda laughed. "Now that sounds like you, Hank."

"That's because you keep moving everything around," Hank commented, sounding relieved that the subject of their house surviving the storm had been temporarily put aside. He tasted a spoonful of chili. "For instance, you moved all the spices and I couldn't find the new can of chili powder."

Linda waved her hand in front of her mouth in a cooling motion and then took a swallow of wine. "There was more than enough in the old can."

Katherine grinned, wishing she and Sloan could have at least one conversation that sounded settled and easy and comfortable. "I better go and get the candles before he destroys the kitchen. I'll be right back."

In the kitchen most of the drawers hung open and Sloan had begun on the cabinets. The odor of sulfur hung in the air as Sloan lit matches in the dark.

"The one beside the refrigerator," she said calmly.

"Why didn't you say so before I came out here."

"Because you didn't ask me."

Sloan took a deep breath, not wanting to argue. At least make an effort to lighten up, he told himself. He had no right to blame her for their being in Chelsea Beach, or his fear that she meant more to him than any woman ever had, and certainly not the storm. Even as angry as he'd been about Hank and Linda staying the night, he had to admit he liked the position it put he and Katy in. Since withdrawing from her had not killed his feelings for her, perhaps he should just release the tension that dragged at him. Maybe it was time to try talking instead of silence.

He pulled open the cabinet door, felt around for a few seconds and took out some unopened packages. Running his hand over them, he said, "Don't we have any regular ones? These are too skinny. They'll burn in no time."

"Sorry, the tapers are it."

He tore open one of the packages. "We'll be lucky to get an hour out of each. I wonder who bought—"

She took the candle from his hand before he broke it. "I bought them. I saw them when we went shopping. I thought the burnt orange color would add interest to my autumn flower arrangements." Autumn, she thought. Almost five months from now. How she hoped all would be normal by then. She'd be back at work, Gerald would be arrested, Jennifer would be home with Danny, Sloan would be gone. She shivered, feeling a sweep of self-pity. Again she'd be Katherine Brewster, alone and perhaps pregnant....

Stop it, she scolded herself. You're descending into melodrama as if you were some ignorant woman. Shaking off her mental meanderings, she reached into the same cabinet and took out a candle holder.

Beside her, Sloan lit a match. "Most women wouldn't want to take anything home that reminded them of hiding from a baby-snatcher."

Most women in comparison to who? Angela? But she wisely didn't ask that. And she knew she would have a more permanent reminder than a few candles if what she'd been thinking about became a reality. "I'm not most women."

"Yeah," he muttered. "I'm finding that out."

"Is that why you've been so distant and cool? You've been trying to slot me into some type?"

Her question surprised him. But it also told him that she was right. He had been looking, no, desperately searching, for a way to separate himself from her.

He stared at her in the flickering light. She wondered if he was so stunned by the question he didn't know how to answer or if he was trying to find something to say that wouldn't hurt her.

She concentrated on setting the three candles into the tri-angle-shaped holder. The sudden chill in the kitchen, the darkness and his lack of response made the silence all the more damning. He'd moved behind her, and now reached around in front to strike another match. She could feel his chest against her back, her bottom against the cove of his thighs. Her breathing felt reedy, and she tried to concentrate on the tapers.

He lit the first one. "Too bad we're not alone," he murmured as he lowered his head and kissed the side of her neck. The touch of his mouth stunned her, sending her stomach plummeting.

Katherine didn't move, using all her willpower not to tip her head back. It was the first time he'd touched her this intimately since they'd made love and she found herself wondering why. A distraction, she decided. He didn't want to answer her question. She wasn't sure if she was disappointed or relieved. "You shouldn't do this...."

"Shouldn't do what? Kiss you? Find out where you like to be touched?"

"Sloan..." She closed her eyes and tried to find a reason to push him away. "This is going to make sharing a bed very difficult later."

He lit the second candle, shook out the match and skimmed his hand beneath her sweater to find her breast. "Later I intend to make love to you."

She caught her breath when he worked his fingers inside the cup of her bra. After his coolness and distance, his directness astonished her. Her mind scrambled to find a reason. "Just because you bought the condoms doesn't mean you have to do anything."

"Sweets, the protection is for you. Something I should have made sure I had the other night. And as far as having to do this," he said while his thumb searched for her nipple, "making love to you isn't a duty."

"It's just that I was the one who got us into this with Linda and Hank, and I know you never wanted us to be involved and after I sort of forced you the other night..." She ran out of breath.

"Forced me?" he asked in astonishment. His thumb had finessed her nipple into a sensitive tightness that suddenly made her bra uncomfortable. He eased his hand out and turned her so that he could see her face. "Forced me?" he asked again as if it were an outrageous concept.

Her breast felt tingly and itchy. "Well, you did keep saying no."

He grinned. "I love it." He gave her a quick hard kiss. "Sweets, it was the best sex I've had in twenty years. Why in hell did you think I've been avoiding you? I promised myself we weren't going to get into a personal relationship, and I don't break my promises. But that night I lost it. I'd hoped that if I kept my distance I could put what happened behind us. But coming into your room with the sweater this morning made me feel like a drug addict just presented with an endless fix. I wanted to tumble you onto the bed and forget about everything but how we could make each other feel. Didn't I tell you that once it happened it would happen again and again?"

"But it hasn't happened again and again...." Too late, she realized what she had said. She lowered her head, feeling the slash of color on her cheeks.

He tipped her chin up, but she kept her lashes down. "Look at me, sweets."

She shook her head. "You must think I'm some sex-starved—"

He kissed her again, this time sweeping his tongue deep into her mouth. "I think you are dazzling and so desirable that if Hank and Linda weren't in the other room I'd take you to bed right now."

She felt torn between what she should do—walk away from Sloan now relatively unscarred—and what she wanted to do—accept the promise of being saturated during their remaining time together with hot, hot passion. From one standpoint she would be lonely and unhappy after Sloan was out of her life, but she was going to feel that way no matter what. Maybe she was rationalizing, or maybe she simply wanted an excuse to once again sink into all of those evocative sensations.

He lit the third candle. Tossing the matchbook aside, he slid one hand to the back of her neck and slid the other to her hip. She moved closer, curling her arms around his neck while she continued to bask in his earlier comment.

She felt a little light-headed. No one had ever said she was the best at anything, not since she'd beaten Pudge Peterson in a marathon Monopoly game when she was twelve years old. Watching Sloan's eyes now for any sign of teasing, she asked, "The best sex you've had in twenty years?"

"Absolutely." He nuzzled his mouth into her neck.

She closed her eyes and tried to ignore the question that threatened in the back of her mind. Did that include the sex with Angela? Maybe he wasn't counting her since it wouldn't be just sex with his wife, it would be making love. She decided to press him a little. "Even though it was reckless and foolish and—"

"Dazzling, sweets."

She nodded finally and pushed aside her misgivings, the possibility that she could be pregnant and the realistic fact that later all she would have were these memories of him. She would view all that had happened between them in the context of the role they had assumed. Very simple. In that light she couldn't *really* be hurt because she didn't have to *really* trust him with her heart.

She pressed closer to him.

He grinned and lowered his mouth.

Her eyes fluttered closed and her lips parted.

Sloan had intended only a quick kiss, but it had either been too long or his resistance level had reached a danger level. Whatever the reason, his mouth folded around hers with a devouring intimacy. Her soft moan followed by her hands clutching at his waist and memories of those same fingers unbuttoning his jeans and threatening to tear open the zipper had him swelling with a painful urgency.

He moved his hands to her back and unhooked her bra. Freeing her breasts, he tested their weight. He wanted to taste her skin by candlelight, watch the moisture from his mouth make her nipples pout and peak. She moved restlessly against him, her fingers skimming across the front of his jeans.

"Hey, you two!" Hank called from the living room. "Did you get lost out there?"

Katherine sprang away from Sloan as if she'd been caught doing something naughty. Her hands flew up to her freed breasts in disbelief that she'd allowed him to go that far.

"Take it easy. They think we're married, remember."

"We'll be right there," she called back, and then in a hurried whisper to Sloan, "What did you think you were doing?" She fumbled with her bra.

"Trying to take your bra off."

"Shh, they'll hear you." She concentrated on trying to fit her breasts back in the cups.

"I want another kiss."

She shook her head, her hands struggling beneath the sweater.

"One more and I'll behave."

She gave him a skeptical look.

Sloan ignored that, pulled her hands out from under her sweater and tugged her back into his arms. "We'll be a few minutes," he called out. "We're in the middle of a heavy necking session."

"Sloan!" She peered around him when she heard laughter to see if the Rowens were watching. Thankfully, the chuckle of amusement came from the living room.

"See," he said reasonably. "They understand."

He drew her leg up so that he could press his thigh against her softness. She melted around him and he took advantage by tugging her sweater up and lowering his mouth to her breast.

Katherine caught her breath at the spiral of sensation when he cherished her nipple.

Kissing the inviting swell, he lifted his head and once again took her mouth in a greedy kiss. On an unsteady breath, he muttered, "Enough, or this is going to go way beyond necking."

Straightening, he set her away and picked up the candle holder. She licked her lips, feeling daring and wonderful. "You go on in. I need to do some repair work."

She got her bra rehooked and her sweater back in place. Running her fingers through her hair, she then touched her fingers to her cheeks. Necking, for heaven's sake, like a couple of teenagers. She grinned, feeling a surge of wonderful confidence.

She felt feminine and desirable. Her anticipation for later when they were alone suddenly took on a larger dimension. Perhaps she was a total fool, but she knew it was too late to keep Sloan out of her heart.

"Oh, hell." Sloan shook his head in disgust when his roll of the dice landed him on Park Place.

Hank took a sip of beer and settled back with his head on Linda's lap. "Looks as if Katy finally got you, buddy."

"It's about time," Linda chimed in. "I never saw anyone as lucky with dice as you are, Sloan."

"Too bad this isn't craps," he muttered, looking at the numbers he'd rolled. Mentally he added up what he owed.

Katherine sat cross-legged on the floor, her smile reminding Sloan of a landowner who had just been told her property had increased two hundred percent in value. In the candlelight her cheeks were a soft peach, her eyes sparkling with victory. "Let's see, three hotels, six houses, that's—"

"I know how much it is," Sloan growled. Now he wished he'd followed his gut and said no when Katherine suggested the game. He would have preferred pleading exhaustion and going straight to bed. After they'd finished dinner, the electricity still hadn't come back on and Katherine had suggested Monopoly. Linda and Hank had quickly agreed. Katherine had gone to the closet for the board game, left by a former tenant. After checking to make sure all the pieces were there, she'd talked Sloan into playing. The two women had decided the floor would give them more room to spread out, so after laying out the game, getting cushions from the couch and setting the candles at strategic places for maximum light, the Monopoly game had begun.

Sloan hadn't played in years and it showed.

His losses, his meager pile and his midpriced real estate, proved his ability at the game had rusted markedly. Katherine, on the other hand, was not only winning, but doing it with such serious fervor, Sloan found himself fascinated. Perhaps it *was* greed, he decided with new interest. Greed such as she'd demonstrated the night they'd made love, or in the way she'd melted in the kitchen. Now that kind of rapacious approach, he could get very accustomed to.

Katherine had volunteered to be the banker, an innocent suggestion at the time, but as the game wore on, he concluded that the lady not only played as if losing meant dishonor, but she banked as if the paper were genuine green.

Sloan laid out his money and pushed the pile toward her. Grimly he passed the dice to Linda. "Your turn."

"Not so fast," Katherine said, counting out the bills, frowning and counting again.

Sloan lifted his brows. "Don't you trust me?"

She glanced at him. In the candlelight her amber eyes met his squarely, lighthearted skepticism in their depths. He had the damnedest urge to tangle his hand in her hair, pull her against him and kiss her. She, however, said coolly, "Trust you? Of course not. You cheat. Evidenced by the fact that this is short two hundred dollars."

He slid over and did try to kiss her, but she was having none of it. Sighing, he muttered, "Come on, what's a couple hundred between a man and his wife?"

She didn't miss a beat. "An I.O.U. This bank doesn't accept them." She reached across him and tried to take a small pile of bills that he had hidden beneath his knee.

He trapped her hand on his thigh. "That's my nest egg."

"Not allowed. You either pay or you declare bankruptcy."

Sloan tucked the bills further under his knee, and glanced at Hank and Linda. "Do you believe this?"

Linda grinned. "She's right."

Hank nodded. "A tough businesswoman."

Sloan muttered, "A merciless woman."

Katherine grinned, unfazed. She lifted her hand from his thigh and gave his stomach a pat. To the Rowens she said breezily, "As you can tell, Sloan and I don't play games together too often. If he can get away with it, he tries to cheat, and he hates to lose.''

Sloan glanced at his small cache of money. Maybe he could con or bluff his way around her. There was something disconcerting about just flat out losing. "How about a deal? If I can get around the board three times without landing on Park Place we'll be square.''

She gave him an incredulous look. "What kind of deal is that? I lose both ways.''

He groaned inwardly. She was too damn smart. He decided to try another tack. "Call us square and I won't make you sleep on the couch.''

This time she laughed. "Me! I have news for you, Sloan Calder, you'll be the one out here on the couch.'' Once again she reached across him and made a grab for his money. He gripped her arms and hauled her onto his lap, wrapping his arm across her breasts.

To Hank and Linda, he complained, "See, what did I tell you? The woman is merciless. She not only takes all my money and refuses me credit, but she's going to send me to the couch, where I'll probably get a backache and a sore neck.''

Hank got to his feet, and pulled Linda up with him. "Let's get some fresh beers while these two make their deal.''

The moment the Rowens disappeared into the kitchen, Sloan lay back on the floor and hauled her on top of him. He instantly decided he preferred this kind of playing. With her nestled between his thighs, Sloan adjusted her upper body so that he could slide his hands under her sweater to her breasts. Then in his best car salesman's voice, he growled, "Have I got a deal for you....''

She eyed him suspiciously. "Considering where I am, I can only imagine.''

He rubbed his hands on the lace of her bra, feeling her already responding nipples. "You forget about the two hundred and I'll make it worth your while later.''

"Later when we make love?''

"Yeah. When you're naked and hot and wet.''

He thought she was going to make some comeback comment, but she only pressed her palm against his mouth while she turned around to see if they'd been overheard.

"What am I going to do with you?" she asked, her hand still in place. At the sudden light in his eyes, she shook her head in exasperation. "Never mind. Don't answer that."

She lifted her hand and he tunneled his fingers into her hair. "You could do your wifely duty and take me to bed."

"Hmm."

"That sounds ominous and not encouraging."

"There's still the two hundred dollars that you owe me."

He raised an eyebrow. "For God's sake, it's just a dumb game."

Suddenly serious, she said, "I know, but it isn't any different than the one we're playing with each other, is it?"

An hour later Sloan wasn't sure if they were playing or stalling, but it seemed to take forever before Linda and Hank finally took one last walk outside and pronounced that the rain had finally quit. They discussed getting up early and going to see how much damage was done, then said good-night and went into Sloan's room.

While Sloan waited for Katherine to finish her shower, he took the flashlight and checked to see if any trees or electrical wires were down. With no streetlights, and only an occasional siren, the distant sound of the pounding surf gave a sense of isolation.

Other than a tree limb in the yard, the badly whipped rosebushes Katherine had been nurturing and a neighbor's rolling garbage can, Sloan couldn't find any major damage. He hoped Hank and Linda were as lucky.

After making a final check on Danny, Sloan headed toward her bedroom, trying to ignore the cold chill that prickled the back of his neck. *Sleeping with Katy is just for tonight,* he reminded himself. *This isn't forever. Nothing's been promised beyond physical satisfaction.* Coming from the guy who'd promised himself he wouldn't get into *any* relationship with her, he concluded ruefully, a promise at this point wouldn't have much substance, anyway.

He paused at the closed door. He could sleep on the couch. Realistically, he knew Hank and Linda would be too preoccupied with how their house fared in the storm to give a hoot in hell why Sloan hadn't slept with his wife.

Just a few more days and this role-playing marriage and family routine would be finished. Drummond had said they were just days away from arresting Gerald. Then, Sloan thought, he and Katherine and Danny could all go back to Harbor Bay, back to their separate lives. The incident in the kitchen would be considered just a slip, a moment when their role-playing was plunged into reality.

Disappointment swept through him and he scowled. God, he wanted her. Wanted her in ways he'd never desired any woman, even Angela. He let the two words lodge in his mind. He didn't ignore or dismiss or deny his feelings, but neither did he like them. There was no such thing as a desire that couldn't be satisfied, couldn't be slaked, wouldn't eventually become routine.

But what if his need for Katherine . . .

Ridiculous, he told himself. He wasn't in love. He might have been caught off guard by the sexual attraction, but no way in hell would he allow himself to fall in love with her.

He rubbed his hand across the back of his neck. Yeah, hadn't he said no way in hell would he get involved with her sexually? Yet here he was with a pocket full of condoms, an arousal that wouldn't quit and a woman he desired more than he'd ever desired his wife.

A lethal mixture, Calder. A combination that had his common sense saying, "Take the couch and play it safe."

He stepped into Katherine's bedroom and closed the door, ignoring the inner voice. She stood in front of the dresser, her eyes wide as she watched him in the mirror's reflection. She wore the satin robe, and his thoughts instantly tapped into the fantasy of the other night. The lady was lethal, indeed, he thought. If he stood here long enough, he could get off just watching her. Slowly he walked toward her.

Her lashes lowered and he wondered if she could read his thoughts. He wondered if he would shock her. He wondered if he could hold out long enough to watch her lose all control in his arms.

"I thought you changed your mind," she said softly as he came to a stop behind her. How different he seemed now. More willing, less withdrawn and distant. She realized with a warm glow of insight that she was about to experience more than a fantastic sexual encounter, more than a banquet of sensual pleasure. Tonight their lovemaking would come from their hearts.

"And miss this?" His gray-green eyes were warm and intimate as he lowered his head. He pushed her hair aside and kissed the back of her neck. "I checked on the damage outside. Minimal. Then I took a quick peek at Danny. He's out like a light."

She closed her eyes as the flutter of sensation stole from her neck in a continuous ripple down to her spine. Amid a slew of scattered thoughts, she managed, "Did you lock all the doors?"

"All locked." He moved his mouth to her ear, whispering, "You sound like a wife."

"I do?" She wasn't sure how he meant that.

"That wasn't an insult nor was it a comparison to Angela," he said, anticipating her questions. When he felt her relax, he added, "Tonight was nice, Katy. It felt normal and relaxed. I had a hard time remembering why we're in Chelsea Beach."

She went very still for a moment. "Maybe I should see if Hank and Linda have enough blankets."

He pressed his hand on the front of the robe, toying with the knot on the sash. "Katy, they're fine."

"But the wind makes it so chilly."

He dropped his hands and stepped back. "Look, sweets, you don't need an excuse to say no. Just say it. I'm not going to call you a tease."

He plowed a hand through his hair and walked to the bed. Pulling his shirt off, he flung it aside.

She took a few steps toward him and stopped. "I guess I'm nervous. I don't know what I'm supposed to do. Before was spontaneous and natural and . . ." She paused, her heart thumping and her knees unsteady.

"And what, sweets?"

She met his eyes, seeing his desire, and remembering how bold and uninhibited she'd been before. "... Just fun."

Sloan sprawled on the bed and gazed at her, contemplating her words. *Just fun.* Maybe that was the key. Nothing serious and permanent, just a full exploration of their senses. Maybe he was the one putting all the heavy-duty meaning on something that to her was just fun. A shot of dissatisfaction went through him that she didn't feel more serious about him. Quickly he dismissed his disappointment.

He stacked his hands behind his head and mused aloud, "The Katy Calder approach, huh?"

She stared at him, the bubbles in her spine suddenly warm, the memory of what she'd done that first time feeling like practice compared to the maelstrom of new emotions that swirled in her heart. What she wanted to do had much to do with making love, but it also had to do with allowing herself the freedom to love, unhindered by her unease about the future. Her fingers itched to unsnap his jeans. "How did you know?"

"Because beneath the lonely and mistrustful of men Katherine Brewster lives a very innovative Katy Calder. I think the two have been merging together since you—" he grinned with delight "—forced your attentions upon me the other night."

She crossed to the side of the bed, hoping her sudden nervousness didn't show. "I don't understand how it happened. Sometimes I feel like I'm two people."

"Most of us have a lot of sides to our personality."

She scowled. "Maybe I'm a freak."

"How about normal? I've seen a lot of different sides. Your mothering side with Danny, the intuitive side when you talked Linda into leaving her house, the desperately protective side when you thought that guy on the beach was Gerald. The uninhibited side when we made love in the kitchen."

"My parents and Jennifer would be shocked...no, not shocked, they would never believe I could do such a thing on a kitchen counter."

He reached for the sash of her robe and tugged her closer. "I promise to keep it our secret."

Her eyes wandered over him, from his bare feet to his denim-covered thighs, her gaze resting a moment on the button at his waist. She wanted to capture every detail about him so she would have a treasure chest of memories. But it went further than that; she wanted to assure herself that she didn't expect more. Only in that way could she protect herself from getting hurt.

Then, with an ease that amazed even Sloan, she slipped the button from its hole, bent down and kissed the spot where the denim gaped. He sucked in a long breath, not daring to move. He wanted to let her explore, let her find her way. She kissed his stomach, the middle of his chest, lingering.

Sloan closed his eyes, the tactile sensation sending his blood pumping. "You're a dangerous lady, sweets."

She moved her mouth lower.

"Nice . . ."

And lower. When she reached the open button on his jeans, Sloan thought the top of his head would explode. He tangled his fingers into her hair, his inclination to let her continue so thick he had to fight his way through it.

"Sweets, no . . ."

"I want to."

He wondered if he'd gone crazy. No man in his right mind refused that kind of pleasure. He was amazed at her innocent skill, at her passionate enthusiasm, but he wanted all of her. He wanted the side of her that didn't trust him so readily, the woman the Irwin sisters called lonely. He wanted the woman he'd promised himself he wouldn't get involved with.

"Katherine Brewster . . ." he said softly.

She paused and straightened, her eyes searching his face.

"Not shy and scared, are you?"

She shook her head.

He touched her breast and then slid his fingers to the knot of the robe. "Take it off, sweets."

For what seemed like an eternity she didn't move. Then, with her eyes steady on his, she worked the knot loose.

A single candle burned on the dresser, close enough to allow them to see each other, but far enough away that the light around them was muted and shadowy.

Softly he said, "I had a fantasy about you doing this."

She stopped, the knot loosened, the satin gleaming like silver in the night. "Taking my clothes off for you?"

"Just the robe. You were naked and . . ."

She parted the folds and slowly lowered the fabric off her shoulders.

"God . . ." Sloan watched the robe, nearly hypnotized by the sight of it floating off her naked body. He made his hands stay still, cutting off his urge to lift her astride him. Barely breathing, he drank in the sight before him. Her breasts rose in rich fullness, her waist slender, her hips showcasing the pretty amber triangle between her thighs. In his fantasy it had been Katherine Brewster that had taken off her robe. Katy Calder could easily be tucked into a role, a mock marriage, an ending. But Katherine was reality; she represented what he'd fought against since Angela's death. A woman who would mean too much, who would exact too high a price.

And yet he couldn't deny that Katy was Katherine. A part of Katherine that might have been dormant until that night in the kitchen, but Sloan knew that he couldn't separate the two. Just as he had parts that were cold, distant and terrified. With Katy he'd discovered that he could relax, he could compromise and, like these moments, he could show her that he wanted the entire woman; the sexy Katy and the not-so-trusting Katherine.

Deep inside, the yearning to know Katherine spilled and overflowed. And despite the warnings he should heed, he knew he couldn't let the moment pass.

He swung his legs off the bed in one smooth motion. She took a step back, startled.

"Come here," he urged even as he reached out and drew her between his thighs. His hands roamed up the sides of her legs, and he felt her fingers bury themselves in his hair. He mouthed kisses across her stomach, his tongue gliding into her belly button before moving lower.

She gasped when he tipped her hips and touched his mouth to her sweetness.

"Oh, Sloan, please..."

"That's it, baby, call my name. I know Katy, now let me know Katherine...."

For a single moment she froze, her hands still, her voice husky and unsure. "Katherine wouldn't..."

"Katherine will.... Katherine won't hold back...." Sloan tasted her fully then, the rich sweetness, the soft swollen folds, the delicate pearl. He felt her arch, and to his own astonishment he felt a satisfaction unlike anything he'd ever known before. His body raged, and right there, in that timeless moment of the utmost in intimacies, as she hung on the verge of release, Sloan felt the final door of his soul burst open.

He held her as she rose, as she crested. He gripped her hips, his mouth hot and gentle and rapacious on the amber curls. Held her with tender fierceness as she called out his name with a breathless pleasure.

He loved the sound of his name on her lips, the urgent press of her fingers into his shoulders. Nothing in his experience could match the burst of effusive wonder that swept through him.

Her taste, her warmth, her evocative response folded around and wound through him with an enduring permanency.

"Sweet, sweet Katherine..." Murmuring love words whose meaning was lost in the chasms of exquisite pleasure, Sloan urged her higher, reveling in her whimpers, her whispers of abandonment.

She arched higher. "Oh!"

Her cry of satisfaction broke over Sloan and his already shredded control collapsed. He hauled her down to the bed, tucking her beneath him in a sheltering embrace, and covered her mouth in a devastating kiss.

"You're incredible," he whispered, not wanting to leave her even long enough to get out of his jeans.

"I want you. I want you to make love to me." Her amber gaze was drowsy and replete, yet filled with a new desire. He rolled away from her and stood, peeling the jeans down while Katherine watched. Her eyes gloried in his hard, muscular body that was capable of an enduring gentleness.

She'd told him before that making love was fun. But the word was shallow and superficial; not even hinting at the thousand facets of intimacy that Sloan had given her. Not just by making love to her, but by virtue of his involvement with her and Danny and their safety.

"You look all languid and lazy," he whispered as he finished with the foil packet and tossed it aside. Then he settled on the bed and tugged her back into his arms.

"Your fault," she said softly, thinking she could just stay here the rest of her life. She tangled her arms, her legs, her whole being around him like curls of sleek ribbon. "Please don't wait...."

"I can't. I can't wait any longer...." Sloan slid deep inside her, the burst of feeling so incredible it transcended the ordinary senses. With his arousal encased by her wet amber curls, he felt her respond as though he'd spilled honey.

"Ah, baby, you're so sleek, so hot...."

"Oh, please, please..." She was damp and warm, her breath reedy, her eyes glazed anew by the sweet heat of their joining, by her need for mutual pleasure with him.

He balanced his weight on his elbows so he wouldn't crush her even as she tried to gather him closer. Their bodies moved with an eternal rhythm and when Sloan felt her once again begin to peak, he instantly stopped moving.

For a fragmented moment, they stared at each other. Despite the dark room, and the lack of moonlight outside, each saw the other with a new clarity. Not with the eyes of sight, but with the eyes of their souls.

"Welcome, Katherine Brewster," he whispered, "welcome...."

Then he took her open mouth in a deep and erotically hot kiss. Her arms tightened around him as her breasts pressed against his chest.

Katherine arched and soared into the bursting pleasure, grasping Sloan and knowing, amid the smolder and the satisfaction, that Katherine Brewster had fallen desperately in love.

Chapter 11

"Hey, man, look. We can take a shortcut through this yard."

"What a helluva mess, but the city editor will freak out when he sees the dynamite shots I'm going to get."

"Man, you're gonna love the beach. I heard one of the locals at the diner say entire houses were washed away."

Katherine heard the unfamiliar voices outside as they died away. She opened her eyes and immediately closed them again at the bright sunlight that attacked her. The bedroom window was open and a light breeze moved the curtains. She pushed back the bed covers and then instantly realized she was naked. As that thought registered, the next came quickly.

Sloan.

After years of being wary of men, she knew that falling in love with Sloan Calder was clearly a mistake that would only hurt her. She'd known from the beginning that he wanted nothing from her. Yet she'd allowed him into her heart. Katherine had not only made love with him, but had done it totally and willingly as Katherine Brewster. The emotional safety of her Katy Calder role had been obliterated.

His side of the bed was empty, the sheets cool. She winced at the tenderness in her thighs and breasts as she swung her feet off the bed. Reaching down to the floor for her robe, she pulled on the satin garment and walked over to the window. Whoever had been talking was gone, and she squinted into what promised to be a day as fantastic as her own euphoric memories.

The calm after the storm, she mused, thinking of both the night's weather outside and their lovemaking inside. She pushed back her tangled hair. Despite the stiffness, her body felt replete and her senses more acute. Definitely a day to stand on a mountaintop and announce to the world that she was in love. A smile tugged her lips upward. Well, since there wasn't a mountaintop available, one of the sand dunes would do. Or the deck. Or maybe she would just fling herself into Sloan's arms and drag him back to bed.

She turned and gazed at the closed door. And where was he, anyway? Perhaps he was preparing some marvelous romantic breakfast. He'd told her last night he'd fantasized about her. Surely that fantasy included the next morning....

She crossed to the dresser and peered at herself in the mirror. Expecting to look exhausted, she was amazed to find her cheeks flushed and her eyes bright. The aura of a woman in love. Or satiated from lovemaking. She giggled and hugged herself.

The door opened and in the mirror's reflection she saw Sloan.

Feeling a little shy, she quickly clutched her robe tightly around her and tied the sash. Certainly she could wait until he kissed her or swept her back into bed before she told him how wonderful she felt. However, after she turned and had a closer look at him, her smile died. He wasn't regarding her with love or even lust, he wasn't looking at her at all. Recalling his distance after that first night, she wondered fitfully if she was in for a repeat.

"Morning, sweets," he said casually, still without fully paying attention to her. Admittedly he was friendlier than the last time, but congenial wasn't exactly what she'd had in mind.

He was dressed in boots and jeans and a blue T-shirt with a beer logo. She recalled kissing his chest, his stomach, opening his jeans... Jeans that hugged him now with a too-sexy snugness. She felt a little dizzy as she contemplated the decadent direction of her thoughts.

"Good morning," she said, wondering if he could hear the "I love you" she'd mentally hidden in the greeting.

He propped his hands low on his hips as his eyes surveyed the floor. "You didn't see my keys around, did you?"

She blinked, then sighed with exasperation. "Danny had them last night after we got back from the drugstore. Sloan?"

"They're probably under the couch. Oh, by the way, Danny's awake and he's been fed. Linda got him dressed. She put him back in the crib, but he's looking for you. And the electricity is still off, plus no phone, which is why I want my keys. I'm going to stop in town and see if I can find one to call Drummond and let him know we're okay."

Katherine realized she hadn't thought of Gerald once since she'd awakened. But despite a lessened fear of Danny's father, her happy and expectant mood collapsed. She jammed her hands into her robe pockets and frowned.

He wasn't going to be cool and distant, but he wasn't rushing over to kiss her, either. Just an ultra-casual approach as if the night they'd spent was nothing special. But then to him it probably wasn't. Or else he'd been through the "next morning expectation" with other women. Perhaps complete with pleas for commitment or a relationship or a heartfelt confession of love. Yes, she had no trouble imagining that he'd been the object of all three and had dealt with them accordingly. No doubt he'd expected one or all from her, too. That would explain his entrance; casual, light and friendly, with no touching. She was sure to get the message.

"Hank went out and brought back coffee and fresh doughnuts," Sloan said, not meeting her eyes. He gathered up his stuff, including a leather case and his daily expense reports, which he'd taken from his room the night before.

Katherine regarded him with coolness, but inwardly she berated herself. Maybe she'd been expecting too much from him. She wondered if in his own way, he, too, didn't know how to deal with what had happened between them. She'd felt something far more profound when they'd made love, but she should have known better than to expect anything from him. Sloan had been clear about not wanting involvement from the beginning. She was the one who had allowed herself to hope. She had no right to blame him for being charming and unconcerned. Perhaps, to him, their lovemaking was indeed a finality. Wonderful and satisfying, but also a bittersweet goodbye.

Folding her arms, she watched him put the leather case down on a nearby chair and toss the reports on top of it. Feeling more hurt, more anguished than she'd been the morning after they'd made love in the kitchen, she decided to pretend indifference. "I don't want coffee and I never eat doughnuts."

He glanced up, his brows raised as if she hadn't followed the proper script. Carefully and deliberately, he said, "Look, I know you probably want to talk about last night, but don't you think it would be better if we gave it a few hours or even a day? That way neither of us will say anything that we might regret."

Like saying I love you? Obviously he was afraid she'd blurt it out. Or had she already? During the night in one of those bursts of passion?

Katherine gripped the dresser when her knees suddenly weakened. Oh, God, had she spontaneously declared herself, and now he wanted to pretend she hadn't? Now was not the time to show that she was hurting; or worse, humiliated.

Gathering the shards of her heart together, she asked in what she hoped was a convincingly light tone. "Regret? What would I possibly have to regret?"

He looked relieved, as if he'd been let off the uncomfortable hook of potential commitment. His face relaxed. "Sweets, you were fantastic."

She noted he didn't say dazzling. Despite reminding herself she had no right to be annoyed, she clamped her teeth together to prevent any burst of later-to-be regretted words.

Instead she smiled. "Thank you. So were you. Perhaps we can do it again sometime."

Sloan scowled. His own attempt to be casual had either backfired or he was seeing another side of Katherine Brewster. Perhaps he was. After all, how well did he really know her? Intimacy might provide knowledge, but making love didn't automatically reveal all the facets of human nature. Maybe their lovemaking hadn't been as extraordinary for her as he'd thought. The fact that he felt a crushing disappointment at this rattled him.

"Katy—"

She lifted her chin. "Katherine. I would prefer you call me Katherine."

"I don't want you to misunderstand—"

She pressed her hand to her chest in a melodramatic fashion. "Misunderstand? Why I don't know how I could possibly do that, Sloan. You couldn't mean I might misunderstand because you came in here and greeted me—after we made love all night long—with a question about your car keys?" She hoped her sarcasm made an indelible point. "If I were into pop psychology, as you like to accuse me of, I might suspect that you hunting for car keys is actually a deep-seated need to escape from me."

"Damn," he muttered.

She turned her back to him and gazed out the window. She would not cry. She would be strong and coolly indifferent. Far be it from her to force her feelings on him or expect him to share in the wonderful sensations that he had created in her. In all honesty she'd wanted to shout the words "I love you" at the top of her lungs, but now she wouldn't say them if he crawled across a crab-infested beach and begged her. Maybe it wasn't love, anyway. Maybe it was something light and casual, as easily dispensable as good satisfying sex. No doubt he assumed she would mistake the two. Since she was hardly an expert on either, perhaps she had.

He wanted light and casual, well that was just fine with her. "Have Linda and Hank heard anything about their house?"

After a hesitation in which Katherine was sure she heard him draw a deep breath of thankfulness at the change in subject, he said, "They've gone on over to take a look. I told Hank I'd be over as soon as I talked to you."

She resisted the urge to tell him, he'd have said more by simply not talking. "Why don't you go ahead. I'll get dressed, and Danny and I will be along in a little while."

"You're sure?" He wanted her to say she needed him to stay with her. Terrific, Calder. On the one hand you don't want her close and on the other hand you don't want to ever be away from her.

"Yes." She heard him take a step and then stop.

"We shouldn't be here much longer. From what Drummond said the other night they should be wrapping things up anytime now."

"Wonderful. Then we can get back to our real lives," she said breezily, despite the sudden pain in her stomach. "I can't wait to get home and get back to work." She fussed with getting clothes out of the drawers and when she didn't hear him move she slanted a sideways look in his direction. "Was there something else?"

His eyes had darkened, as if her attitude was both upsetting and angering him. He was no longer matter-of-fact or distantly friendly; even the casualness had disappeared. Katherine tried to ignore the shiver that slid down her spine.

In a slow dangerous saunter he approached her, his eyes never leaving her face. "Yeah, there's a helluva lot else."

She didn't move, but her heart sped up and her pulse clamored. "Well, whatever it is we better wait till another time to discuss it. I certainly wouldn't want us to misunderstand one another."

Before she had a chance to turn completely away, he'd gripped her shoulders and swung her around to face him. Their eyes met, his filled with angry frustration. Whether it was directed at her, himself or their situation, she couldn't tell.

Studying her for too long a moment, he said darkly, "Damn you."

She peered at him, her chin steady. "Just exactly what I wanted to hear. Let go of me."

But he only tightened his grip. "Stop being so casual."

"Casual!" She quit struggling. "You're the one who's been acting like nothing happened, like what we did didn't—"

He crushed his mouth down on hers, his hands sliding under the lapels of her robe in search of her breasts. Katherine's desire leaped as if all she'd needed was the smallest of encouragements. Damn the man and his effect on her. She should be pushing him away instead of rubbing against him. He slid one hand between her thighs.

"Ah, Katherine," he groaned when he encountered her readiness. This was exactly what he didn't want to happen, he thought desperately as he coveted the now familiar feel of her amber curls. Sure he'd been the first one to be cool and aloof, but he hadn't thought she would be. He'd only wanted to ease them through the awkwardness of those first morning-after moments. He'd feared that if he came into the bedroom, drew her into his arms and kissed her as he wanted to, that she would have assumed more than he could offer.

He kissed her again, long and deep, trying to garner the will and discipline to step away from her. Now was the time to leave. Now before he couldn't. But she brushed her hand across him, lingering too long on the swell of his zipper.

"It seems you have the same problem," she said with far too much delight and satisfaction. Slowly she worked his zipper down.

He moved his hands on her breasts, cupping them, finessing her nipples into tight peaks. "You know I can't leave you, don't you?" he muttered as he lowered his head and kissed her neck.

He didn't see her grin, but her silence answered his question. Sloan knew he wasn't going anywhere except deep into her body.

He backed up to the bed and sprawled down on the mussed sheets, taking her with him. His hand groped on the night table for what he needed, tearing open the packet with unsteady hands.

She sat astride him, her robe bunched up around her hips. He fumbled with the protection, finally getting it set, and then lifted her to slide down on him. He gritted his teeth, gripped her hips and gloved himself with such ease he wondered if she'd been made just to fit him.

Katherine moaned, rocking and swaying.

"I didn't come in here for this," he murmured with a deep shudder.

"I know," she whispered, feeling very much in control and deciding that she liked it.

"You're enjoying this, aren't you?" he asked before his breath threatened to evaporate. He closed his eyes and shuddered when her mouth took a light nip on his chin. He groaned. "Hell, you could be addictive."

"Was that a compliment?"

"No, damn it, just an obvious fact."

She rose up and then slid back down loving the power she had over him. "My, such flattery could turn my head."

He growled, "Katherine . . ."

She rocked forward and smiled broadly as his restraint began to shatter.

He clamped his hands on her hips, his voice low and a little desperate. "I don't want or need a woman who makes me think about things I don't want to think about."

She leaned down and kissed him. "Sloan, I would never want to control your thoughts. Especially since I have such wonderful control over your body."

He swore amid a shattering release.

Around noon, with Danny propped on her hip, Katherine picked her way through what was left of the sand dunes that lined the upper edge of the beach. The same dunes where she and Sloan had picnicked, where she'd run from the stranger who she thought was Gerald. Sloan had left the cottage earlier to go and help Hank. With no electricity and the phone still out, Katherine was not only bored, she felt too isolated. Besides, she wanted to see Linda and how the Rowens' house had survived the storm.

Katherine had told Linda she would help her after the storm, and now the thought of an afternoon without the distraction of Sloan appealed to her. If she could just keep her mind focused on getting him out of her thoughts, or at the very least putting him in some sort of perspective, she knew that saying goodbye would be much less painful.

Now, coming down onto the beach, Katherine stared in wide-eyed astonishment. Hundreds of curiosity seekers, local media people with cameras, looters scavenging for any valuables from the badly damaged homes, swarmed along the shore from the parking lot at one end all the way to the seawall at the other end.

Trucks bit through the wet-packed sand, two backhoes worked to clear debris and a panel truck from a Boston TV station was trying to set up for a live report. Near where Katherine stood, a woman screamed and then fainted in her husband's arms when she saw what was left of her house; part of a chimney with a soggy mattress snagged in its bricks.

The waves rolling onto the beach were still powerful and high. Surfers dotted the racing spray-swept whitecaps, a stark contrast of summer fun in the midst of a pile of destruction.

Katherine searched the seawall area for Linda's house. The water and wind had destroyed and moved the landscape so that parts of it were level where there'd been sand dunes and broken where there'd been rocks. Much of the area was no longer recognizable.

"Katy! We're over here," Linda called, waving frantically.

Katherine waved back. She'd gripped Danny and had begun to work her way through the crowd when a man in chinos and a dark shirt stopped her.

She froze when she realized who it was. He immediately began to back away and lowered his head sheepishly. Keeping his voice low, he said, "I ain't gonna hurt you, ma'am. I been hopin' you'd be down here. I jus' want to tell you 'bout the other day."

She stared at him. Up close she could see he bore only the barest resemblance to Gerald in size and coloring. This man was older, definitely not as forceful appearing and the ravages of years of drinking showed on his face. She could smell alcohol now. Seeing him here he seemed little more than a poor misguided drunk, and yet that afternoon her imagination had filled in a hundred frightening possibilities. "You're the man who scared me on the beach."

He pulled off his bill cap, the same one he'd worn that afternoon. His hair was thick and uncombed. He twisted his hat in his fingers. "Yes, ma'am, and I ain't been able to sleep thinkin' about it. I didn't mean you no harm. Just wanted to see your little boy. Cute little fella." He reached out to touch Danny's foot, but Katherine stepped back and Danny tightened his hands around her neck.

In a steady voice, she said, "Well, whatever your intentions, you did frighten us. Why did you keep coming after us when I was obviously trying to get away?" The man stared down at his feet and Katherine regretted her sharp tone.

"Didn't mean to scare you," he said again. "Your little boy, I thought—" He shook his head and crumpled his bill cap tighter. "Ain't no use. Ain't never gonna see him again." He shuddered and turned away, mumbling another apology.

"Wait," Katherine said, feeling more sympathetic now than scared. Whatever the man's reasons, they were obviously not harmful ones. "Who aren't you going to see again?"

He raised his head, his eyes sunken deep and tired. They were blue and she imagined that at one time they'd been lively and clear. "I'm a little drunk and when I'm a drinkin' I get to rememberin' and regrettin'." For a moment his face seemed to relax. "You take good care of that little boy, ma'am. You watch him close. Don't you let him too near the water." His eyes filled with tears and he reached into his pocket for a brown flask. He tipped it to his mouth and drank as though the liquid were his only friend. Wiping his hand across his lips, he shoved the bottle back into his pocket. He shook out his twisted cap and stuck it on his head. He touched his fingers to the bill, nodded to her and lumbered off.

Katherine stared after him, not noticing that Linda was there until she touched Katherine's arm. "Oliver didn't bother you, did he?"

"What? Oh, he was just—"

"Telling you that Danny reminded you of his son?"

Katherine shook her head. "Actually, he only told me to keep Danny away from the water."

Linda nodded. "Some of the locals think he's crazy. He wanders the beach all year round, mostly drunk. His son drowned here one summer about five years ago."

Katherine watched his slouching figure as he walked a few steps and then stopped. "My God. How horrible."

"It was one of those freak tragedies. His wife had left him with the boy while she walked to the refreshment stand with the daughter. Apparently, or so the story goes, he got engrossed in a conversation with another man and forgot about the toddler. The baby wandered off and they found him later in a small tidal pool. He had dark hair like Danny and was just about his age."

Katherine noted that the man had again taken the flask from his pocket and raised it to his mouth. "The poor man." Then in a thoughtful voice, she added, "He must have been drunk the other day."

Linda frowned. "What happened the other day?"

"Oh, I saw him on the beach and he acted like he knew us," she said vaguely. "His guilt about his son must be overwhelming."

"His wife divorced him, took their daughter and disappeared. He hasn't seen them since. He's harmless, but when he's been drinking he tends to forget his son is dead. It's really sad."

Katherine hugged Danny fiercely. With a kind of foresight, she understood the man's grief and desperation. She thought of Gerald and how she would feel if he'd succeeded in snatching Danny. Jennifer would certainly blame her, but no more than she would blame herself. Perhaps, like this man, she'd be looking for Danny in every little boy, struggling with her guilt, desperate for anything that would make the memory go away.

Someone urged Katherine aside and she stepped back behind Linda.

Linda was speaking to a woman reporter holding a microphone. "Thank God, my house is still standing," Linda was saying. "Precariously, and with a lot of damage, but at least it's not at the bottom of the Atlantic. My husband and a friend are looking at how to brace one corner temporarily. We were fortunate. Some of our neighbors lost everything.''

Katherine juggled Danny, who wanted to get down. She tried to calm and distract him by shifting him to her other hip. The beach was too littered to allow him on the sand.

Linda nodded to a question about evacuation. ''Yes, we did evacuate. The height of the water was terrifying. Fortunately we had some wonderful friends to stay with.'' Linda talked on, answering questions about the area and how long they'd lived in Chelsea Beach.

Katherine paid little attention. She was caught in her own thoughts about Oliver losing his son. Those thoughts soon spilled into ones about Sloan and his own loss.

He'd lost his wife and baby, and he'd blamed himself. He, too, had been gripped by guilt, only he hadn't let it destroy him the way Oliver had. Sloan was mentally and psychologically whole and incredibly stable. So stable that he'd taken an assignment to protect another woman and another baby. She realized all over again why her hysteria that day on the beach had so affected him. My God, she thought, no wonder he was so dead set against any kind of personal involvement. Emotionally, he'd geared himself for one objective; their safety from Gerald. Sloan simply hadn't prepared himself for anything that involved more than his expertise as a private investigator.

Katherine glanced up to see a video camera pointed in her direction. ''Do you have a house here on the beach, ma'am?'' the woman reporter asked.

''No, we don't.''

The reporter immediately lost interest. She gestured to the video cameraman. In a crisp voice, she said, ''The woman who fainted has recovered. Can you get a shot of her with the chimney and mattress in the background?'' The crew made their way to the grieving woman and her husband.

Linda took Katherine's arm. ''Come on. Sloan and Hank will be wondering what happened to us.'' They wove through the crowd, stepping carefully over wood and rocks that had been thrown onto the beach by the powerful surf.

Moments later Katherine saw for herself that the Rowen house was indeed still standing, although the foundation at one corner had been substantially weakened by the pounding water.

For the next few hours Sloan, Hank and a crew of other men worked to brace the weakened corner. A friend of Hank's brought in a backhoe to level off the ground and fill in the ruts with rocks. Water damage inside the house had left much of the first floor in need of major repair. Katherine and Linda salvaged what they could, including the painting of the fishermen, which remarkably still hung on the wall.

By five o'clock Katherine was exhausted. The temporary support was in place and most of the men had left. Hank and Linda stood with their arms around each other, staring at their now fairly even house. Sloan had taken off his T-shirt and rolled it into a long, thin band so that he could tie it around his head to catch the dripping sweat. Katherine found him sprawled in a lawn chair with a can of soda in his hand. Danny slept soundly nearby in an old rowboat one of the men had dragged close to the house that Linda had filled with bed pillows.

Sloan glanced up when Katherine sat down on the edge of the boat.

"You look beat."

"So do you," she said. "I don't think I saw you sit once all afternoon."

"The house needed to be secured before dark," he said matter-of-factly as he tipped the can to his mouth.

She stood up and stretched. "Well, anytime you're ready to go, we are."

Sloan crumpled the can and heaved himself out of the chair. He untied his shirt, shook it out and pulled the badly wrinkled garment over his head. He went to the rowboat, intent on picking up Danny. Hank and Linda came toward them.

"You guys leaving?"

"Yeah. Katy's tired and I'm running on empty."

Hank offered his hand to Sloan. "How can I ever thank you?"

Sloan gripped his hand. "You just did. Did I hear that your insurance man is coming in tomorrow to take a look?"

Hank nodded and the two men discussed the extent of the damage while Linda hugged Katherine. "Oh, Katy, how I wished you lived here all year round. If it hadn't been for you, I don't know what I would have done."

Katherine's eyes misted. She would miss Linda. It was on the tip of her tongue to say let's keep in touch, but she stopped herself. She couldn't. Not until all this business with Gerald was concluded. In a few weeks. Sloan would be out of her life by then, Jennifer would be back to take care of Danny. Once again, she'd have only the flower shop to take up her time. Strange, she mused, even the possibility of being pregnant with Sloan's baby seemed remote.

She smiled now, sidestepping Linda's request to exchange addresses. "I may—I mean we may be moving. Let me get in touch with you."

"You won't forget?" Linda asked worriedly. "Hank and I would like another chance to beat you at Monopoly."

Katherine laughed. "Sloan still owes me two hundred dollars."

Sloan had walked over and draped an arm around her neck. "You can take it out in trade, sweets," he murmured.

They all laughed, but Katherine's held a tinge of sadness. It was no longer just around Hank and Linda. Most of the time now, she didn't feel as if she and Sloan were playing a role. She really did feel married to him. Yet Sloan's teasing only served to remind her that they wouldn't be together long enough for her to "take it out in trade."

Sloan awakened Danny, who flailed his arms and scowled fiercely at being disturbed. After a promise to stop in the following day, Katherine and Sloan walked back to the cottage. He closed and locked the gate at the deck steps before they went around to the front yard where they both came to a sudden stop.

Parked at the curb was a police car with its red and blue roof lights flashing.

Katherine stared, her fingers digging into Sloan's arm. "What do they want?"

Sloan swore. "I can only think of one thing. Drummond sent them."

"G-Gerald . . ." She could barely get out his name.

"The son of a bitch must have gotten tired of waiting for you to come back with Danny and split." Sloan handed Danny to Katherine and scowled with fury. "Unless somebody involved in the investigation screwed up big time."

Katherine felt a numbing fear. Her eyes darted around the darkening evening as though she expected Gerald to leap out at her. She watched Sloan take long strides toward the police car. An officer got out, said something, and Sloan swung around and glared back at her.

She'd moved to the corner of the house near the rosebushes. Danny pointed to the flashing lights and wiggled to get down, but she barely noticed. The police officer nodded, got back into his car and drove off.

Sloan stalked over to her, his eyes cold and angry. "Just what in hell did you think you were doing?"

She blinked in confusion. "I don't know what you're talking about."

"Television. The Providence affiliate of a Boston station used live storm-related interviews. You and Danny, along with Linda, were on the twelve o'clock news."

Chapter 12

Katherine stood speechless, then turned away, fighting tears of self-reproach.

Sloan watched the police car drive away, then dragged a hand through his hair. "They had storm problems in Harbor Bay, too. The cops had their hands full trying to keep the surf lovers and gawkers away from the beaches. Gerald apparently took advantage of the confusion and disappeared." Sloan paused, then added wearily, "We're going to have to get out of here."

"But Gerald can't know exactly where we are," Katherine said, desperate for any possibility that what she feared hadn't happened. "I mean, it isn't as if Danny and I were identified as being residents of Chelsea Beach."

"The camera was on you, Katherine. How likely is the possibility that you would have traveled from another town to stand on a beach? According to what Drummond told the Chelsea Beach police chief, you were seen during the time the interviewer got Linda's name and learned that her house was on the seawall. God knows how long before that the camera had been panning the area for file pictures and filler shots. It could have picked up you and Linda talking before the interviewer ever began."

Everything he said made her realize that no matter how careful she'd been while they were at Chelsea Beach, no matter how realistically she'd played the role of Katy Calder, and no matter how her feelings for Sloan had evolved from wariness to love, nothing would matter if those few moments on the beach helped Gerald find Danny. . . .

Katherine hugged the toddler to her, trying to ward off the sudden chilling possibilities.

Sloan took a few steps toward the front door and then stopped. Staring back at her as if astonished all over again, he said, "I can't believe you wouldn't have considered the ramifications of a TV camera." Then after a brief pause, he added succinctly, "We might as well have called Gerald and invited him over for Monopoly."

Katherine shifted Danny and gave Sloan a caustic look. "Damn it, Sloan! Do you think I deliberately stood there like some kid who wants to be on TV? I had my mind on something else." That something else being Oliver and her discovery—through Oliver's story—of the contrast between Oliver and Sloan's ability to deal with tragedy. However, she wasn't about to say anything about Oliver now. No doubt Sloan would accuse her of dabbling in more pop psychology when she should have been dodging a TV camera. "Besides," she added. "Once the interviewer determined I didn't have a house on the seawall she lost interest. Our conversation lasted all of three seconds."

Frustrated and angry at himself rather than her, he asked, "You talked to the TV reporter?"

"I answered her question. Would you have preferred that I scream and say she couldn't talk to me because I was in hiding?"

"Hell, no. I would rather you'd been more aware of what you were doing."

She caught Sloan's arm as he pulled his keys from his pocket to unlock the front door. Why hadn't she thought of it before? Perhaps Gerald hadn't seen her; perhaps he'd seen Sloan! "And what about you?" she asked. "How do you know you weren't on TV?"

He stared at her as if she had two heads. "What! Don't be ridiculous. No one was shoving a camera at me."

"There were Camcorders everywhere," she said staunchly. "And a lot of people with them were milling around where you and Hank were working. You know the TV stations encourage amateurs to send in tapes of disasters or anything that would be provocative and newsworthy. Maybe a Camcorder buff got some really good tape and sold it to the Boston station. And maybe Gerald saw you and not me. You're fairly well known in Harbor Bay. Seeing you on TV in Chelsea Beach may have had Gerald putting two and two together."

For a long moment he stood silently, considering what she'd said. Finally he replied, "That's about as farfetched as I've ever heard."

She stood her ground. "Why? Is it because you don't want to believe that if Gerald finds us the reason could as easily be you as me?"

He looked away, but not before she saw that his face had gone pale. Suddenly she realized that he hadn't heard what she'd said as a mere possibility. By raising the question, he heard her saying that he hadn't protected her and Danny. Just as he believed he hadn't protected Angela and his baby.

Juggling Danny, she stepped in front of the door he was about to unlock. "Sloan, I didn't mean that the way it sounded."

He took Danny, and then pushed her aside, but this time she knew the anger was self-directed.

"Didn't mean what?" he asked grimly. "That I fouled up this case? Well, I did. Never mind the TV cameras or some Camcorder. I was hired to be with you and Danny, and if I'd been doing my job instead of getting a good neighbor award, we wouldn't be standing here wondering where in hell Gerald is."

Inside the cottage less than five feet from the locked front door, Gerald Graham smiled in the darkness. He moved swiftly through the interior, deftly sidestepping an inflated red ball. He'd been careful not to disturb anything. He didn't want to raise any suspicion until he was ready to make his move.

He'd entered the house through a loose unlocked window in Danny's room. The weak window frame had disturbed Graham. If the wind from the storm had hurled in toward that side of the house, the glass could have blown in and shattered all over his son.

His son. He'd liked the way that sounded from the moment he'd heard that Danny had been born. He'd told everyone at his restaurant that he had a son. Gerald didn't like the word kid. "Son" sounded soft and close and connected. And Gerald had always felt very connected to Danny, despite Jennifer's refusal to marry him. Gerald could never be like those men who saw their sons or daughters as burdens or traps. He'd been about Danny's age when his own old man had disappeared. Gerald was determined that he would be a good father; he would know his son.

A good father beginning tonight, he decided as he peered through the glass back door. Beyond was the path across the dunes he intended to take. Once clear of the cops and Katherine, he and Danny could start over somewhere. Maybe out west or even down in Texas—he'd always wanted to go to Texas....

Jennifer would be sorry then, he thought with a rush of satisfaction. She'd be sorry that she hadn't agreed to marry him, that she hadn't believed him when he said he'd gotten out of the blackmail business. Very soon now she would regret that she'd try to deny him his rights to see Danny. If she'd only cooperated, Gerald knew he wouldn't have been forced to do something so permanent. It was all her fault....

He listened now to the voices on the other side of the front door, reminding himself there were plenty of days ahead to enjoy his revenge against Jennifer. Plenty of days ahead to wonder if she was sorry for rejecting him that day in her office. She'd said she hated him, said she'd never let him see Danny again. He smirked to himself now. He'd fix her. He'd fix her good.

Enough. He had to concentrate on his final plan.

Gerald had dressed in dark clothes and running shoes. He'd spent three weeks getting his body in shape. He'd even quit drinking. After he'd botched things up at Katherine's house, he'd convinced himself that if he'd been cold sober and in better physical shape, he would have gotten Danny that night.

Tonight he didn't intend to fail.

He'd been inside the cottage for more than an hour, which had given him an opportunity to map out his strategy. He'd already put diapers and a few of Danny's sleepers into a bag, which he'd stashed some distance away. Gerald felt confident and totally focused on the future, having used the weeks the cops had him under surveillance to plan his escape from Harbor Bay. Danny had been the missing piece, the one thing that had kept Gerald from running sooner. During the days after Katherine had disappeared with Danny, Gerald had called in every marker owed him, every favor, talked to every contact he had, in a search of information. He had learned that the cops were hiding her and that she was in southern New England, but her exact whereabouts had remained a secret.

Until earlier today.

Gerald credited himself for his own stroke of genius. It had come a few days ago; a brilliant idea that had worked so well, he'd almost had second thoughts.

Hearing that Katherine and Danny were in Chelsea Beach had been too good to be true. In fact, he'd been instantly suspicious. It had come so easily, he'd suspected it might be a trap. Once here, he'd asked around about new arrivals and easily located them. But now, knowing he'd found Danny and he was moments away from getting him, he still wasn't completely convinced Drummond hadn't set him up. That was the trouble with Drummond, Gerald decided with a sudden pang of nervousness as he made sure he'd unlocked the door to the deck. The chief had a reputation for never allowing an investigation to get completely out of his control. Drummond liked those commendations and plaques from the city. No doubt he wanted to add Gerald's arrest to the list of successes.

The arrival of the cop a little while ago had given him a few moments of panic until he realized the guy was gonna sit in the cruiser and study his fingernails.

But hearing Calder's voice had sent a cold shot of sweat down Gerald's back. The P.I. was obviously Drummond's ace, his master stroke.

Gerald knew about Sloan Calder. He knew all about the hit-and-run that had gotten Calder's old lady instead of him. And he knew all about Calder's methodical and obsessive hunt for Suggs Mello. Calder hadn't failed.

But master stroke or not, he wasn't about to let Calder shake his mood tonight. Gerald took a long steady breath, already feeling a sense of victory. Finally he would get his son and no one would stop him.

"Not you, Calder," he muttered under his breath. "Drummond might think you can do the impossible, but I've got a nice surprise for you."

Gerald slipped his hand beneath his sweatshirt and wrapped his fingers around the butt of the revolver tucked into the waistband of his pants. Lifting the weapon smoothly, he raised it, took a practice aim and smiled broadly. He then repositioned the weapon to give him the best advantage. A trickle of sweat inched down his temple. Adrenaline pumped through his body. When he heard the front door lock click open, he flattened himself against the wall just inside Katherine's bedroom.

Sloan shoved the front door open wide to let in as much of the moonlight as possible. No streetlights were on and the neighbors' homes were all dark except for the flicker of candles near some of the windows. He held Danny and urged Katherine inside.

Still carrying Danny, Sloan went into the kitchen and returned moments later with a candle in a holder. "Phone's still out, too." He continued on, tapping the red ball so that it rolled toward the couch. He went into Danny's room with Katherine following.

After putting the child into the crib, Sloan lit the candle. He pushed Danny's truck out of the way so she wouldn't trip in the dark. "Just get enough stuff for tonight. Once I talk to Drummond in the morning we'll know exactly what he wants us to do."

"I don't suppose the police are going to take some of the blame for this?" She opened a drawer and felt around for clean sleepers. "If they'd arrested Gerald when I reported the snatching attempt, we wouldn't be in this mess."

"He would have been out on bail within twenty-four hours," Sloan said flatly. At the doorway he said, "I'll get your stuff and mine and put it in the car. I want us to be away from here in ten minutes."

Katherine scowled. Something should be done about the bail system, she decided, when baby-snatchers can run around loose. She opened another drawer—automatically searching for what she hadn't found in the first drawer—but still found no sleepers. Planting her hands on her hips, she frowned at the open drawers as if they were playing some trick on her. She'd been certain she'd emptied the dryer, but with all that had been going on maybe she'd just thought she had.

The candle flickered and she was about to blow it out while she went to check the dryer when Danny giggled. She reached inside the crib to ruffle his hair and saw the teddy bear. Katherine blinked in momentary confusion. Where had that come from? With a mental shrug, she decided it was probably from Sloan. She could tell by the thickness of the artificial fur that the toy animal hadn't come cheap. Just as cost hadn't been a factor in the purchase of her ring and the heavy fisherman's sweater she wore.

Days earlier she'd accused Sloan of spoiling Danny when he bought the red truck. Now she assumed he'd probably gotten the stuffed animal at the same time and rather than cause another ruckus, had sneaked it into the child's room this morning.

She handed the teddy back to Danny, who hugged it fiercely. She heard a noise behind her and turned with every intention of telling Sloan that despite the problems between them, she appreciated his generosity toward Danny.

But her thoughts scattered and for a few frozen seconds, nothing registered but disbelief.

"Nothing like the element of surprise is there?" Gerald commented confidently from the doorway.

The flickering candlelight underscored the eeriness of the moment rather than illuminating the dark of the room. She wanted to grab Danny and run, but there was nowhere to go. He blocked the door.

Then, as if enjoying her predicament, he slouched against the doorjamb, his hands in his pockets. He wore dark slacks and a loose sweatshirt. And Katherine had seen enough cop shows on TV to know that the lump beneath the shirt at his waist was probably a gun. The very fact that he saw no need to wave it at her frightened Katherine even more. This wasn't the reckless, slightly drunk baby-snatcher who had invaded her apartment. There was something more dangerous, more sinister and controlled about this Gerald Graham.

She tried to relax. Any moment now Sloan would loom up and grab Gerald. Katherine's eyes searched expectantly, but nothing lay beyond Gerald save silent darkness.

She was about to call Sloan's name when she realized that he was probably only inches away, out of sight and waiting for the best moment to strike. Katherine thought shakily that right now would be terrific, but pulled herself together. If Sloan was sneaking up, she didn't want Gerald to know.

Katherine recalled her hysteria that day on the beach when she'd thought Oliver was Gerald. Now she faced the real Gerald and she wasn't screaming or falling apart. She chanced a sideways glance at Danny. The toddler, facing away from the door, was lying down with the teddy bear.

Now is not the time to examine why you're not hysterical, she reminded herself. *Just keep Gerald from turning around.*

Katherine's thoughts jumped fretfully in a hundred different directions before she asked, "How did you get in here?"

"The window was unlocked," he said as though she shouldn't have asked such a stupid question.

She started to tell him the wood had been swollen, but decided it might be safer for him to continue to think she was stupid.

"Pretty dumb, Katherine, but I can overlook that." He glared then, his voice holding just the slightest edge. His eyes bored into her, chilling her. "The danger to my son I can't overlook. If the glass had blown in, Danny would have been cut and hurt badly. If that had happened . . ." His words trailed off ominously, letting her mind conclude the worst.

Katherine damned herself for forgetting to mention the window to Sloan. She had no excuse, she'd noticed the window the night before when she'd excused herself during the chili supper. She found it ironic, however, that Gerald would take his fury out on her for Danny being hurt when she was the one who wanted to keep the toddler safe.

Her eyes darted again to the darkness. Please, Sloan, hurry. Nervously she asked, "How did you find us?"

He laughed, apparently feeling very much at ease. Too much so, Katherine thought suddenly.

"Those two dumb broads who live upstairs from you."

"The Irwin sisters?" she asked incredulously. "But they didn't know where we, uh, where Danny and I were." Inwardly she cursed the near slip. If he didn't know about Sloan, then Sloan would have even more of an edge.

"I know they didn't and that was why my brilliant idea worked so well. I called them a few days ago and told them I worked with Jennifer and that she was missing. I needed their help in locating you. They told me you had gone away for a few weeks, but they didn't know where." Katherine held her breath hoping Marion and Nina hadn't mentioned Sloan. Gerald continued, "I gave them a number and told them to call me if they heard from you." He chuckled, obviously enjoying his own strategy. Then, with the flourish of a final jab, he added, "It seems they saw you and Danny on the twelve o'clock news."

Katherine let her eyes close briefly, her heart pounding. Not in a million years would she have thought Marion and Nina would be the ones who innocently gave away Katherine's location. She'd been so focused on Gerald being watched by the police, she hadn't considered other factors. Of course he wouldn't have been just waiting for her to return as if he'd been frozen in time. He would have still been planning his revenge against Jennifer, still planning to snatch Danny, and most of all, still searching for a way to accomplish both.

Suddenly Katherine knew, with a sense of draining defeat, that no matter how far she ran, or how deep she hid, Gerald would have eventually found them. In a strange though twisted way, he possessed the same obsession about having Danny as Sloan had had about finding Angela's killer. The difference being that Sloan hadn't broken the law and the man who'd killed Angela deserved to be caught and imprisoned.

No matter that Gerald was Danny's father. Katherine knew that Danny deserved better.

She shivered, realizing that Gerald believed he was being perfectly rational and logical. He'd been denied his son. His obsessive determination had simply taken over, blocking out the fact that he was a kidnapper, a liar, a man on the run and the worst possible influence on a child.

Katherine felt a waving edge of panic as the minutes slipped away and Sloan didn't appear. The cottage was totally silent. Had Sloan gone to the car unaware of Gerald? Maybe a neighbor had delayed him to ask about the police car. Although the fast-burning taper had barely melted, it seemed as if she'd been trapped by Gerald for hours.

Keep talking, she told herself. And try to think. If Sloan's been hurt... She sucked in a breath.

Oh, God. She glanced furtively at the lump at Gerald's waist. Had Gerald... But she would have heard. Sloan is too smart, but Gerald had been in the house all along...and he had a gun. Sloan didn't....

She stopped her rambling thoughts. She couldn't do this. She had to stay calm if she wanted to protect Danny. In what she hoped was a controlled voice she asked, "The Irwin sisters just believed you when you said you worked with Jennifer? No questions?" She found that suspect, recalling that Sloan had mentioned their immediate suspicion of him.

Gerald straightened. "I can be very convincing. A few buzz words, a little authority and those two broads were eating it up. Plus I mentioned we had fallen in love." He preened a little, his mouth curled into a smug smirk.

Katherine closed her eyes in defeat. Marion and Nina were suckers for romance.

Gerald boasted, "Jennifer always thought I was sexy and charming. Even those rookie cops thought I was their best friend. It all comes down to how you present yourself." He scowled. "At your place I forgot about presentation. A major mistake, if I'd done it right I would have gotten my son then." The scowl broke into another smirky smile. "And we wouldn't be having this charming conversation."

"I find nothing charming about you and you won't take Danny." She'd automatically stepped in front of the crib.

Gerald grinned confidently. "Back away from him."

Danny rolled over then and sat up. He clutched the bear, but his eyes widened as Gerald came closer to the crib. The candlelight threw distorted shadows.

"See, he likes my present. Don't you, Danny-boy?"

For an instant the comment didn't register, but when it did Katherine wanted to snatch the teddy bear from Danny and fling it at Gerald.

His eyes narrowed as he moved threateningly closer.

"You and Calder seem to be having some difficulties with your relationship." He waved his hand dismissively. "Whatever. The old broads mentioned an engagement but I figured you were just trying to cover your ass. Anyway, if I'd known Calder was going to be your bodyguard..." He grinned as if Sloan had gotten the worst of the deal. "I would have warned him you're nothing but trouble. Just like your sister."

Katherine covered her disappointment when he mentioned Sloan. He knew she wasn't alone. She let him talk, using the precious moments to plan her way out. She knew he was toying with her, treating her as if she were no more than a wisp of dust that he would flick out of his way. He could easily prevent her from grabbing Danny so she had to do something else. Katherine curled her fingers into tight fists to keep her hands from shaking.

Her mind raced. She strained to hear any sound. Sloan wouldn't have left her, she knew that, and yet Gerald acted as if Sloan were no threat. Her gaze touched on the lump at his waist. No, she would not think about that possibility. She couldn't. Sloan couldn't be...

As though sensing the direction of her thoughts, Gerald grinned, "Calder can't help you. Now get away from the crib."

She didn't move, her fear steadily growing. "Where's Sloan?"

Moving forward, Gerald gripped her arm and Katherine winced, remembering the last time. She also recalled how furious Sloan had been that she'd excused the bruise.

She tried to jerk away. "Take your hands off me, you bastard. I asked you a question. Where's Sloan?"

He shoved her sideways. "Forget your boyfriend. I already took care of him."

A thousand black-and-white spots swam before her eyes. "Took care of him . . . ?"

He looked at her, then leaned forward, shoving his face close to hers, smirking. "Yeah, I shot the sonofabitch and splattered his blood all over that mussed-up bed where you and he were gettin' it on." He shoved her aside again and she stumbled as his words sliced into her like jagged cuts of raw reality.

She couldn't take it in. Her mind simply refused, the terror slowly changing into an anger that boiled with a ferocity that left no doubt she could kill this man.

He reached for Danny, but the toddler's earlier calm had disappeared. "B-bad m-man," the baby cried, straining for Katherine.

"Shh, Danny-boy, I'm your daddy. You and I are gonna get to know each other," he murmured as he tried to cradle the boy and stop his crying.

Sloan's face swam before her. Blood where they made love. Blood on him, oh, God . . . Katherine shook. Danny. She had to protect Danny.

Frantically she looked around for something to hurt Gerald with, but everything was soft, everything except . . .

She inched down and reached for the truck that Sloan had pushed aside, the one he'd bought for Danny. Her fingers closed around the solid metal body. She rose slowly, raising her arm back to get momentum.

He turned suddenly, catching her in the act. "Bitch," he snarled, then backhanded her, sending the truck flying through the air to crash through the window.

Katherine slammed back against the crib, her head exploding with pain. Stunned she clung there, fighting the nausea, the black spots of dizziness. A tiny clear part of her mind kept saying, "He's escaping. *He's taking Danny.*"

Pulling on the strength and desperation the frantic terror gave her, Katherine staggered from the room. She saw Gerald at the sliding-glass door to the deck. Danny was struggling. He arched and strained to get loose until finally Gerald shoved the toddler roughly under his arm. Danny screamed.

Katherine tasted despair. She had to stop him. She started forward when a hand grabbed her arm from behind. For one crazy moment she was sure her body went in one direction and her heart in another.

"Get back," Sloan ordered. He shoved her against the wall near her bedroom where he'd flattened himself. He held a revolver, and it was pointed straight at Gerald.

Katherine went weak with relief. "He said you were dead."

"Not quite," Sloan muttered. She could see blood on his face that trickled from a nasty cut on the side of his head. "Put the boy down, Graham."

She clutched Sloan's arm, the one with the gun. "For God's sake, don't shoot," Katherine said frantically. "You might miss him and hit Danny."

"Thanks for the vote of confidence," Sloan said dryly. Gerald turned then, illuminated by the moonlight. Danny struggled weakly now, his cries mere whimpers. Gerald waved his own gun menacingly.

"I should have finished you off, Calder."

"Yeah. Mistakes are costly. Don't make a major one now. Let Katherine have Danny."

But he squeezed the baby even tighter. Then, to Katherine's horror, he aimed the barrel of his weapon near Danny's chest. "He's mine. Goddamnit, he's mine!"

Sloan's voice was so calm, Katherine was stunned at his control. Her eyes were riveted to Gerald's gun. "I know,"

Sloan said. "He's your son, Graham. Part of you, but you're hurting him."

Gerald straightened, shouting, "No! I would never hurt him. I love him. I want him to love me. I want to be his father."

Katherine pleaded, her eyes swimming with tears of terror for Danny. His face was so red. "Gerald, you're strangling him. Please . . ." She tried to run toward Danny, but Sloan hauled her back.

"Graham, listen to me," Sloan said soothingly. "You are his father. That will never change."

"She said I could never see him again. I had to do this. She made me." His voice faltered. "She made me. . . ."

"But this isn't the way, man. If you care anything at all about Danny—"

"I love him!"

"—Then you'll do what's best for him."

Still Gerald held the gun too close to Danny for Sloan to make any charging moves. Katherine was afraid to breathe, her ears straining to hear even a whimper from Danny. Gerald kicked the screen door, shoving it back on its track. He backed onto the deck, his eyes darting around every few seconds to see how close he was to the steps.

"Get behind me," Sloan muttered to Katherine. He moved forward, his revolver held in a pre-firing position.

"Oh, God, no. Sloan, please . . ." Her whole body was rigid and weak and shaking all at the same time.

Sloan moved onto the deck. He took a step forward for every one Gerald took back. Danny now hung limp.

In a terrified voice Katherine pleaded, "Gerald, please, you're killing your own son."

Gerald's head jerked up and then down to look at Danny's limp body. He'd halted just before the steps, just before the gate that Sloan had closed earlier.

His pause was all Sloan needed. "Gerald! Look out!"

He whirled, but the momentum threw him off balance and he crashed into the gate. Startled, he flailed, the gun waving menacingly in the air. Suddenly the weapon fired, the sound roaring through the windless night. Katherine's heart plummeted to her feet.

Sloan dropped his own weapon and dove into Gerald, launching him backward. The gate splintered, its hinges ripping as Sloan's hold on Gerald took the three of them down the steps onto the softer sand. Gerald's gun flew from his hand to land a few feet away. Sloan twisted at the last second so as to cradle Danny from the impact of the fall. Katherine rushed forward.

Sloan extricated Danny and then got to his feet, his own breathing labored.

"Oh, Danny," Katherine cried. "Sloan, is he all right?"

"A little scared and shook up, but okay. Aren't you, tiger?" Sloan brushed sand from the toddler's cheek. Danny gulped for air and reached for Katherine. His whimpers broke into furious cries. She took him in her arms, holding him close, a look of thankfulness on her face for his tears.

Sloan watched them, grateful that they were both alive and out of danger. He suddenly remembered why he'd taken this case, remembered his need to make up for Angela and his own baby. In a factual one-for-one, he'd done what he'd set out to do. He should be filled with an inner sense of vindication and peace, yet all he felt was a cold premonition that the days ahead were going to be very empty.

Perhaps that's the price of guilt, he thought. It's never replaced with peace and freedom for the soul, only with a yawning emptiness.

Wearily he glanced from the joyous scene of Katherine and Danny down to the defeated Gerald, who had rolled onto his side, groaning softly and holding his arm.

Sloan felt more like a spectator now. Their roles as Sloan and Katy Calder were finished. No need to continue, he realized with an almost painful sadness. He decided the only way to do this was to make the end clean and precise, like the dropping of a final curtain. Time to go back to real life in Harbor Bay.

Sloan reached down for the man still crumpled in the sand. "Come on, Gerald, on your feet."

Spitting sand out of his mouth, he snarled at Sloan, "I should have hit you harder."

"As I said before, mistakes can be costly." To prove it Sloan had a headache from the dull grind of pain when the butt of Gerald's gun bore into the side of his head mere seconds after he'd walked into Katherine's bedroom. He'd had a millisecond of a glimpse of a smug Gerald, but it had been enough for Sloan to turn so that the weapon didn't hit his temple. He didn't know how long he'd been out, but he'd heard the crash of breaking glass. By the time he'd gotten his revolver from the leather case, Gerald had Danny.

Thank the Lord he'd been able to grab Katherine before she tackled Gerald. In a crazy kind of way, Sloan had felt sorry for Gerald. He outweighed Katherine by at least ninety pounds, he had Danny and he had a gun, yet Sloan knew that she would have given the guy one hell of a fight.

Now he glanced at Katherine as she rocked and soothed Danny. Reflectively he said, "If you'd killed me, Graham, you would have had to deal with Katherine."

"She's just a woman. What in hell was she gonna do? She didn't even have a gun."

"Yeah, but she stopped you. She made you have second thoughts when she told you you were killing your son. That stopped you."

Gerald glared, his confusion evident. "That's a lot of garbage." He scowled in confusion at the broken gate, muttering, "I know I opened that gate."

"And I closed and locked it. Habit. Katherine didn't want any accidents like Danny falling down the deck steps."

Gerald scowled at Sloan as if he thought Sloan was making some point. "You messing around with my mind, Calder?"

Sloan said, "Just something for you to think about while you're cooling your heels in prison."

Gerald swore and lowered his head in defeat.

The neighbors began to gather. "We heard a gunshot," one of them shouted. "The police are on their way."

In the distance came the sound of a siren.

Later, after Sloan explained everything to the police, Gerald was taken away. The neighbors had returned to their homes when the electricity came back on.

Katherine sat on the couch, still holding Danny, who blinked furiously at the sudden light.

Sloan had sprawled down beside her, his head back, his eyes closed. "He really is okay, isn't he?"

"He's wonderful. What about you?" She reached up and touched the bloodied bump on the side of his head.

"Apart from a headache, I'm okay." He turned to examine her cheek where Gerald had backhanded her. He brushed his knuckles across her skin. "First you scratched it with the shell and now it's swollen. Good thing the electricity was off when Gerald was still here. I would have loosened a few of his teeth." He closed his eyes and sighed. Then talking with little emotion, he said, "Phone's working. I called Drummond. I also called Linda and Hank and said I wouldn't be over tomorrow."

Suddenly she knew they were leaving, and very soon, but then, what point was there in staying? Katherine reminded herself that she had prepared for this. She'd known that it would happen. She wasn't going to be depressed or sad and she would not cry. Swallowing hard, she asked, "Did you tell them the truth about us?"

He shook his head. "I was afraid they'd want to come over. I told Linda you'd call her." He sat forward, his head lowered, his hands braced on his knees. "Guess that about wraps everything up. We can get things packed and head home. You feel up to it tonight, or do you want to wait until morning?"

She wanted to sleep with him, to hold him once more, to steal away into that dazzling world where she and Sloan were one. Suggesting it frightened her, though, for she would be mortified if he refused. Certainly if he wanted to spend this final night together, he would say so. She waited through long seconds of silence, then finally allowed the reality to settle in. He didn't want anything more between them. Perhaps just leaving was best. Break it off while there still weren't any arguments, no second thoughts, no despairing final night of lovemaking. God, she couldn't bear that kind of goodbye.

"Do you feel up to driving back tonight?" she asked.

"I'm so wired I doubt I'd do much sleeping."

"Me, too." She managed a smile, glad that her shattered heart wasn't visible. "I guess it's time to get back to our real lives." My empty life, she thought to herself.

She pressed her hand against Danny's back and thought of her own possible pregnancy.

In a few days she'd know for sure.

Chapter 13

"Gerald tried to snatch Danny?" Jennifer Brewster's perfectly made-up hazel eyes widened with shock and disbelief.

"Twice." Katherine took a sip from her cup of hot tea.

"My God."

Jennifer collapsed on the couch in a loose heap. Dressed in khaki slacks and a safari-style jacket, her face paled to a pasty shade of gray as Katherine related a condensed version of Gerald's escapades.

In the week since she and Sloan had returned to Harbor Bay, Katherine had selectively chosen exactly what she wanted to tell Jennifer. She didn't want to share the intimate details of her relationship with Sloan, or that she'd fallen in love with him. Nor did she want to admit that once again she'd allowed herself to choose a man who didn't want her.

Katherine had remained decidedly composed during the recounting of the snatching attempts. Her calm hid a newly-realized anger at her sister, which arose from Jennifer's cavalier attitude regarding Danny. Sloan had been purposely sarcastic when he'd called Jennifer a paragon of motherhood, and though she undoubtedly loved her son,

Katherine thought her sister's affection was far too careless, too automatic and assumed far too much.

As for Katherine, the two encounters with Gerald had changed her. And after having faced the numbing terror of those moments when she'd been convinced he'd killed Sloan, well, in effect, it made all other things, like her sister's shock, not terribly important.

Jennifer had been in the apartment less than fifteen minutes. Her luggage, camera equipment and a huge koala bear that she'd brought from Australia for Danny were just inside the door where the taxi driver had dropped them. The flight had been delayed two hours by weather turbulence. After trying numerous things to keep Danny awake, Katherine had finally given up when the toddler fell asleep in the playpen. She'd tucked him into bed just before Jennifer arrived.

"Danny is here, isn't he?" Jennifer asked suddenly.

"He's asleep."

"I brought him a present...." She went to get the stuffed animal. Katherine bit down on saying that Gerald, too, had brought his son a teddy bear. That, she decided, would be unfair. Gerald had tried to gain Danny's trust. Jennifer had done what any mother would do and brought her son a souvenir.

Jennifer hugged the koala bear much as she'd done with a favorite dolly when she was little and had been naughty. "You're angry with me, aren't you? I can tell you blame me for this. Your voice is clipped and you're being really distant."

Just what she'd so often accused Sloan of being, she realized grimly. Katherine made herself stay seated, despite her sisterly urge to get up and reassure Jennifer with a hug. Forgive and forget had always been the pattern of the past. Jennifer's problems, whether real or imagined, always ended up on Katherine's shoulders. Now she steeled herself against offering solace and allowing Jennifer any opening to duck through. Perhaps she was being too harsh, but she knew that what could have happened to Danny could not be easily shrugged off or dismissed. She didn't want to take the chance of Jennifer burrowing behind tears and apologies.

"Angry and disappointed," Katherine said flatly. "I tried to reach you before I left, but you had gone off into the outback without leaving any clue with the hotel as to when you'd return. Then when I got home I was sure there would be a bunch of concerned messages from you since I was supposed to be here and I wasn't." Katherine glared at her. "Eight messages, Jennifer, and only one of them was yours. That's when I got angry. You never even called the Irwin sisters to find out if Danny and I were all right. And the message you left sounded like a talking postcard." Katherine mimicked, "'Hi, the scenery is fabulous. Got some great shots. And guess what, my guide is to die for. Sexy and hunky and yummy. I'll tell you the good stuff when I get home. A ton of kisses for Danny. Thanks, Katy. See you in a few weeks.'" Katherine paused a moment, then asked, "Did I leave anything out?"

Jennifer's sheepish look was genuine. "Okay, I know it sounded shallow and dumb, but be fair. I had no reason to worry about Danny. He was with you. In fact, I did call a couple of other times but when I got the machine I didn't bother to leave a message. To be honest with you, I was so involved . . ." She peered at Katherine, who raised her eyebrows. "Not with the guide," Jennifer replied with lofty indignation. "With my assignment. Anyway, how was I to know that Gerald would go berserk?" But before Katherine could say anything, Jennifer looked as if she wanted to pull back her question. She glanced at the floor, her tone self-accusatory. "But I should have. . . . Damn him. . . ."

Katherine frowned, her mind sorting the questions about Gerald that she wanted answered.

Still holding the bear, Jennifer sat down beside Katherine and promptly changed the subject. "So tell me about the guy who helped you and Danny?"

Katherine wanted to discuss Gerald. Just the mention of Sloan made her insides tighten. She had deliberately avoided his name, wanting to focus on the break-in at the apartment and then the one in Chelsea Beach. She'd skimmed through the other events because Sloan was tied to all of them.

Katherine glanced toward the kitchen as if willing the phone to ring. It felt like eons since she'd called Sloan and left a message that she wanted to talk to him.

As the hours had passed she'd gotten worried. Maybe his answering machine wasn't working or her message had somehow been erased.

And she'd gotten scared. Perhaps he dreaded returning the call because he thought she was going to suggest they get together, or he'd assumed she had some other ulterior motive.

Now she put her empty cup on the table and stopped the topsy-turvy direction of her thoughts. To her sister, she said, "His name was Sloan Calder. He's a private investigator hired by the police—"

"Wait a minute." Jennifer frowned thoughtfully. "Sloan Calder. Calder. That name is familiar." Then her eyes blinked and widened knowingly. "Isn't that the same guy that you practically went to the ends of the earth for to get some out-of-season flowers for his wife's casket?"

"Yes."

"And you personally delivered them to him at his office the day before the funeral because he wanted to make sure they were the right ones?"

"Yes."

"The same guy who did something that so affected you that you refused to talk about it."

Katherine took a deep breath, recalling those poignant vulnerable moments with Sloan. "Yes."

For a long tense minute Jennifer simply stared. Then as if she'd forgotten why Sloan had been hired, she snapped, "And you took my son and went off with him? My God—"

Katherine leaped to her feet, her hands planted on her hips. "Don't you dare say anything against him, Jennifer Brewster! There is not another man in the entire world like Sloan. If it wasn't for him, Gerald would have Danny right now and be God knows where."

Jennifer sagged back and stared up at Katherine in astonishment. "If I hadn't heard this with my own ears I wouldn't have believed it. You've never been that defensive of anyone."

"Sloan's different."

"Ah," Jennifer said with a confident smile. "Then there can be only one other explanation."

Katherine sat back down and tried not to look at her. She reached for her cup to keep her hands from trembling. "Why don't you go and see Danny?"

Her sister sat forward, studied Katherine's profile for a few seconds, then stood, her voice composed and firm. "And when I come back, we're going to have a long talk."

Katherine wasn't about to be bullied into saying more than she wanted to say. "Yes, we can talk. About Gerald and some questions I want you to answer."

Jennifer didn't walk away, but said in a sympathetic whisper, "You're in love with this Sloan Calder, aren't you?"

Tears gathered in Katherine's eyes. Damn. Damn! She didn't want understanding, and for sure she didn't want to admit how foolish she'd been.

Jennifer tossed the bear aside, sat back down and put her arm around Katherine. "Oh, Katy, he hurt you, didn't he?"

"No." Again she put the cup down, this time for fear of dropping it. She let herself sag into her sister's support. Katherine realized that as upset as she'd been, she'd missed Jennifer's unfailing loyalty.

Katherine swallowed, feeling the whole story rising to her lips and wishing she had the tenacity to just lift her head and say he can't hurt me because I don't love him. But she couldn't. She did hurt and she did love him and she had no one to blame but herself.

Finally, speaking in a soft murmur, she said, "Sloan doesn't know how I feel."

"And you never tried to tell him?"

She shook her head. "He doesn't love me, so there was no point. It would have been awkward for him. He was with us because of Gerald. In fact, I never would have gone along with the police's plan if I had thought Sloan had other intentions. He was clear and careful about reassuring me as any professional would. Of course, we talked about some personal things, but I'm sure a lot of that was because we were stuck together. He went through a bad time when he lost his wife. He adored her and I don't think any woman will ever replace her."

Jennifer listened, nodding occasionally, but Katherine knew by the patient looks that her sister wasn't fooled by Katherine's attempt to avoid what had *really* happened with Sloan. "Katy...?"

"Don't ask me," Katherine warned, feeling a flush of heat in her cheeks.

Jennifer's eyes filled with concern. "Now I don't have to." She hugged Katherine fiercely. "But I bet you weren't as reckless and careless as I was. At least you would insist that he use protection. I remember how concerned you were when I told you I hadn't with Gerald."

Katherine sat rigid and still. She couldn't tell Jennifer. Not yet. She managed a smile. "Go on in and see Danny. I need to get a fresh cup of tea."

Jennifer picked up the bear, eyeing Katherine with lingering concern. "You and I do manage to love the wrong men, don't we?"

She took a deep breath. "Go on. I'm all right. Oh, wait," she said as Jennifer headed for the nursery. "Danny's in my room. Since that first night he's had some nightmares and so I moved his crib."

Jennifer gave Katherine a grateful look. "You're a pretty terrific sister, you know that?"

"Danny's a pretty terrific little boy."

The two women smiled at each other before Jennifer went on in to see her son.

Katherine went into the kitchen, filled the kettle and set it on the burner to heat. She sat on one of the counter stools and fiddled with the phone cord while her thoughts once again slipped over the past few days.

Since she'd returned home, she'd spent a week denying that her relationship with Sloan was really finished. A week of sudden tears followed by annoyance at herself for not accepting the inevitable. A week of staring at the pregnancy test kit she'd bought but had put off taking.

This morning she'd awakened to the wonderful sounds of Danny happily playing in his crib.

She'd lain in her queen-size bed with its plump, down-filled pillows, its white satin comforter, its lace-trimmed sheets and wished Sloan were there with her. She'd daydreamed of how it would feel to tumble their bodies in the lace and satin of sensual luxury. Yet her sudden pleasurable shiver had come not from the romantic surroundings in that fantasy, but from the very real memory of her legs gripping Sloan's hips when he'd made love to her on the cottage kitchen counter.

Impulsive and dazzling, yes, but it had also been reckless. She now faced the reality that her period was three days late.

Of course, emotional upheaval could account for a disruption of her cycle, and if that were the reason, the pregnancy test would be negative. She wasn't even sure what she feared—that she'd be like Jennifer, pregnant when a modern sophisticated woman of the nineties would be constantly aware of the dangers of unprotected sex? Or did she fear she wasn't pregnant? Katherine Brewster wanted to have Sloan Calder's baby.

Despite the ramifications.

Sloan's word, she'd thought with a shudder of realization that she couldn't escape the powerful and lasting influence he'd made on her life. Having his child would forever connect them. She'd told herself her motive for continuing a pregnancy came from love, but was it that simple? Perhaps she was selfish, making an attempt to keep ties to Sloan when he clearly didn't love her or want any ties to her. That wasn't love, it was the same feeling Gerald had for Danny. Obsession.

Earlier in the afternoon Katherine had decided that she could not continue her self-imposed limbo. Wasn't there some saying about today being the first day of the rest of your life? And since living life was making decisions, she'd marched into the bathroom, closed the door and taken the pregnancy test.

She'd pressed her hand against her stomach when she saw the positive test results. She carried his child, and with that knowledge came another decision. Whether it was practical or logical or smart didn't matter any longer. She had to tell Sloan.

Katherine intended to be methodical and calm about this. No tears or emotions. She wouldn't pressure him, she didn't want anything from him. Not marriage or money or some fake relationship because of a few moments of reckless passion.

She sighed. She could hear Jennifer's laughter and Danny's squeals of delight coming from the bedroom. Katherine stared at the kitchen phone as though that would make it ring. She glanced at the phone cord wound around her left hand and how it obliterated the nakedness of her third finger.

The day they'd returned to Harbor Bay, Sloan had refused to take the diamond ring back when she'd tugged it off her finger and tried to press it into his palm. She'd insisted until finally he'd relented and jammed it into his pocket as if the piece of jewelry were worth about twenty cents.

He'd scowled in exasperation when she'd tugged the fisherman's sweater over her head and tossed it to him. She'd known from his dark grimace that he'd recalled the night she'd pulled off his shirt in the kitchen in Chelsea Beach and thrown the garment at him while he'd stared back at her.

She closed her eyes briefly now at the searing memory of her being naked and hot and wet....

But this time there'd been no such reaction. He'd balled the sweater up and flung it back to her, his tone cool and even. "What next, Katy? You want me to take back the red truck I gave to Danny?"

She couldn't look at him. "No, of course not."

"Keep the sweater. Besides, I haven't paid you the two hundred bucks from the Monopoly game. The sweater should just about square us."

"All right," she replied brightly, determined she wasn't going to make a fool of herself and ask him to kiss her goodbye. "Thank you for everything."

"You're welcome."

"I know you're glad it's over and—"

He interrupted her. "I'm not glad it's over. I'm glad you and Danny are safe."

"Yes, well . . ." she said, her thoughts fumbling for the right words. "I guess, there isn't anything else. . . ." Her voice trailed off and she ducked her head for fear he would see how hard this was for her.

He stepped closer to her then, cupped her chin and lifted her face. For a long moment, their breaths blended, their eyes gazed deeply into one another's.

Katherine felt her blood pound hot and thick. If she just raised up on her toes she could kiss him.

Sloan didn't lower his mouth to hers, but she saw a flash of something cross his face.

"Kiss me," she whispered. She couldn't stand to have him just walk away, just smile and say goodbye. She knew her pride was in shreds, but she wanted to bask in one final taste of him.

His thumb pressed into her bottom lip, his voice just husky enough so she knew he was fighting back his own impulses. "You haven't forgotten what I told you, have you?"

She had. She couldn't think about anything except that she'd never be this close to him again. "What did I forget?"

He hesitated as if even talking to her was difficult. "That you kiss too hot, sweets."

"So do you," she murmured. "So do you. . . ."

"We shouldn't. . . ."

"I know." But she wanted to, and since she feared he would release her without kissing her, she brushed her mouth against his and felt a moment of joy when his lips caught hers in a fierce, tongue-plunging, taste-absorbing kiss that Katherine didn't want ever to end.

But of course it had. He kissed her again, softer and sweeter, then he walked to the door. He paused and glanced at her for a moment. Katherine wanted to believe she saw regret in his expression, but she feared it was only relief. ·

She'd almost wished their departure had been as dramatic as their beginning the day he'd come to take her to the Cape.

He'd arrived dressed in leather and denim and with a distant, but laid-back authority that was unlike any of the men she'd ever known. She'd been wary, but intrigued. And that intrigue had grown from curiosity to attraction and passion and finally to love. But there was no happily ever after. Their relationship was simply finished. No dramatic heart-wrenching departure. Just a low whisper of "Goodbye, Katy Calder," and the gentle closing of the door.

Unwinding the phone cord now, she rubbed her finger. Calling him was probably a mistake. Maybe he didn't want any messages from her, maybe she shouldn't be adding oh-and-by-the-way-I'm-pregnant to their nonrelationship. Maybe he wouldn't want anything from her. Not even his child. Maybe...

Jennifer leaned against the doorway. "I have to tell you something."

Katherine blinked at the change in her sister's demeanor.

Jennifer shoved both of her hands through her dark heavy curls, and swallowed nervously. Katherine couldn't recall ever having seen her so undone.

Pushing aside her erratic thoughts about Sloan, she led the way back to the living room. When they were once again seated on the couch, she asked, "What is it?"

"I think this is all my fault. I mean from the last time I saw Gerald and he... I should have known he wouldn't just go away," Jennifer said in a nervous, edgy voice. "At first he was so furious that I'd rejected him, but then he got so calm and controlled those last few moments. I mean, he'd even helped me pick up.... And then I was so swamped with the last-minute details for the Australia assignment.... Oh, God..." She began to tremble.

Katherine put her arm around her sister comfortingly. "Slow down. I can't follow you. Take a deep breath."

Jennifer gathered in a gulp of air. "I said awful things to him, screaming at him to get out of my life, that I'd never let him see Danny...." Then she wiped at her eyes, her voice cracking. "I want you to tell me exactly what Gerald said about me."

Katherine wanted to say it didn't matter. Gerald had been arrested with bail denied because of his mob connections.

He would probably go to prison. Danny was safe. But she knew Jennifer needed to get this all out. And Katherine reminded herself that she still had some unanswered questions of her own. In a softened voice, she said, "He blamed you for why he was taking Danny. Gerald wanted to hurt you, to take revenge for what he perceived was your rejection."

"It wasn't perceived. I did reject him."

"But that had been true since before Danny was born."

"Yes, but I hadn't completely closed the door. He was Danny's father and, I don't know..." She lowered her head into her hands. "God, Katy, sometimes I felt like a wicked bitch for denying him even visiting rights. Sometimes we talked and a few times I let him see Danny."

"I had no idea you'd been seeing him."

"I didn't tell you because I knew you'd flip out and give me a long lecture. You made it clear from the day I brought him home after I met him in Atlantic City that you didn't approve," Jennifer said, but without rancor.

"Jennifer, it wasn't a matter of approval. You hardly need that from me. I just didn't trust him. Maybe because of Robert, I don't know, but it seemed to me that Gerald had that same smooth, too-many-smiles style."

"You were always up-front about how you felt. I know it's hard to believe, but I really loved him at first. Only after we'd been involved for a while I caught him in a few lies. He told me once he was going to Chicago and I learned later he'd been down in Atlantic City with some rookie cop, showing him a good time. There were other things like telling me he made a lot of his money from his restaurant, when in reality he made it from his connections with the mob."

Appalled, Katherine asked, "You knew about his illegal dealings and still you continued to see him?"

"By that time I was pregnant. I was furious about the sleazy stuff he was pulling. I told him I couldn't see him anymore and that I wasn't about to let him influence my child. He immediately launched a romantic campaign to get me back, as if flowers and expensive dinners could make me forget what he was. But Gerald can be very convincing and most of the time his explanations were so logical.... I know

now they appeared to be logical because I didn't want to face the truth."

Katherine wasn't sure she wanted to know. "What truth?"

Jennifer shuddered. "Oh, God..."

"What!" Katherine felt a sinking sensation in her stomach. Whatever Jennifer was about to say, she knew instinctively that she wasn't going to like it.

"He came to see me before I was to leave for Australia. He said he was getting out of all the illegal activities. That included some scheme he was involved in that had to do with police recruits. He was afraid the cops were on to him. He wanted to go away and start over with me and Danny. He begged me to marry him and give him another chance."

"And that was when you rejected him completely."

She shook her head. "A few days before Gerald came to see me, I had found out that one of the rookie cops that Gerald had taken to Atlantic City committed suicide."

"Yes, that was what prompted the police investigation. Sloan told me about it, but the police kept it out of the newspapers."

"One of the women I work with knew the family. She told me. Anyway, I asked Gerald about it because I knew he had befriended a lot of the new cops. Dinner at his restaurant when they were on duty, and he'd taken a few to Atlantic City. When I heard about the suicide, something inside me clicked and I was positive Gerald was involved. I think I wanted him to deny it. A silly soft spot inside me that wanted to find some particle of worth in a man who I'd been so involved with that I'd had his child. So I asked him if the rookie who'd killed himself was one of the ones he'd taken to Atlantic City." She laced her fingers together in a tight clench.

Katherine held her breath.

"He totally freaked out, screeching that nothing ever worked out the way he planned it. He called me names I won't repeat, told me the stuff with the cops and the mob was all in the past, that he'd changed. I was the only woman he'd ever loved and I had no right to deny him being a father to Danny. He was off the wall."

Katherine knew that her face had gotten paler with each revelation. "He hit you, didn't he?" she asked, recalling how he'd backhanded her in Chelsea Beach when he'd freaked out.

"He tried," Jennifer said grimly. "But I swung my purse at him and then the weirdest thing happened. He just stopped. The clasp on my purse broke and the stuff went all over the floor. He apologized and then helped me pick everything up. He told me to have a good time in Australia and then he left. I never saw him again."

Katherine leaned back on the couch, drained and exhausted. "Why didn't you ever tell me any of this?"

She lowered her head. "Now it sounds dumb and foolish, but I wanted to handle Gerald myself. I've always run to you whenever I got into a mess and this time I wanted to prove I could bail myself out. When he left my office he was calm and I thought 'this is the end of it.'" She paused. "When you were telling me about the break-in here you said you had no idea how Gerald got in. There'd been no sign of forced entry." She looked up at Katherine with guilty eyes. "I think he used my keys. When the stuff in my purse went all over the floor, Gerald helped me pick everything up. Later when I got in my car, I couldn't find my keys. I figured they were under the desk, but the office was already locked so I used my spare car key. You were home so I didn't need the door key. I looked the next day, but couldn't find them. Then I left, and just forgot about my keys."

"Sloan was right," Katherine muttered with a sigh. "Before we left for Chelsea Beach, Sloan asked me if Gerald had a key. I was outraged and told him you would never have given Gerald a key. I never considered that he might have stolen it from you."

"Katy, I'm so sorry. I should have told you what happened, but I honestly thought he was out of my life. And I never thought he would do anything like try and snatch Danny." She lowered her head. "Now I know."

Katherine hugged her. "Of course you couldn't have known. And Danny is safe. That's what counts. Everything turned out all right."

Except for the endless pain in her heart.

* * *

Three weeks later Sloan sat at his cluttered desk at the Calder Investigation Agency. He scowled at his scrawled shorthand on an expense sheet from one of his pre-Chelsea Beach cases.

Since he'd returned to Harbor Bay, his mind had been so preoccupied with Katherine, that he could barely concentrate on clear English never mind his scribblings.

Hell. Pre-Chelsea Beach. Preoccupied with Katherine. Like it or not he couldn't rid himself of her and those days with her. It had gotten so bad that she'd become a pre-and-post focal point in his thoughts and conversation. Like last week.

To a potential client, he'd said, "Before the Brewster case, I was mostly involved in security and white-collar investigations." And just this morning when he'd stopped for coffee, he'd mentioned that after the Brewster case he'd taken a few days off to relax.

Some relaxation, he thought now as he rubbed the back of his neck, attributing the tension to lack of sleep. At least he'd told himself that was the problem. His nights had been awful. Sporadic sleep, often coming awake suddenly and too often reaching for Katherine. One damn night they'd slept together, he thought ruefully, and his subconscious had clung to the memory as if it had been a thousand nights.

Sloan was still kicking himself for allowing that final kiss in her apartment. And he'd been responsible for it. He'd walked up to her instead of out the door.

And then there was the message she'd left on his machine. "Sloan, this is Katherine Brewster. I want to talk to you about something. Could you give me a call?"

He'd played and replayed the message, at first annoyed that she would think she needed to give him her full name. Then he'd wondered if by doing so she was saying something significant. Had she assumed that he'd forgotten her just as he would most names after he'd concluded a case? Then he tried to discern what she wanted to talk about. There he drew a total blank. Hadn't they tied off all the loose ends right down to his taking the ring and her keeping the sweater?

"Damn pop psychology," he muttered in disgust when he realized he'd been analyzing the phone message as if it were in code.

He'd lifted the receiver a dozen times to return her call and then changed his mind. He'd gone so far as deciding it would be better to casually stop into her florist shop. Or he could go to her apartment....

Now, two weeks later, he'd still done nothing about the call. She hadn't called him again and that bothered him.

Swearing succinctly, he flung the stapled sheaf of papers across the room. Why was he fighting so hard to forget her?

He leaned back in his chair, propped his booted feet on the desk and faced the truth. He was scared. Just like when he'd walked into the police station to take the assignment of protecting her and Danny. Then he'd been scared he'd fail as he'd failed Angela.

But Katherine and Danny were safe. Although Sloan had reconciled with himself that he would never feel totally guiltless for what had happened to Angela and his unborn child, Katherine had helped him put it in perspective. During those days with her he'd turned a major corner in his life and yet today, he felt worse than he'd ever thought possible.

He scowled at the diamond ring Katherine had returned. He'd tossed it into the tray of paper clips to prove to himself it was worthless to him, but he knew it that were true, he would have pawned the damn thing.

Damn it, he was *not* in love with her. Absolutely not. What he felt was something else. Like physical pleasure. Hadn't he told her that sex with her was the best he'd had in twenty years? Or admiration at the way she handled Danny. He'd told her she was a better mother than Jennifer. A hundred other moments flitted through his thoughts from her terror on the beach to her letting herself go when they'd made love.

She'd trusted him with her life and she'd trusted him in the bedroom. Oh, he knew she was wary of men, but she'd made herself put aside that caution and let herself go. He'd seen that in her Katy Calder role, but more importantly he'd seen it when she was plain Katherine Brewster.

He glanced at the chair on the opposite side of his desk. Katherine had sat there after he'd given her the news that Robert was involved with another woman, and she'd sat there the day before Angela was to be buried....

Sloan straightened suddenly in the chair, bringing his feet to the floor with a clunk.

Katherine had sat in that chair the day before Angela was to be buried? He repeated it again while the color drained out of his face. How in hell could he have forgotten it was her? Sure there were memory gaps from those days, but why this one? Why would the florist who delivered the jasmine and tulips have escaped his memory? He should have recalled it any number of times. The roses at the cottage. The conversation with the Rowens' about her being a florist. God, he'd even told her about how Angela had died...about the baby. Katherine had come through for him when every florist he'd called had told him the out-of-season flowers would be impossible to get.

But she'd gotten them.

And he'd forgotten. Naturally or deliberately?

Why hadn't she told him? Just as he'd had a lot of opportunities to remember, she'd had more than enough time to remind him. Her motive for remaining silent gnawed at him until he realized he had the perfect excuse to call her.

He picked up the receiver, then changed his mind and set it back on its cradle. Face it, Calder, you want to see her about as bad as you've ever wanted anything. And this is as good an excuse as you've got.

Just as he rounded the desk, he spotted the ring among the paper clips. Not wanting to think about *his reason* why, he scooped up the diamond-set gold band and hurried out of the office.

Chapter 14

"Come on in," Katherine called out, responding to a knock on her workroom door at Stems 'n Petals. She stood behind a counter, where she was arranging daisies, carnations and delicate ferns in a milk glass vase. Her eyes widened in surprise as Sloan entered and firmly closed the door behind him.

Her spirits soared as if on cue and she reminded herself that the role-playing was finished. Reality was that more than three weeks had passed since she'd called him. Whatever reason Sloan had for not wanting to see her or even return her phone call had saddened and pained her. His unannounced appearance now fanned a whole range of emotions—from anger to anticipation to euphoria. She took a deep breath and made herself remain calm.

However, her decision to tell him about the baby hadn't changed. Despite that decision she had felt no obligation to seek him out until she was ready. She wanted to be sure she could see him without getting emotional about it.

But perhaps now that he was here this was the best time. At least she wouldn't have to go through those hours of turmoil she would have had if she'd set up a meeting with him.

He said nothing, staring at her as if he were trying to decide to stay or leave. Katherine hated the thick silence and yet she was at a loss as to what to say herself. Why was he here?

She did note the distant expression on his face, the one she'd become accustomed to while they'd been in Chelsea Beach. In spite of his obvious hesitancy, her own heart reached for everything that she loved about him. From the tousled, slightly overlong black hair on his head to the peek of chest hair at the opened shirt placket to the snug jeans. From the way he'd spoiled Danny with the red truck to soothing away the baby's nightmares. From sharing his guilt over Angela to his buying the diamond wedding ring so she wouldn't have a green finger. Her stomach did a little flip-flop as he drew closer.

To cut the heavy silence, as well as disguise any emotion he might detect, she said breezily, "Sloan, how nice to see you."

"Why didn't you tell me?" he asked in a low voice.

Taken aback, she almost upset the vase. Her mind immediately leaped to the baby, but how could he already know? My God, did she have a pregnant look? She glanced down. This morning her slacks had felt a little snug, and she'd left the closure open, but her work smock covered that.

He studied her as though unsure whether he wanted to continue. She'd never seen him look quite so rattled, but then as she saw the grimness around his mouth she was reminded that she had indeed seen him that rattled. That day on the beach when she'd refused his comfort and accused him of leaving her and Danny.

Finally he said, "You could make this a lot easier if you answered my question."

Katherine felt more than a little annoyed at being put on the defensive. "We are no longer playing the role of the Calders. I don't have to make anything easy for you. In fact, I wanted to talk weeks ago. I called you and—"

"I didn't return your call because I didn't want to talk to you and I didn't want to see you," he said flatly.

Katherine wasn't prepared for the shredded slices of pain that went through her heart. She glanced down, but the flowers on the counter all blurred together. In a choked voice, she said, "Well, I certainly can't fault you for not being honest, can I? But then you always were." She turned away so he wouldn't see her wipe away the tears. "I have two more arrangements to do before three o'clock, so if you'll excuse me."

He rounded the counter, and turned her to face him. "You didn't answer my question."

She forgot the sheen in her eyes and stared at him. His hands gripped her arms and she was reminded of the day he'd said he was terrified of kissing her.

But before she could frame a response, he murmured, "About the flowers."

"What?" she asked in confusion.

"The jasmine and tulips. Why didn't you ever say anything?" His gray-green eyes bored into her, but more for answers than in anger.

She closed her eyes and sighed. He'd remembered, but how much? Then again, perhaps it didn't matter. It was painfully obvious that he hadn't come here to declare his love or sweep her up in his arms as if the past weeks had been hell for him. She thought of her doubts that she could never live up to Angela, but then she realized that like the Katy Calder role, trying to replace Angela would have been no more than a fantasy. She was herself and Sloan had adequately reminded her of that the night he'd made love to Katherine Brewster. Cautiously, she asked, "Didn't I? I was sure I'd mentioned it."

"You never mentioned it and you know it. Why?"

She swallowed. "You were so sad that day." She paused, a little unsure as to how much he'd recalled. *You're still trying to spare him*, she admitted to herself. *Despite everything that has happened, you want to allow him to keep that most vulnerable of all moments to himself.* In a soft voice, she continued. "The few times you talked about Angela in Chelsea Beach, you made it clear you didn't like discussing anything about her death. I didn't see any point in bringing up such a difficult subject."

He spoke as if he hadn't heard her. "You went to a lot of trouble to get those flowers, didn't you?"

She started to shake her head, but he framed her cheeks with his hands and stopped the motion. His expression shifted to something else. Gratitude? Astonishment? Love? Oh, God, how she wanted it to be love.

The pads of his thumbs brushed the fragile skin beneath her eyes. She murmured, "No, I..."

"Don't deny it, Katherine. I just talked to one of your more than competent saleswomen. She told me you had the flowers specially flown in from California. You personally drove to the airport in Providence to meet the plane. You wouldn't allow anyone to help with the arrangement. The saleswoman said you guarded those blossoms as if each one of them was priceless."

Her eyes never blinked while he spoke. Yes, she'd done all those things, but she'd never heard them all listed as if she'd made getting the funeral flowers a mission. Now that she thought about it, perhaps that's what she had done. But it hadn't been her intent to make her effort into some masterpiece of kindness. She'd simply responded to a man who'd requested a funeral spray to drape his wife's casket. "I wanted to make sure the flowers were exactly what you specified on the phone. Fresh and not damaged in any way."

"What else did I say?"

She felt her throat close up and she tried to pull away from him. He held her fast. In a husky voice, she said, "I don't remember."

The carnations scented the air around them and Katherine thought of the irony of the beauty of flowers and the ugliness of death. Sloan pulled her forward, clasping her to him as if he needed support to stay standing. Her hands felt the hard warmth of his back through his shirt.

"I remember," he murmured, and she knew from the catch in his voice that the memory was difficult. "It's a funny thing about memory gaps. Once one is filled in, the others tend to follow. I told you I wanted flawless and perfect blossoms to cover the casket because she was so broken and so bloody."

Katherine shivered and tightened her hold on him. "Sloan, please, you don't have to say any more...." Her own voice broke as she recalled how bluntly explicit and distraught he'd been.

Relentlessly he continued, as though he needed to spill out the painful details of seeing Angela after the accident, to wash out the dark places in his heart. When he'd finished, he tipped her head back and asked quietly, "Why did you go to so much trouble simply for one customer's funeral flowers?"

"Because you called me and—" She gulped, then continued in a whisper, as if even now she wanted to keep this just between the two of them. "You sounded so desperate, I couldn't tell you that the order would be very difficult to get on such short notice."

His expression was grim and filled with self-recrimination. "But you got them, sweets. Katherine Brewster bails out a drunk widower who calls and demands out-of-season flowers because he knew his wife loved jasmine and tulips. Or perhaps because the flowers covered up all the horror and the guilt. But you . . . God, Katherine, you came through just like you do for Jennifer when she needs you, and for Danny when he was almost snatched. Even for Linda Rowen. And when I wanted those flowers, *you came through for me.*"

"I knew you loved her." Then in a softer voice, she said, "You were so kind to me when you found out what Robert was doing. I could tell that when you had to reveal Robert was a cheat that it was as hard on you as it was on me. You were supportive, and yet so careful to spare me from feeling a sense of total humiliation that Robert preferred other women to me. I never forgot that. When I heard about Angela's death, I was stunned. I wanted to call you to express my sympathy, but I wasn't even sure you'd remember me. When you called about the flowers and I heard the pain in your voice, I felt that this was a way I could do something for you. I knew then that I would get the jasmine and tulips that you wanted no matter what the cost."

He studied her face for a long time. "No matter what the cost," he murmured. Then after a long pause, he muttered something about not seeing love when it was there all the time. He tugged her into his arms and she went without hesitation. "I was drunk when you came to the office with the flowers, wasn't I?"

Katherine remained perfectly still against him, but she felt the pounding of his heart. This is the hardest part for him, she realized. "Yes, you were drunk."

His voice seemed to come from far away. "I even remember your exact words. 'There's a time to be strong and a time to fall apart.'" Then in a whisper, he added, "You let me fall apart without making me feel weak." He shook his head, still astonished that he'd done what he'd done and that she'd seen him that vulnerable. "Crying in front of you was what got me through the funeral the following day. I must have sensed that you wouldn't try to comfort or offer sympathy and you didn't. You just let me cry. God, Katherine . . ."

Katherine thought her heart would burst. "Oh, Sloan, you needed to cry. You needed to let all your emotions go. I cried with you, you know. I couldn't help it. It was so plainly obvious how much you adored her." She tightened her arms and heard him draw in a long breath.

They stood together, silently letting the tragedy of those days settle and in a poignant way draw them closer.

Finally Sloan said, "You know, I agreed to take you and Danny to Chelsea Beach to vindicate myself against the past. I was sure once I proved to myself that I could keep a woman and a child safe that the guilt I'd been carrying for so long would lessen."

"Did it? Lessen, I mean."

He shook his head. "It hasn't lessened as much as it's leveled off and become a part of my past, thanks to you. I can't change it and I can't make it go away, but I can see it in a different light now. Remember when I told Gerald that mistakes can be costly?" At her nod, he said, "There's something even more important. When you don't make a mistake and do the right thing it can be life-changing."

She felt a sudden surge of hope. "And what was the right thing for you?"

"Agreeing to take you and Danny to the Cape."

"And that changed your life?"

He gave her a long intense look, shaking his head slowly. "No, sweets, you changed my life because you broke through all the locks on my soul."

Tears slipped down her cheeks, coupled with an intense burst of love for him. "Oh, Sloan, no one has ever said anything quite so wonderful to me."

He waited a few seconds and then he said, "These past weeks have been hell. I haven't slept worth a damn. I keep thinking about you and what we had." He dipped his fingers into his jean pocket and pulled out the diamond ring. Glancing at her, he said, "I couldn't even take the ring to a pawn shop."

Startled that he still had it, she said, "A pawn shop. The ring wasn't listed as part of your expenses?"

"Are you kidding? The gate for Danny wasn't a problem, but Drummond wouldn't have sprung for a diamond ring. Besides, it never occurred to me to list the ring. I bought the ring for you." Then after what seemed like an eon of silence, he said, "When you insisted that I take it back, I felt like I'd been divorced."

"I did, too," she admitted. "Perhaps we played our parts more realistically than we realized."

"Perhaps. Most probably some of your pop psychology at work." He grinned. "I knew you liked the ring and I wanted you to have it. If you recall, you didn't want much from me. You weren't exactly happy about going to the Cape as my wife. You didn't even really trust me. And you didn't like your own tendency of being honest about your feelings toward me. Like in the jewelry store when you said you couldn't forget the kiss. Remember?"

"Yes, and I wish *you* didn't remember. I was mortified." She gave him a quizzical look. "And you never did say if you were paid to kiss me." She held her hand over his mouth. "Before you answer that, it's okay to lie and say no."

He snagged her wrist and kissed her palm. "Sweets, I couldn't put a price tag on your kisses."

"Really?"

"Really. Just like the price of the ring. It's worthless to me unless it's on your finger. I vowed after I lost Angela that any kind of commitment that involved love carried too high a price. But after those days with you in Chelsea Beach and then the days without you back here, I knew the price of being *without* you was worse. The ring has been lying in a tray of paper clips on my desk as a daily reminder that the longer I waited to tell you I love you, the more lonely I was going to get."

Suddenly she felt a burst of dazzling wonder. *He did love her.* He loved her and he wasn't saying it because of the baby, because he felt obligated to her. She raised her lashes, intent on telling him about their child. "Sloan . . ."

He scowled. "You're not going to tell me you've found someone else, are you? Is that what your phone call was all about?"

"No, of course not. But there is something. . . ."

"You don't want me."

He looked so devastated she had to suppress her giggle. "I want you forever. In fact I've loved you since before we came home."

"You have?" He scowled as if that surprised him and then he looked hopeful. "That's what you called to tell me."

She laughed. This wasn't going anything like she'd thought it would. She'd been sure she would have to tiptoe into the subject. "No. I didn't call you to tell you I loved you."

His disappointment was so acute, she wanted to ruffle his hair. "You look like Danny does when he doesn't get his way." She slipped her arms around his neck. "After I tell you this, I want you to kiss me and tell me you love me again."

He kissed her first. Tongue-deep and hot. Then with a frown he asked, "Am I going to like it?"

"Yes, I think you're going to love it as much as I do." She waited another five seconds, then whispered in his ear. "We're going to have a baby."

For just a second he looked totally stunned. He gripped her shoulders and studied her face for so long she felt as if he'd memorized every pore. Then the smile came, a wonderful satisfied smile that sent her heart soaring. He hauled her close, sliding his hand down to her waist and under her smock to her stomach. He splayed his fingers and rested them against her while he sought her mouth. "The night in the kitchen . . ."

"Yes."

Suddenly Sloan realized that he could very easily have not known if he'd continued to deny he loved her. "I should have called. It wasn't that I didn't want to see you or talk to you. . . ." She felt the tension roll out of him. "I was just so afraid to let myself love you." He stared at her, his confession making his eyes shimmer with wonder. "A baby. Ah, sweets. The ring and now a baby. Maybe they both mean that from the very beginning I wanted forever with you before I even knew I loved you."

New tears glistened in her eyes. "I love you, too."

Long deep kisses were followed by a thorough investigation of her waistline that she finally called a halt to when he bent to kiss her tummy where their child lay.

He let her go enough to slip the diamond ring on her finger. "Will you marry me for real, Katherine Brewster?"

"Oh, yes," she said as she pressed her body close to his. "Katherine Brewster accepts with love and happiness."

* * * * *

HE WHO DARES

Starting in July, every month in **Silhouette Sensation**, one fabulous, irresistible man will be featured as *He Who Dares*. When Silhouette Sensation's best writers go all-out to create exciting, extraordinary men, it's no wonder if women everywhere start falling in love. Just take a look at what—and who!—we have in store during the next few months.

In July:
MACKENZIE'S MISSION by Linda Howard

In August:
QUINN EISLEY'S WAR by Patricia Gardner Evans

In September:
BLACK TREE MOON by Kathleen Eagle

In October:
CHEROKEE THUNDER by Rachel Lee

He Who Dares. You won't want to miss a single one, but watch out—these men are dangerous!

SILHOUETTE

Sensation

YOU'LL BE INTRIGUED BY OUR NEW SERIES

Intrigue, the new series from Silhouette, features romantic tales of danger and suspense.

The intriguing plots will keep you turning page after page as the gripping stories reveal mystery, murder and even a touch of the supernatural.

4 titles every month, priced at £1.95 each, from July 1994.

COMING NEXT MONTH

MACKENZIE'S MISSION Linda Howard

He Who Dares

Joe "Breed" Mackenzie was the best of the best—a colonel in the U.S. Air Force, he was responsible for a revolutionary test plane that someone on the inside was trying to sabotage. Joe suspected everyone, but civilian Caroline Evans—blonde, beautiful and aggressive—was the most likely candidate. Consequently, Joe was taking personal charge of this investigation!

EXILE'S END Rachel Lee

Under Blue Wyoming Skies

CIA agent Ransom Laird hadn't expected to find a woman he could grow old with when he came to Wyoming. Now that he had found her, he certainly wasn't going to lose her to an unknown assassin, someone who wanted Ransom dead. Whoever it was, they were going to have to go through him to get to Mandy...

THE HELL-RAISER Dallas Schulze

Mitch Sullivan was known to be trouble in the small-town where he and Jenny Monroe lived. But he'd always been tender with her and she wanted him. Wanted him as no good girl should want a hard-as-nails nobody from the wrong side of the tracks. Ten years on, older and no wiser, Jenny still wanted him. This hell-raiser was going to be her own piece of heaven...

THE LOVE OF DUGAN MAGEE Linda Turner

The ghosts of Sarah Haywood's past were resurrected as a serial rapist stalked the city. There was only one man she trusted—police detective Dugan Magee. Dugan felt the heat crackling between them as soon as they met and knew what such intimacy would cost Sarah. He wanted to heal her, but first he had to protect her from a madman...

COMING NEXT MONTH FROM

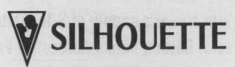 **SILHOUETTE**

Intrigue

Danger, deception and desire—
new from Silhouette...

NIGHT MOVES Nora Roberts
TIGER'S DEN Andrea Davidson
WHISTLEBLOWER Tess Gerritsen
MURDER BY THE BOOK Margaret St George

Special Edition

Satisfying romances packed with emotion

SALLY JANE GOT MARRIED Celeste Hamilton
HE'S MY SOLDIER BOY Lisa Jackson
WHEN STARS COLLIDE Patricia Coughlin
MARRY ME KATE Tracy Sinclair
WITH BABY IN MIND Arlene James
DENVER'S LADY Jennifer Mikels

Desire

Provocative, sensual love stories for the
woman of today

WILD INNOCENCE Ann Major
YESTERDAY'S OUTLAW Raye Morgan
SEVEN YEAR ITCH Peggy Moreland
TWILIGHT MAN Karen Leabo
RICH GIRL, BAD BOY Audra Adams
BLACK LACE AND LINEN Susan Carroll

HEART  HEART

Win a year's supply of Silhouette Special Edition books ABSOLUTELY FREE?

Yes, you can win one whole year's supply of Silhouette Special Edition books. It's easy! Find a path through the maze, starting at the top left square and finishing at the bottom right. The symbols must follow the sequence above. You can move up, down, left, right and diagonally.

Please turn over for entry details

HEART ♡ HEART

SEND YOUR ENTRY NOW!

The first five correct entries picked out of the bag after the closing date will each win one year's supply of Silhouette Special Edition books (six books every month for twelve months - worth over £85). What could be easier?

Don't forget to enter your name and address in the space below then put this page in an envelope and post it today (you don't need a stamp). Competition closes 31st December 1994.

HEART TO HEART Competition
FREEPOST
P.O. Box 236
Croydon
Surrey CR9 9EL

Are you a Reader Service subscriber?   Yes ☐   No ☐

Ms/Mrs/Miss/Mr _____ COMSE

Address _____

_____

_____

                            Postcode

Signature _____